THE STRANGEWORLDS
· TRAVEL AGENCY ·

The Secrets of the Stormforest

By L.D. Lapinski

THE
STRANGEWORLDS
· TRAVEL AGENCY ·

THE
STRANGEWORLDS
· TRAVEL AGENCY ·

The Edge of the Ocean

THE
STRANGEWORLDS
· TRAVEL AGENCY ·

The Secrets of the Stormforest

THE STRANGEWORLDS

· TRAVEL AGENCY ·

The Secrets of the Stormforest

L. D. LAPINSKI

Orion

ORION CHILDREN'S BOOKS

First published in Great Britain in 2022
by Hodder & Stoughton

1 3 5 7 9 10 8 6 4 2

A CIP catalogue record for this book
is available from the British Library.

ISBN 978 151 0 10596 6

Printed and bound in Great Britain by Clays Ltd, Elcograf S.p.A.

The paper and board used in this book are made
from wood from responsible sources.

Orion Children's Books
An imprint of
Hachette Children's Group
Part of Hodder & Stoughton Limited
Carmelite House
50 Victoria Embankment
London EC4Y 0DZ

An Hachette UK Company

www.hachette.co.uk
www.hachettechildrens.co.uk

For Alice and
Avery

and
for everyone who
has joined Flick,
Jonathan and Avery on
their adventures

'Cowards die many times before their deaths;
The valiant never taste of death but once.'

William Shakespeare
Julius Caesar
(Act II, Scene II, Line 34)

PROLOGUE

Little Wyverns
November 1873

The evening the stranger arrived ought to have been a dark and stormy night. That would have been more appropriate for our story.

But in reality it was the calmest night Henry L'Estrange had known for weeks. It was, however, a suitably bleak hour; the gas-lamp on the other side of the street glowed half-heartedly in the early winter evening. Henry found himself suppressing a yawn, though closing time was still several hours away.

It had been a busy day, by his standards. He'd

sold a rather marvellous cruise to one of his regular clients, and arranged train tickets and passage for several others. Henry was looking forward to closing up for the day and heading home. A few dark shapes occasionally passed in front of the bay window; office workers and clerks leaving their jobs. Henry didn't hold out a great deal of hope of making a sale at this hour – clerks did not tend to make many voyages abroad. He went back to the book he was reading.

The bell chimed as the door opened. He looked up to see a well-dressed young woman, wrapped in a travelling cloak and carrying two suitcases: one, a brown cardboard affair that looked as though it had been dragged through several hedges and back; the other glossy red and small, with shining gold fastenings. The woman looked well-dressed, and her hair was in a sort of bun under her hat. She closed the door quietly behind herself, and Henry stood, giving her a salesman's smile. 'Good afternoon, miss.'

She did not smile back, but gave him a piercing look, then spoke without so much as introducing herself. 'The room upstairs. May I sleep there tonight?'

Henry was so astounded he actually sat back down

in his chair. Such a question! And asked as if it were the most natural thing in the world! He hardly knew how to answer. 'I – I'm not sure if—'

'I can pay you,' the woman said, taking out a heavy-looking purse.

'Are you in some sort of danger, miss?' Henry blurted out. There was no other way of asking.

'Yes,' she said. 'I am.'

'I see,' Henry lied, quite mystified. His day had been upended by this strange young woman, and she had only been in the shop for a minute. The suitcases, the money . . . something was afoot. The young woman's clothes were too fine to belong to a servant, but they were travel-worn. There was dirt and loose threads on the hem of her dress. She was clearly running away from something.

Henry was trying to think of what to do, when the woman's gaze was caught by the maps framed on the walls of the travel agency. 'Are these yours?' she asked.

'Yes. Well, we bought them,' he explained, his train of thought completely derailed. 'We have a cartographer in Hay-on-Wye who does all the map-work. He's rather good, isn't he?'

A small smile crept on to the woman's face, and stayed there. 'He has a little skill.'

'A little, miss?'

The woman put her suitcases down, unfastened the worn cardboard one and slipped a gloved hand inside to pull out a leather-bound portfolio. She handed it to Henry, who opened it on his desk.

He gasped.

The portfolio contained maps. Pages and pages and pages of maps. Maps of towns, of countries, of the world, of coastlines Henry didn't recognise. Each one was meticulously detailed, colourful and practically dripping with rich ink.

He looked up. 'Who made these?'

'I did,' she said simply. 'I'm a cartographer. Amongst other things.'

Henry lifted one of the maps by the edge. It was the city of Edinburgh. 'This is exquisite, miss. Who taught you?'

The young woman hesitated.

Henry sensed the question was unwelcome and moved on. 'I don't suppose these are for sale? I would be happy to take some of them off your hands, if you need money.'

'I don't need money,' she said. 'Not yet, anyhow. But I do need a place to stay.'

The implication was clear. Henry was torn between

his desire to own some of the maps and the sense of unease he felt about this whole meeting. He laid the page down as he tried to come to a decision. In the corner of the map, in fine black ink, was the name *Elara Mercator*.

She was watching Henry with tired eyes that seemed empty of hope. He knew from her face that she would not ask a third time.

He cleared his throat. 'I . . . should think a single night would be acceptable, Miss Mercator,' he said. 'The upstairs is in some disarray, but I am sure we could—'

'Thank you,' she interrupted, her shoulders dropping in relief. 'I can sleep anywhere with a floor.' She took the portfolio back, save for the map of Edinburgh, which she left on Henry's desk. 'I would appreciate it if you did not tell anyone I was staying here.'

'I understand.'

'I hope so,' she said, her voice fearful for the first time. 'The people looking for me can be terribly persuasive.'

Henry felt a shiver race over his skin. He had the feeling that since he had agreed to give this woman shelter his world had shifted slightly, or perhaps widened, but the change had been so swift and imperceptible that he couldn't say exactly what was different.

He led Elara up the stairs, where she settled herself quite comfortably in the front room, waving Henry and his lamp away.

'Remember, I am not supposed to be here,' she said, looking up from her position on the floor. 'You should lock up as usual, and I shall keep the place in darkness. Everything you do must be as you normally do. Give no one any reason to suspect I am here.'

*

By closing time, Henry had almost forgotten about his strange lodger.

But just before the clock struck for seven, the bell over the door clanged as someone came in, and Henry looked up from his account-book.

A man and a woman came in, and something about the sight of them chilled Henry to the bone. He couldn't say precisely what it was. Perhaps it was their height (both of them towered over him), or perhaps it was their overly bright eyes (which flickered eagerly around the room as if searching for something). Or perhaps it was their skin, which was smooth and without wrinkles, but seemed worn-out, like crepe, thin and almost transparent.

'Good evening,' he said, getting warily to his feet.

Like Elara, neither of them returned his greeting. The man moved his head and neck like a snake looking for a mouse. The woman walked over to Henry and took a photograph from her bag. 'Have you seen this girl?' she asked, thrusting the picture at Henry's face.

Henry took it, knowing before he looked that it would be a photograph of Elara. And indeed it was. A formal picture – Elara's hair scraped back off her face, her back rod-straight as she looked to the right of the lens. She was wearing fine clothes, there were a number of glassy-looking ornaments on the shelves in the background, and beside her was a suitcase.

He lowered the picture. A lifetime of telling untruths to his father about a great many things had made him an accomplished liar. 'I'm sorry, madam,' he said, his voice a bored drawl. 'I haven't seen this person.'

The woman did not even blink. 'Look again,' she ordered. Behind her, the man had drawn out a magnifying glass, and was peering through it as though he fancied himself a detective from a story.

Henry frowned and looked at the photograph again. 'I'm sorry, I haven't seen her. Is she a relative of yours?'

The woman's nostrils flared. Her eyes seemed to brighten even more. 'She was seen coming in here.'

Henry made a confused face, but his back was starting to sweat. 'She came in here? When? I have a lot of customers.' He gestured at the account-book.

The woman slammed her hands down flat on the desk between them. 'Tell me what you did for her, and where she went.'

'I don't care for your tone,' Henry said firmly, meeting her eyes and hoping he sounded braver than he felt. 'I'm going to have to ask you to leave.'

There was a *bang* from upstairs.

The man and woman looked at each other.

Henry, his blood draining into his legs, opened his mouth, but the woman shoved him hard into the wall behind the desk before he could come up with an explanation. The man was already running up the stairs. Henry coughed, winded. Heart racing, he waited for the moment Elara would be discovered and dragged down the stairs . . .

The man's heavy footsteps thumped around on the floorboards above, and then there was a snarl of anger. 'She's not here, Sephie!' He stomped back down the stairs.

The woman seethed through her teeth.

Henry wheezed, trying not to look shocked. 'I told you,' he croaked. 'I haven't seen her. Now get out of my shop, before I call for a constable.'

The couple looked as though they would have very much liked to stay and make Henry's life a misery, but with a shared glance, seemed to decide against it.

Henry watched them sweep out of the shop and disappear down the street. He was trembling from head to foot, and there was a throbbing pain in his back from where he'd hit the wall.

He wasn't foolish enough to rush upstairs to check on his guest. Those people might yet be watching him through the window. He dusted his waistcoat off, rubbed some life back into his chest, and went to lock the door. If these were the people Elara was running from, he could certainly understand why she was doing so.

It was quite a while later that he heard footsteps on the floor above.

Henry left his desk and went into the small

room at the back of the shop to find Elara Mercator hovering halfway down the staircase. 'Are they gone?' she asked.

'For an hour or more, now,' he said, filling the kettle from the copper tap. He set it on the stove and lit the flame.

'Did they hurt you?' she asked.

'Not much,' he said bravely, though his back did still ache. 'Who are they?'

Elara bit her lip. 'They're dangerous, that's all you need to know.'

'The man went upstairs. How did you hide from him?'

'It's a long story.' She came into the kitchen and helped herself to a chair, sitting down with a sigh. She suddenly looked exhausted.

'I have time to listen,' Henry said, 'if you want to tell me.'

'It's quite unbelievable,' she said.

'And full of secrets, no doubt,' Henry replied with a small smile, taking the remaining chair at the table.

Elara nodded. She looked into his eyes and seemed to make a decision. 'Those people,' she said, 'they aren't . . . people. Not as you know them.'

Henry, thinking of their too-bright eyes and papery, smooth skin, thought this wasn't so unbelievable after all. 'What are they?'

Elara took a deep breath and then began.

CHAPTER ONE

'We are called the Seren,' Tristyan said. 'And it is my people who created schisms.'

These words had been echoing through Flick's mind for what felt like an eternity – though in reality it had only been seconds. But in those few seconds, sitting in Tristyan's apothecary shop in another world, everything she thought she knew about herself, about her world, about magic and the multiverse, had all been turned upside down in a flash.

She looked over at Jonathan, standing beside her, looking as shocked as she felt, and then back at Tristyan. She realised her mouth was hanging open, and tried to remember how to speak.

'They – you – created—' She shook her head. It felt extremely full.

'Schisms are natural phenomena,' Jonathan said. 'They have always existed, they weren't created by anyone. Although' – he gave Flick a look – 'I suppose we do know that new ones can be torn, by some people.'

Flick, meanwhile, continued to stare at Tristyan. Until a few minutes ago, she had thought this tall, elf-like man was nothing more than a kind apothecary, who sometimes helped out travellers from other worlds. But now, she was cradling the revelation that he was her grandfather. Her own dad's dad was from another world. And therefore, so was she. In a way. Her whole life had been turned upside down as quick as winking.

Felicity Hudson and her friend Jonathan Mercator were part of The Strangeworlds Travel Agency – custodians of a very powerful magical travel system contained within the dozens of suitcases stacked in an old and dusty shop. Within each suitcase was a schism – a gateway to another world – and to travel from one to another, all you had to do was step inside.

Schisms didn't only exist within suitcases, however; they occurred naturally everywhere. At least, that is what Flick and Jonathan had been led to believe. To hear that the rips and tears in the fabric of the multiverse had been *created* was like learning that someone coloured in the sky every morning. It seemed too far-fetched to be true.

'I don't understand,' Flick said. 'What is a Seren? Am I part Seren?'

Tristyan shook his head. 'Let me explain properly. Please?' He indicated the chairs, and they each carefully took a seat.

Jonathan was still clutching the piece of paper in his hands that had given him hope that his missing father was still alive. Daniel Mercator, the true Head Custodian of Strangeworlds, had been missing for months, and presumed dead. But Tristyan had shown them with this scrap of paper that Daniel could still be alive, somewhere out there in the multiverse.

'The Seren are not a species,' Tristyan said, lacing his spidery fingers together. 'They are an organisation, not unlike The Strangeworlds Society. The difference is, once you are one of the Seren you are expected to remain one for life. They become your family, your whole world.'

'And where does inventing schisms come into this?' Jonathan said, clearly not in the mood for sentimentality.

Tristyan gave him a small, sad smile. 'Contrary to what you've been told, young man, schisms have *not* always existed. There was a time, thousands and thousands of years ago, when the worlds of the multiverse were free of schisms and tears. The worlds existed alongside each other, but without any knowledge of one another, and certainly no travel between them. And in a world on the other side of reality from yours, there were the Seren.

'They were not a bad people, not in the beginning. They consumed magic to survive, in the same way you consume food and water. Since living things also produce magic simply by existing, there was plenty of excess magic to keep their world spinning happily. At first.'

'I think I know where this is going,' Flick said. 'It's like natural resources in our world, right? They got greedy. That's what happened with the Thieves in Five Lights – they bottled so much magic that their entire world was damaged almost beyond repair.'

'Exactly. The Seren are just like the Five Lights Thieves, only on a much larger scale.' Tristyan gave a sigh. 'They began to use magic to make other things – spells, and so on – and, as they grew more ambitious, their consumption of magic grew. Eventually, they were using it up faster than it could ever be replenished. And the walls of their world became thin.'

Flick sat up. 'And a schism tore?'

'The first schism,' Tristyan said. 'The first, and the largest. The schism tore their world to pieces, and the aftershocks of that opened up schisms across the multiverse. When it happened, a few of the Seren tumbled into another world and survived. The rest of their people were lost.'

'That's a sad story,' Flick said.

'Don't be fooled,' Tristyan said. 'Their story does not end there. Rather than learning from their mistakes and beginning their lives again peacefully in this new world, using magic in moderation, the surviving Seren simply picked up where they had left off. They would move from world to world, using magic to extend their lives, escaping through schisms as each world they touched died in their wake. The Seren are no longer a people – they are a virus. I am certain that it is they who caused the initial damage to the City of Five Lights, and I am positive it was they who were taking the magic of The Break in such frightening quantities.'

Flick tried to process what she was being told. 'They destroy worlds? On purpose?'

'That's right,' Tristyan said. 'Though they have been quiet, for a long time. I thought they might even be gone forever. Wishful thinking. What happened in Five Lights and The Break shows that they are back. The Seren are the biggest threat to the multiverse there has ever been.'

'And you were one of them?' Flick asked, incredulous.

'Not by choice,' Tristyan said. 'As the Seren's power grew, they . . . took, for want of a better word, children who were magically gifted, children who could help them harness even more magic. They raised us within the Seren and taught us to be one of them. I knew no better. I thought I was on the side of the good guys, until I met Aspen Thatcher, from The Strangeworlds Society.' He smiled sadly. 'She showed me what the Seren really were.'

'So, you escaped?' Jonathan asked.

'I did.' Tristyan nodded. 'Though I was not the first person to do so.'

'Other people have run away from them?' Flick asked. 'Who?'

Tristyan gave her a wry look. 'Can't you think of anyone who was extremely magically gifted? Whose powers seemed to come from nowhere? Someone who did everything they could to keep the worlds of the multiverse safe from danger?'

Flick put a hand to her mouth.

Jonathan sat up sharply. 'You don't mean to say that . . .'

'Yes,' Tristyan nodded. 'The first person ever to escape the Seren was your very own Society founder, Elara Mercator.'

CHAPTER TWO

Four Months Later

Felicity Hudson pulled her hat down further over her curly hair as the sleet blew her along the path from the school doors out towards the school gates. It was a wet and freezing January, but Byron Hall's uniform policy meant that only smart black shoes could be worn – no boots – so the icy water flecking up from the pavement soaked into her socks. Winter had arrived in a great slosh of sleet, and in places the walk home was now like paddling through the North Sea.

It was a Monday, so Flick didn't have to run across Little Wyverns to collect Freddy, her baby brother, from nursery. He could walk now, sort of, which meant he hated the buggy with a passion bordering on insane rage, and Flick burned with humiliation pushing him home three days out of five with him screaming blue murder. He had also mastered the word 'Help', which he wailed pitifully at strangers as though his sister was kidnapping him.

Flick was mooching up the school drive, enjoying the freedom of not having a screaming toddler with her and thinking vaguely about the essay due at the end of the week, when she heard something that made her stop in her tracks.

'. . . kid with a suitcase? What's he come dressed as? He looks like Doctor Who.'

She raised her head, and immediately caught sight of the person who fitted that description.

Jonathan Mercator, looking extremely uncomfortable, was standing at the top of the driveway of Byron Hall, clutching a suitcase in one hand. As always, his eccentric dress sense made him stand out like a sore thumb. He was wearing a deep plum frock coat, cherry-red Doc Martens boots, and what looked like two or three different plaid scarves. There were fingerless gloves on his hands, and his rectangular faux-tortoiseshell glasses had been replaced by ones with rounder steel frames. His wavy black hair was, as usual, all over the place. His face looked grim, and he was doing his best to avoid eye contact with the students, some of whom were giving him weird looks.

Flick felt a jolt in her stomach. Something had happened. Jonathan was not in the habit of appearing at her school gates unannounced. Or at all, for that matter. But, in a way, it wasn't a complete surprise. She had been expecting something like this would happen, sooner or later. Ever since they had found out about the Seren, the world had seemed different. It was as though knowing about them had made it more likely that things would start happening.

Of course, things had been going wrong in the multiverse for some time. People had been disappearing, as had whole streets. Worlds were being abandoned – like the eerie lighthouse world that still haunted Flick's memories.

It seemed to Flick that she had become a part of The Strangeworlds Society just when it needed her the most.

'Hey,' she said, as she got close to Jonathan. 'What's happened?'

'Things have . . . escalated,' he said. 'Can you come back with me?'

Flick nodded, and they started walking quickly

away from her school, down towards the village high street. 'Is it the Seren?' she asked.

'Yes. And Tristyan is at the travel agency. He says he guessed this would start happening.'

At the mention of Tristyan, Flick's stomach did a funny sort of clench. 'He guessed *what* might start happening?' she asked.

They crossed the road, and Jonathan paused as they went into the old stone-built shopping arcade, which stole what little warmth Flick had worked up on their walk, and made her shiver.

'When you destroyed the world of The Break,' Jonathan said quietly, 'you cut the Seren off from their source of magic. And that has made them desperate.

'They need magic to live. So, they're on the hunt for another world to devour. Mori and Hudspeth, some of my older Society members, they say there have been disappearances from Palomar, where the Laughing Dog Travel Station is based. That's how it started in Five Lights and The Break. It happened there, and it's happening again, now.'

Flick trotted after Jonathan. 'What is Tristyan doing at Strangeworlds?' she asked.

'Mr Golding, one of my Society members, sent word the Seren were seen in the world of Inniss, where

Tristyan lives. He got a message to Tristyan, and he didn't feel safe staying there, after that,' Jonathan said. 'After all, he did run away from the Seren – and they don't sound like the sort of people to forget that.'

They exited the shopping arcade into the grey dying light of the afternoon, and Flick saw The Strangeworlds Travel Agency ahead of them. It looked the same as ever, nestled crookedly between an alleyway and a closed-down bookshop. There was a thin snake of smoke whisping from the chimney, and the leaded bay window was steamed up with the warmth of the fireplace inside. As they approached, Flick could make out the huge wall filled with suitcases that pulled out like drawers, and the piles and stacks of suitcases in the window seat and on the floor. Each one a gateway to another world.

Jonathan pushed the door open, and the empty bell over the doorway shook silently as it always did. Flick followed him, smiling without realising it as the familiar warmth and old smell of the travel agency washed around her. It was the first time she had been there since Christmas. It felt so much like home – the armchairs, the fireplace, the dozens of clocks on the mantelpiece, the black and white photographs of Strangeworlds explorers on the wall. Flick noticed that one of the armchairs had an unfamiliar coat draped over the back and a leather bag stuffed full of glowing magical bottles on its seat.

As the door shut behind her, Tristyan came into the front of the shop from the tiny kitchen at the back. His face was tight with worry, and his long, greying black hair was tied back in a plait, exposing his elf-like pointy ears. He was wearing his brown shop apron.

He gave her a nervous smile. 'Felicity.'

'Tristyan,' she said, not bothering to keep the relief out of her voice. 'Are you, um, are you all right?'

'Better for being here,' he said. 'I was too visible back in Inniss. The Seren would only have had to offer a description of me and anyone in that city could have pointed them in my direction. It's been so long since the Seren have had enough magic to travel that I got complacent there, arrogant, thinking they couldn't get to me. But now they've been seen, and in more than one world . . . I wasn't safe there.'

'How come they didn't have enough magic to travel, before?' Flick frowned.

Tristyan wrung his hands slightly. 'Travelling via schism comes at a great cost, as you know. It is fatal to most people. The amount of magic needed would take up entire rooms, buildings even. And less than forty years ago, the Seren had just that. Incredible stores of magic, heavily guarded, extremely secret.'

Flick rubbed her thumb between her eyebrows. 'Had? What happened to it?'

Tristyan took a deep breath. 'I destroyed it.'

Flick's mouth dropped open. 'You . . . destroyed it?'

'I freed it, back into the multiverse,' Tristyan clarified. 'Broke the glass bottles and released the magical energy back where it belonged.'

Jonathan took his glasses off and started cleaning them frantically.

Flick stared at Tristyan, not really knowing what to say. 'Um. I bet they weren't happy about that.'

Tristyan grinned, and Flick thought there was pride in his eyes. 'I imagine not,' he said. 'Though I didn't wait around to find out.'

Flick stepped forward, interested despite herself. Now they were back in the travel agency, and she could see Tristyan was safe, the sense of urgency had dropped, and his story was intriguing. 'Can you tell us what happened?' she asked.

'It's really the end of one story, and the beginning of another.' Tristyan glanced out of the bay window; the day had fully faded now but the street was golden with the orange of the old street lamps. 'It happened forty years ago. In another world. And it starts with your grandmother, Felicity.'

'Aspen Thatcher,' Flick said, remembering the name of the woman she had never met, but whose Strangeworlds *Study of Particulars* she owned. It was odd, that this name she had stared at and wondered about was connected to her. It didn't feel quite real. It was the same with Tristyan; she knew that he was her grandfather, but she didn't have years of memories to make it feel real. Not yet. At the moment, he seemed more like a new friend, albeit one who was older and had a lot of secrets.

Tristyan moved his leather bag off the chair before taking a seat, and then started his story properly. 'I was a Seren, through and through. I'd been assigned to watch Aspen, like a spy, I suppose. They wanted to see if she – as a Strangeworlder – might be brought around to being on our side, become a Seren. But the opposite happened, and I ended up on her side. She opened my eyes to why it was evil to drain magic from other worlds. I vowed to do what I could to stop the Seren after that.' He looked pensively into the empty fireplace for a moment. 'I had always known what we were doing, but I never thought it was wrong until Aspen showed me it was, and who we were hurting. So, before leaving through a suitcase with her, I smashed every single bottle of magic the Seren had stored.'

Flick imagined broken glass flying in the air, and magic rushing upwards to freedom. 'So the Seren were trapped? They didn't have enough magic to leave?'

'Exactly,' he said.

'Where?' Jonathan asked, from where he was perched up on the desk. 'Where were they trapped?'

Tristyan gave a rueful smile. 'In a half-rotten world that they had mostly drained. They called it Serentegra. They were only using it to store their magic, but they had arranged to assemble there before moving on to another world. I waited, to catch them when they were all in the same place.'

'Did they know it was you who destroyed their magic?' Flick breathed.

'Oh, yes,' Tristyan said grimly. 'They would have figured it out as soon as they realised I was missing.'

'But how did you end up in Inniss?' Jonathan asked. 'Aspen was from our world. Why didn't she bring you back here?'

Tristyan's eyes saddened. 'She did,' he said, 'but Nicolas Mercator was furious she'd brought me back.

The Society rules state you must never bring anyone or anything back with you. Nicolas never really forgave her for breaking her oath, and the other Strangeworlds members felt the same way, particularly Aspen's sister. We decided to make the best of it in another world, away from here, together. And . . . the rest you know.'

Jonathan was picking his thumbnail. He looked extremely uncomfortable. 'You should have had a happy ending,' he said suddenly, jumping down from the desk and going into the kitchen at the back of the shop. Flick heard him running water noisily into the kettle. When in a crisis, or at risk of showing emotion, make tea. That was Jonathan's knee-jerk reaction.

Tristyan sighed, then gave Flick an even look. 'Are you angry with me, Felicity? For what happened with your father? I promise you we had no idea that Nicolas' dislike of people from other worlds, his . . . xenophobia, would extend to our son.'

'It's Flick,' she corrected. Only Jonathan was allowed to call her Felicity. *Was* she mad at Tristyan? Initially she had been, but now that she knew more of his story . . . 'I don't know,' she said finally. 'It wasn't really your fault. You didn't know he was going to be abandoned, you thought he was going to have a better life. And if none of it had happened, I wouldn't be here.' She swallowed, nervous about what she was about to suggest. 'You could see him, you know. My dad. Isaac.'

Tristyan went white. 'I can't,' he said, sounding choked. 'I – I really can't. Anyway, we don't have time.'

He's scared, Flick thought. But then her father didn't want to find his birth family either – he had often said so.

'If the Seren are on the move again, it's because they are hunting,' Tristyan said, grabbing her attention back quickly. 'And if they are hunting, it is essential that we find it first.'

'Find *what* first?' Flick asked.

Tristyan met her gaze and his expression was afraid. 'The suitcase that contains the end of the multiverse,' he said.

CHAPTER THREE

Flick had often sat looking at the wall of suitcases in the travel agency, and the many cases that were stacked here and there on the floor, wondering what kind of world was inside each one. Though she had been through a lot of them, there were over seven hundred in total and so there were many she had yet to explore. She had dreamt to herself about what joys or horrors might be waiting for her, but never in all her imaginings had she thought up something as awful and bone-chilling as the end of everything.

'Elara Mercator knew that the Seren were the biggest threat there was to the multiverse,' Tristyan said. 'After she escaped from them, she did what she could to prevent their influence from widening. She took all her suitcases with her, so they could no longer travel between worlds with them. And she made other plans. We heard a rumour, in the Seren, that Elara had managed to trap a schism that would, if unleashed, bring about the end of everything.'

'Why would she make something like that?' Flick asked. 'And why wouldn't she keep it here?'

'Because of the danger it contains,' Tristyan said. 'That suitcase was created in case the suffering of the multiverse was so great there was no other option but to use it. And also,' he added, 'I suspect, as insurance for herself too. The rumour of its existence stopped the Seren from coming after her for many years, because there was always the risk she would use it if they did.'

Jonathan was nodding to himself. 'There are pages in the *Study of Particulars* that refer to something like that. Though it's never named, and it's never mentioned where it might be.' He fished his own copy off the bookshelf, and flipped through the pages to the right section:

> . . . *a great many suitcases that are duplicates, particularly to the City of Five Lights. There are also suitcases that contain schisms through which*

travelling would be ill-advised. These include the Wastelands of Darkness, the Cold Emptiness, and one suitcase which is said to contain a great power, only to be unleashed if the anguish of the multiverse is so beyond repair that the holder would be left with no choice but to open it and

'That's it,' Jonathan said, turning the page in confusion. 'The following page is gone. It looks as though it's been torn out. How are we meant to know where this frightful suitcase is now?' He shut the book irritably.

Flick didn't bother suggesting they check her copy of the *Particulars*. She knew it from cover to cover. 'Could it be here?' she asked, looking up at the wall of suitcases that took up one side of the building.

'I don't think it would be the sort of thing you'd leave lying about,' Jonathan said, shaking his head. 'And besides, all of these are accounted for. No, you'd put it somewhere no one could get to . . .' He trailed off, thinking.

But Flick was faster. 'The House on the Horizon. No one can get there. You can get to the desert, but not up to the house itself. It would be the perfect place to store something you didn't want to be easily found.'

Jonathan snapped his fingers. 'Yes, precisely. We

have Avery to thank for that information.' Avery Eldritch was Jonathan's cousin, who had joined them on their last big adventure. The sudden mention of her name made Flick feel as though a few dozen butterflies were flying around in her heart.

Jonathan rubbed his chin as he thought. 'There must be a way to get there. The suitcase we have – the one Captain Nyfe gave to us – only leads to the surrounding desert, but maybe there's another suitcase, a secret one, hidden elsewhere, that might lead us into the House itself. And maybe this Doomsday Case is there . . .'

Tristyan had watched them talk without butting in, which Flick thought was quite unusual for an adult. He was sitting in the armchair, and had his chin resting on his hand as he listened. Jonathan's words had made Flick realise something.

'Tristyan, why would the Seren even *want* a case that could end the multiverse?' she asked. 'And why now?'

'They were deathly afraid of it for years,' Tristyan explained. 'It contains enormous energy. Think of the suitcase as an explosion, waiting to happen. But then the Seren realised they could use the potential energy to make themselves stronger. They could harness it for their own gains. And the Seren with that sort of power . . .' He shuddered.

'Could the Seren have kidnapped my dad to try and get to the suitcase?' Jonathan asked, going suddenly pale.

'Very possibly,' Tristyan said. 'If they have him, things are even more serious. He could, under pressure, lead them here to Strangeworlds, or to another Strangeworlds Society outpost. If the Seren ever got access to all the suitcase-schisms you have . . .' He shook his head. 'You would have to kiss the multiverse goodbye.'

There was an uncomfortable silence.

Flick swallowed. 'The world with the lighthouse . . . until we moved the pirates of The Break there, it was completely empty. Do you think the Seren might have already started to target it? Drain its magic?'

'It would make sense,' Tristyan said. 'And as much as all signs point to Clara, my daughter, having been there, given the photographs you found of our family, I am going to choose to believe she is safe. I cannot think otherwise, my heart does not have the space in it for another loss.' He looked down at the floor.

Flick was thinking furiously. 'If the Seren are already hunting for the Doomsday Case, they might find other

Strangeworlds suitcases scattered throughout the multiverse. Which would lead them back here! We need to stop that happening.'

Jonathan cracked his knuckles. 'Which means that *all* of the suitcases out there in the multiverse need to be found and brought back here, before the Seren find them. And we particularly need to find that Doomsday Case before they do.'

Tristyan looked thoughtful. 'And what would you do with this dangerous suitcase? Hide it further?'

Flick considered. 'Do you think it could be broken?'

'Is breaking a suitcase something you've done before?'

'Yeah,' she said, nodding. 'Back in Five Lights, and once by accident here.'

Tristyan looked admiringly at her. 'Well, it's certainly worth a try, isn't it?'

Jonathan started pacing, as he did when he was anxious. 'It's a huge task,' he said, bouncing on the balls of his feet. 'Phenomenally huge. We'll have to go to every outpost, in every world, and pull every suitcase we find back here.'

Flick stood up. She couldn't sit down either, everything felt too fizzy, and Jonathan's anxiety was infectious. 'Not all of the cases are in outposts either.

Like, there's the suitcase we left with Nyfe and Burnish, there're suitcases dotted across the multiverse for emergencies . . .'

'You have maps, don't you?' Tristyan asked. 'Showing you where they are?'

'So long as the suitcases haven't been moved, yes,' Jonathan said. He looked at Flick. 'I think we should call Avery in to help. And all the other Society members, as well. We can't do this alone.'

Flick nodded. Then frowned, turning to Tristyan. 'Wait. If we pull all the cases back here, then what about Jonathan's dad? What if Daniel is trying to get home and we cut him off?'

'I don't know that we have any other choice,' Tristyan said, not unkindly.

Jonathan made the pinched face he made when he was trying not to show he was upset, and gave a curt nod. 'Protecting the suitcases and schisms is the most important thing right now. We need to make sure that the Seren have absolutely no way of getting back here. And we need to find this Doomsday Case before they do.'

Flick nodded, trying to show she wasn't scared at the thought of the Seren – those world-eating monsters – getting into the place she loved most in the multiverse. 'I think we should go back to Five Lights first. Darilyn and Greysen Quickspark helped us – we should tell them what might be coming. Nicc De Vyce and the other Thieves deserve to be warned too.'

'You're right,' Jonathan said. 'Let's make that our first port of call. Let me find the case, and we can head there immediately.'

*

When they stepped out of the pink and gold suitcase into the City of Five Lights, all three of them stood frozen in shock.

The city was a mess – it looked as though it had recently played host to a violent tornado. The shops and stalls were wrecked. Doors and windows were broken and smashed, the sellers' carts lying broken and ruined on the pink cobbles. The fountain in the square that Flick, Jonathan and Tristyan stepped out into was dry. The fish statues around it were cracked, and the vase that usually had water streaming from it was broken, and brown and green with dirt and algae.

There was a man hurriedly packing away a sheet spread on the ground covered in trinkets – he kept glancing at Flick as though terrified. Flick wondered if it was because he had seen them come out of the suitcase. That had never bothered the people of Five Lights before. They were used to the strange and unusual.

But, clearly, things had changed.

Flick looked across the square and let out a gasp. Jonathan followed her gaze and did the same, and Tristyan put a hand on Flick's shoulder as they all stared up at the horrible sight before them.

The Thieves' headquarters, a huge tower on the north side of the square, was almost unrecognisable. It was blackened and streaked with ash. The roof had caved in and the windows were broken into shards. The mosaics and stained glass were black with soot and there were notices propped on the steps warning people not to enter the building.

'We're too late,' Tristyan said, his voice dry. 'The Seren have already been here.'

'They set the building on fire?' Flick breathed shakily. Jonathan had a hand to his mouth.

'This is what they do,' Tristyan said. 'If they cannot get what they want, they scour the place. This is precisely what they were doing before . . .' He broke off, his breathing catching and heavy in his throat.

Flick stared up at the ruined building, her stomach churning. 'We could have prevented this.'

'You didn't know this was going to happen,' Tristyan said, swallowing hard. 'You came here as soon as you knew the place might be in danger.'

This didn't make Flick feel any better and, by the look on his face, it didn't help Jonathan either. In silence, they turned from the scorched building and headed down the street to the place that their Five Lights guidebook recommended visiting in a crisis – the city Watch Patrol building, which sat like a fat white beetle at the end of a once-busy road.

The building had a domed ceiling and several columns on the front, each of which was carved with various patterns and shapes. When they got closer, Flick realised there was also a red flag fluttering pathetically from a pole outside, with the Thieves emblem – a hand clutching a bag with three coins inside – on it in fading gold thread. Flick felt relieved – the Thieves had gotten away, after all. Some of them, at least. She thought of her friend Nicc De Vyce. She was quick. Surely if anyone had gotten out in time, Nicc would have. Surely?

The three of them quickly went up the stone steps and pushed open the doors, to have their ears immediately assaulted with *noise*. The entrance hall of the Watch building was in chaos. Flick had expected a sort of police station, but instead there was what seemed to be a makeshift hospital in one corner, with beds and hanging sheets just about concealing patients from view. There were three desks with Watch officers sitting at them, and a queue of Five Lights citizens that snaked through the whole room waiting to see them.

There were Thieves arguing with each other in raised voices, and there were others slumped against the walls like dolls. A couple of Thieves were writing in books, others were repairing clothes. Watch officers were filling in paperwork on the floor, and children were skidding on their knees on the polished woodwork. It was chaos, but the sort where people know that it's better than not having it at all.

There was a red sign on the wall with some script on it that Flick couldn't read. But she thought that red probably meant Thieves, and there was an arrow on the sign pointing around a corner, so they all followed it. They didn't have far to go. Two dozen steps further down the corridor was a desk, planted awkwardly in the middle of the walkway, and at it sat a Thief in his forties, typing on what looked like a small electronic tablet, backed in wood. He had a frown between his eyebrows that was so deep it looked as though it had been chiselled in. A handwritten sign propped against a stack of books on the desk said "Overseer Cutpurse".

Jonathan cleared his throat. 'Excuse me, Overseer?'

The Thief looked up at Jonathan. Then down at the suitcase in Jonathan's hand. His dark eyes went wide. 'How in the blazes . . .'

'We're friends,' Flick said quickly. 'We know Nicc De Vyce. And we're the ones who got rid of Glean and her gang.'

The new Overseer got to his feet. Though only about as tall as Jonathan, he had a fierce look in his eye that marked him immediately as someone not to cross. His black hair was even longer than Tristyan's, and plaited back out of his rugged brown face with a skein of scarlet ribbon that fell to his knees. Unlike Glean, who had worn waistcoats and fitted trousers with only hints of red in them, Overseer Cutpurse's garments were like those of the other Thieves Flick had seen – billowy sleeves and deep-red robes fastened tight at the waist with a golden sash. There were blackened burn-marks all over his clothes. 'I know who you are, Strangeworlders,' he said tightly.

'We are . . . so sorry . . .' Jonathan said. He trailed off, clearly unsure what to say.

'Can you tell us what happened?' Tristyan asked. 'Who did this to you?'

'Is Nicc all right?' Flick added quietly.

Cutpurse sniffed. 'We still don't understand half of it ourselves,' he said angrily to Tristyan. Then he looked at Flick and seemed to soften. 'Come with me.' He led the three of them past another makeshift hospital (Flick turned her face away as they passed the curtains), and down a corridor to a room where more Thieves were sitting together around a cluster of low tables. Some were eating, some writing, others haggling with one another for items they had taken. They all looked pretty worse for wear, and some of them wore bandages.

Cutpurse went over to a small group and Flick thought she saw the back of a familiar head. The head turned at Cutpurse's approach and then, before she knew it, Nicc was hugging her tightly and Flick was letting out a breath she hadn't realised she'd been holding.

When they finally separated, Flick noticed Nicc's clothes were black rather than red, with a Watch logo embroidered on the chest – clearly borrowed. A red skein of ribbon worn like a sash across her chest was her only marker of belonging to the Thieves, and there was a strange squishy bandage on her forearm – it looked as though it was made of gel, and Flick guessed it was for a burn. Guilt seared through her. *What had happened here?*

As if echoing her thoughts, Tristyan spoke. 'Can you tell us what happened?' he asked, for the second time.

Nicc looked to Cutpurse, and he gestured for them to follow him over to a quiet corner, where they all sat down on the floor. Then he nodded at Nicc, and she began.

'They appeared in the city a few weeks ago. They came straight to us, which was a bit odd – who comes to Thieves, we wondered? – and said they were travellers, studying the worlds. They gave us trinkets and valuables, and seemed like kind people. So, when they asked for our help, we helped them.'

'What did they need your help with?' Tristyan asked.

'They said they were cataloguing the progress of the large schism,' Cutpurse said. 'All they wanted at first was to watch what happened as we released magic back into it, through their magnifying glasses. Harmless enough, we thought.'

'But then they started asking questions,' Nicc said,

grimly. 'They suddenly wanted to know where Glean was, and Swype, and the others you banished out of this world.'

'They were looking for Glean?' Flick asked. She looked at Tristyan. 'Why?'

'I don't know that name,' he said, 'but I can think of one good reason the Seren, and I think we can assume that is who these people were, would be hunting for someone. Did this Glean person always live here, in this world?'

'No,' said Nicc. 'She and her gang came from somewhere else, but no one has ever been sure of where.'

Tristyan's mouth tightened. 'They might have been escapees from the Seren.'

'That would make sense,' Jonathan said, adjusting his grip on the pink and gold suitcase. 'Back when we met her, Glean was very keen to escape from here without being followed. She said there was more at stake than we knew, and it looks like she was right.'

Overseer Cutpurse snorted. 'These Seren, if that's what they were, didn't believe that we couldn't locate Glean and her gang. And, when we continued to be of no help, they attacked. They used our own stockpile of magic against us and the rest of the city.

It's only fortunate we had released almost all of it back into the air on your instruction. I dread to think what they might have been able to do if they'd had access to more.'

'It wasn't just Glean they were after, either,' Nicc said. 'They were also searching for Darilyn and Greysen Quickspark. We sent someone out to their emporium to warn them, but the Quicksparks were gone. Not a suitcase to be seen. And there was something else the Seren were after, too.'

The Overseer snatched at thin air, and a piece of paper appeared in his hand. 'They spoke often of a box they wanted, though after one of them drew this picture for us it seems they meant *suitcase* rather than a box. They said it contained great power.' He held out the page, which was illustrated with a fine drawing of a scarlet suitcase with brown leather fastenings and gold trim.

Jonathan had gone white. He clenched hold of his own suitcase like it was a lifeline.

'They're looking for it,' Flick breathed. She looked at Tristyan. 'You were right, they're looking for Elara's suitcase.'

'I wish I was wrong,' he murmured, all the colour having drained from his face.

'We should go,' Jonathan said. 'There's no time to waste.'

'You must stop this from happening anywhere else,' Cutpurse said. 'Go back to your home and put an end to this, before they attack again.'

Jonathan dropped the suitcase and undid the catches.

As Flick approached the suitcase, Nicc grabbed her hand. 'If you need us, just get a message to us and we'll do what we can. We don't have suitcases or anything, but . . . if we can help, we will.' She gave Flick a tense smile. 'Be safe, won't you?'

Flick gave her friend's hand a tight squeeze. 'I'll be all right,' she said. 'I promise.'

CHAPTER FOUR

It would be a while before Flick stopped dreaming about the image of the burnt-out Thieves building, or the devastated, once-beautiful City of Five Lights. The Seren had sounded like a story at first, but now there was proof they were really out there, searching for the same thing Flick and her friends were looking for. The race was on.

Jonathan, with Tristyan's help (his bag, full of magical bottles, immediately came in useful as fuel to send enchanted letters to other worlds), contacted as many members of The Strangeworlds Society as he could, including his cousin Avery, to warn them about the Seren. All of the Society members sprang into action, with Mr Golding even bringing his grown-up daughter in to take the Society oath.

'The more the merrier, in this instance,' Jonathan had said, when Cassie Golding looked through a magical magnifying glass and confirmed she could see the golden blur in the air that was magic. Only Flick saw individual magical sparkles when she looked through one of Strangeworlds' magical magnifying glasses, but then there were a lot of things only Flick could do.

*

For the two weeks following their return from Five Lights, Flick hurried to the agency every afternoon after school. Each day, she and her friends made slow progress towards their goal of retrieving all the suitcases from around the multiverse.

At the strange left-luggage outpost known as The Station, they found a number of magical suitcases, which they dragged back to Strangeworlds before setting out again. Next, they revisited the world of an ethereal fae-like people, which only Jonathan amongst them had been to before. The world of Ikara, as it was called, was cold in many ways – the people spoke little – but they showed them to their single remaining suitcase and did not seem reluctant to let it go. In fact, they seemed glad to be seeing the back of it.

The icy, mountainous world of Snowmore, where Jonathan had once come close to cracking his head open, remained impassable. There was supposed to be a Strangeworlds outpost there somewhere, but there seemed to be no safe way down the mountain. Though none of them felt good about it, they simply pulled that suitcase back through with them, and were forced to call that one case closed. They just had to hope that the Seren were as vulnerable to cold temperatures as they were.

'They most likely are,' Tristyan said, as they sat shivering back at Strangeworlds. Flick, wearing two of Jonathan's cardigans, was practically crawling into the hearth in an attempt to warm up. 'The Seren extend their lives using magic, but their bodies suffer as a result. You could easily hurt one badly with a single punch – though you'd be lucky to get that close to them.'

'How come you can't get close?' Flick asked. Along with being cold, she was also exhausted. Travelling through world after world was extremely tiring, and they hadn't given themselves much time to relax and recover. Flick was struggling to keep her eyes open.

'The Seren can use magic to craft weapons and shields,' Tristyan explained, rubbing a hand over his face. He looked tired, too. 'It comes at a cost, of course, but it's very effective. If you're ever unlucky enough to come face to face with one, bear in mind they don't need to be holding a physical weapon to hurt you.'

'I'll bear that in mind,' Flick said. 'Can *anyone* make weapons out of magic?'

'Not, not anyone,' Tristyan said. He stretched his long legs out, and winced. 'Only those with the right training and some natural ability to manipulate magic can make a physical form out of it.'

'Can you do it?'

'I used to do it,' he said carefully. 'It's something I very much hoped not to have to do again, but if I had to . . . I could.' He gave her a strange look. 'Have you ever tried to give magic a physical form?'

Flick flinched. 'No,' she said. 'I've done stuff to schisms, but I've never made anything. You said only people with training could do that.'

'As far as I know, that's true. But I have to wonder, with your extraordinary abilities . . . you have saved two worlds with your powers, Felicity. You may be capable of even more.' He gave her a soft smile, his relatively young face not matching his grey hair or tired eyes.

Flick didn't smile back right away. At his mention of saving worlds, she had gone right back to the moment she had saved The Break – when magic had run through her like she was a conduit – and she had been aware of the emptiness of the space between worlds. The darkness that lurked around the edges of the multiverse.

The Inbetween.

She shuddered. Thinking about the existence of that dark place, and darker magic, scared her, right down to her bones. Magic was a part of who she was, a part of what made her special, but schisms were things to be feared, and in a lot of ways, magic was too.

Tristyan waited quietly for Flick to organise her thoughts, with the patience of someone who has lived for hundreds of years and has time to spare.

One of the smokeless logs in the fireplace splintered, and orange sparks rose into the air, reminding Flick of how magical energy looked when seen through Strangeworlds' magical magnifying glasses.

'I don't want this to turn into a fight if it doesn't have to,' she said. 'I don't want to make weapons. I'm not a soldier.'

'I know,' Tristyan said. 'Hopefully, it won't come to that.'

*

A few days later, on the second weekend of the anti-Seren suitcase rescue mission, Flick was sitting in the front room with Jonathan, while Tristyan was out in the back garden. He had taken up residence in Jonathan's spare room. He was very easy to live with, did more than his fair share of the chores and had even persuaded Jonathan to eat regular meals.

'I'd gotten so used to living by myself I thought having someone here might be intrusive,' Jonathan said to Flick. 'But apart from having to wash an extra set of cups and plates, you'd hardly know he was here. And to be honest, he does most of the washing up.' Jonathan was reading a report from Strangeworlds Society members Mori and Hudspeth – they were currently checking the remote world of Palomar for any remaining suitcases, without much success.

Within three weeks, every outpost listed in the *Study of Particulars* had been visited at least once, with the only exceptions being the House on the Horizon, and Thatcher's Apothecary in Inniss, where Tristyan had fled from. He had brought the only suitcase there back with him, and it had been pulled through and stacked with the others that were rapidly taking over the building.

Flick and her friends also sent a magical note to the pirates of The Break, warning them to be on the alert for anything strange or unusual, and promising to visit them in person as soon as they could. Flick's stomach still jolted when she thought about that world and its abandoned lighthouse, but given that they already had the only way in or out of the place (that they knew of), hunting in it wasn't high on their list of priorities.

As they had combed the multiverse for suitcases, they had cross-referenced their findings against the list they had of Strangeworlds Outposts.

A Comprehensive List of Strangeworlds Society Outposts (correct as of 1987)

Strangeworlds Travel Agency – flagship base, Earth. A custodian is available at all times. Strangeworlds is home to seven hundred and forty-three suitcases – the largest number of any posting. Established by Elara Mercator in 1873.

Contact: The Mercator family.

Quickspark's Travel Emporium – secondary base, Five Lights City. Custodians can be contacted at all times. Home to a small number of suitcases. Established by Elara Mercator in 1880.

Contact: The Quickspark family.

Phaeton's Trading Post – secondary base, Mount Snowmore. Custodians are family in nearby village. A handful of suitcases and supplies available. Established by Nicolas Mercator, 1965.

Contact: Maskelyne.

The Laughing Dog Travel Station – emergency base, Palomar. Custodians may not be available and discretion is advised. Established by Margaret Mercator, 1952.

Contact: Lost.

Thatcher's Apothecary – emergency base, Inniss. No custodians on site. Apothecary, run by T. Thatcher. Established by Anna-May Thatcher, 1985.

Contact: ~~Aspen and~~ Tristyan Thatcher

The House on the Horizon – emergency base, Desert of Dreams. One custodian on site. Established by Elara Mercator, 1895.
Contact: Lost.

The Station – storage room, hidden in plain sight inside lost luggage office, Mandlaus Railway. No custodian at present. Use caution. Established by Nicolas Mercator, 1967.
Contact: None.

Non-Outpost Worlds that Contain Suitcases

Ikara – single suitcase left here for emergencies. Allies of Elara. A Fae-world. Magic and fae rules apply (see relevant guidebook). Contact established by Elara Mercator, 1912.
Contact: Pseida family.

The Break – single suitcase left here as a symbol of inter-world cooperation. Water world of changeable time and societal rules (see guidebook for full details). Accord first established by Henry L'Estrange, 1914.
Contact: ~~Captain Talia Jarvis, The Painted Soul~~
~~Captain Eyrea Doran, Davy Jones' Bride~~
Captain Nyfe Shaban, the Pirate Queen

The travel agency was slowly filling with suitcases and they had begun to use the cellar below the shop for storage as well. Like many of the buildings in Little Wyverns, The Strangeworlds Travel Agency had been built with a cellar carved into the sandstone below it, meaning there was more room below the shop than there was above. These man-made caves were useful, if not ideal – they got damp and sometimes even flooded in winter, so Jonathan was hoping it would be only a temporary solution.

In between their excursions to bring back more suitcases, Flick went to school and Jonathan slept. Tristyan had taken it on himself to sort out the scrubby back garden behind Strangeworlds. None of the Mercators had been gardeners, and for many years it had just been a place for the bins to stand. But Tristyan had picked up all the broken bottles and bricks and litter, and raked up the weeds, so there was a nice plot of earth ready to be sown with seeds. Tristyan was doing battle against the elements – the icy rain and wind was continuing through February, and it looked like his blank patch of garden would remain plantless for quite some time. He had asked Jonathan to order him a seed catalogue, but seemed very disappointed to learn that nothing would grow until spring.

'I think he's doing it to avoid thinking about anything else,' Jonathan said, one rainy evening, as Flick watched Tristyan at work from the back kitchen window. 'Not that I'm not grateful. But he's out there all day, even in this weather.'

Just then, Tristyan spotted Flick at the window and waved. Flick felt herself warming to him more than ever – his obstinate determination reminded her of her brother, Freddy. And of herself, too.

But in all their searching, there was as yet no sign of Elara's dangerous suitcase, or of any suitcase that might lead them directly to the House on the Horizon. Flick, unlike Jonathan, could tell how full of magical power a suitcase was, and whether it had been used recently. All she had to do was look at it through a Strangeworlds magical magnifying glass. None of the ones they had rescued so far had either been used recently or seemed full of world-ending potential.

The idea of such a suitcase being out there somewhere, anywhere, was terrible. Flick felt like she'd spotted a huge spider, blinked, and it had disappeared. It could be anywhere, lurking out of sight. Waiting.

*

Flick came into Strangeworlds after school at the end of the following week to be assaulted by a sharp smell of burning.

'What *is* that?' She propped the door open to let the smell out, despite the cold. 'It stinks, is something on fire in here?'

Jonathan looked up witheringly from the book he was reading. He was wearing a brown tweed suit, with actual leather elbow patches. 'I can't tell you what it is,' he said, with the air of someone who'd had enough several hours ago. 'It's a surprise.'

'Is the surprise that the kitchen has burnt down?'

Jonathan tutted. 'Steady on, I think my sides have split. Anyway' – he nodded at a brown paper bag on the desk – 'happy birthday.'

'Oh!' Flick grinned and blushed, picking it up. She hadn't expected him to remember. Her parents were working late and she'd been expecting a rather low-key birthday. 'Thank you.'

'It's frankly disgusting that you're a teenager,' he said, turning back to his book. 'The first five years are the worst.'

Flick unrolled the bag, expecting the contents to be something Jonathan had found in his junk room upstairs, but to her surprise a soft purple sweater poured out of the paper, the tag from the shop still attached. 'Oh, I love it,' she said, holding it up. 'Thank you.'

'You're welcome. I'm sick of you either shivering or stealing my knitwear.' But he was smiling as he said it.

'It's not stealing, it's borrowing.' Flick folded the jumper up. 'I'll wear it today, as long as we're not going anywhere warm.'

'We're not going anywhere at all,' Jonathan said. He licked a finger to turn a page. 'We're taking the afternoon off in your honour. And also because we're all exhausted, I have to add.'

Flick tried not to show how pleased she was. 'Thanks. So what's with the burning? I'm guessing you didn't try to cook this jumper.'

'Oh, if only it was that simple.' Jonathan lowered his book. He jerked his head in the direction of the kitchen. 'Go and see. And be nice,' he added, in an undertone.

Flick dropped her schoolbag on to one of the armchairs and went into the back of the shop, where the tiny kitchen was filled with a cloud of flour, powdered sugar, and smoke. Tristyan, back in his apothecary's apron, was bent over the table, concentrating hard over an object that looked vaguely like a loaf of brown bread.

'What are you doing?' Flick asked, making him jump. 'Did you bake something?'

Tristyan stood up quickly, standing in front of the table. 'Felicity. Flick. I wasn't expecting you back until—'

'We finish early on Fridays,' Flick said. 'What are you making?'

Tristyan's pointed ears began to go red. 'It . . . it isn't quite . . .'

'Did you bake a cake?' Flick asked, peering round him and feeling her face starting to go as red as his ears.

He sighed. 'In a fashion.' He moved aside to let her see.

A very brown, very crispy-looking cake sat on a plate. A wobbly magnifying glass was drawn on to it in white icing, which dripped down the side in a sort of slug-trail. It was sagging in the middle, like a sofa that had been sat on too many times, and looked worryingly shiny at the edges, as though it had been baked in bacon-fat.

It was very much a cake that deserved a sticker that said, 'You Tried'.

But Flick didn't have to force a smile. She was so enchanted by the effort that she almost wanted to cry. 'Oh, that's—'

'Terrible,' Tristyan finished for her, looking mortified. 'I'll throw it away.'

'No, don't,' Flick said quickly. 'It might be OK.'

They looked at each other with identically dubious expressions. Then burst out laughing.

Flick gazed back at the cake. 'Did you run out of things to do in the garden?'

'Not really,' he said, dusting at his apron. 'Actually, I, er . . . made it for you.'

Flick looked up at him questioningly, not trusting herself to speak.

'Jonathan told me that it's your birthday,' Tristyan said, falteringly. 'I didn't have any money to buy you a gift, and Aspen always used to say cakes were traditional.' He sighed again as the magnifying glass melted further, icing plopping off the side on to the plate. 'I just wanted to . . . do something nice for you.' He looked miserably at the cake.

Flick didn't know what to say. For the first time since she'd found out who Tristyan really was, he didn't feel like just a friend. He felt like more. 'Thank you,' she managed to croak. 'I really love it. No one's ever made me a cake before. My mum always buys them, and – this is special.'

Tristyan practically sagged in relief. 'I'll clean up in here, and we can try it?'

Flick took the cake over to the cleanest bit of the worksurface and looked at it again. A cake, made for her. All right, it was burnt and soggy and possible inedible, but it was for her. Specially. She looked back at Tristyan sweeping up his mess of flour and felt her heart ache. But it was a good ache. It felt right.

Jonathan managed to restrain himself from commenting on the state of the cake when Flick brought it through into the front of the shop, and he even produced a candle (a massive white one saved for power cuts) from the back of a drawer and rammed it into the top. 'Should we sing?' he asked.

'Absolutely not,' Flick hissed. She blew the candle out.

Tristyan cut the cake, and it really wasn't too bad at all with a cup of tea. It was a strange sort of birthday, Flick thought, eating over-cooked cake made by a family member she'd only met a few weeks before, while sitting in a magical travel agency. But, as she glanced first at her best friend and then at her grandfather, she realised she felt completely comfortable and happy.

When it was time to head home, it was Tristyan who took her to the door. 'Many happy returns,' he said. 'I'm sorry it wasn't anything better.'

'It was the best,' Flick said honestly. 'Thank you.' She hesitated, then quickly moved to give Tristyan a hug. At first he flinched in surprise, but after a second he responded, hugging her gently. She stepped back and gave him a bit of a stupid smile. 'See you.'

'Take care,' he said. And it didn't sound like he was saying it in the way people did when they wanted you out of their way and gone. It felt like he actually wanted her to take care. It felt the same way it did when her dad said it to her.

It felt like family.

CHAPTER FIVE

'I would like to go to the lighthouse you spoke of,' Tristyan said, the next day. 'And gather Clara's things – the photographs and books she left there, I mean. She was studying magic, and I would not wish for her work to fall into the hands of the Seren.'

'Of course,' Jonathan said. 'There could be all sorts of sensitive materials there.'

Flick didn't say anything. She didn't like the thought of going back to that world – even though it would now be her fourth trip, and nothing really bad had ever happened to her there. But Tristyan had every right to want to collect his daughter's belongings, and, besides, the place would now be teeming with pirates and mer-people. Still, when Flick thought of it, she couldn't shake off the feeling of emptiness and coldness of the lighthouse itself; nor the memory of that abandoned picnic on the beach, or the drag-marks carved into the damp sand.

And yet, each time she went there, she had learned something important. First, that Daniel Mercator had been there. Second, that Tristyan was the man in the photographs scattered over the desk. And the last time she was there, she had delivered the pirates of The Break to their new home and learned that she was capable of using a magic she hadn't known existed to stretch a schism large enough to sail a ship through. She had even dreamed about the place. She just hadn't planned on going back before she had to. But she could hardly say no to Tristyan's request.

Her quiet discomfort had been noted.

'Would you rather stay here, Flick?' Tristyan asked kindly.

'No, I'll come,' she said. 'It sort of feels like I have to be there, even if I don't want to be. I've never liked it. Maybe it'll be different now the pirates are there, but when I was alone . . . it felt like I was the only person – the only creature – alive in that world. Like everything else had just been . . . wiped away. If it had ever been there at all.'

*

They stepped out of the suitcase on to the sand, which was as dry and featureless as Flick remembered it, at least as far as she could see. The flat, waveless sea barely moved against the shore, making the smallest ripples on the skin of the water. In the distance, Flick could just make out a moving dot, which was likely to be one of the pirate ships she had rescued from The Break. The sight made her feel a little better, and some of the sour-feeling tension she had been carrying seemed to ease.

Jonathan pulled a face at the sand beneath his brogues, picking up the suitcase and dusting it delicately. 'Delightful. I'd forgotten how much I enjoyed my brief stay here.'

Tristyan was looking at the lighthouse. 'Is that the lighthouse you mentioned?'

'Yes,' Flick said. 'Why?'

'Because it's not a lighthouse,' he said softly. 'That is a storm-tower.'

'A what?' Flick asked as they started walking.

'A storm-tower. We have them in Inniss. The globe on the top harnesses lightning.'

'Oh.' Flick frowned. 'I thought it was used to show ships where the cliffs were.'

'What ships?' Jonathan asked her. 'There weren't any here until you brought them.' As they reached the grassy top above the sand, he turned to Tristyan. 'Harnesses the lightning *how*? For *what*, exactly?'

'Storm-towers capture the electricity produced by lightning and store it. It can then be used to power machinery, and so on.' Tristyan shrugged. 'Quite dull, really, but I do have to wonder why one is here, of all places.'

'I didn't see any machinery inside,' Flick said.

'The plot thickens,' Jonathan said, ominously.

They had arrived at the tower, and Tristyan shoved the door open for them all to get inside.

It was exactly how Flick had left it. The papers on the desk, the spiral staircase in the centre of the room, the cold absence of life.

Tristyan went straight over to the desk. He picked up some of the loose photographs and his face suddenly creased in a grimace of grief, which he quickly got control over and erased. 'She brought all of these here,' he said softly.

Flick glanced up the staircase. 'I'm going to go up to the top.'

'Rather you than me,' Jonathan said, looking uneasy. 'Last time I almost went over the railing.'

Flick went up the spiral once again. The cold metal of the handrail was biting, and she tried to use just her fingertips to grip it. At the top, there was a cut-out in the floorboards that she climbed through. Waist-height wood-panelling gave way to a dome of glass, rising high above her head. A locked hatch in the wood led outside to a slender balcony with a brass rail.

The basket of toys she had seen the last time was still there, undisturbed. The rabbit with one eye seemed to be glaring at her, and she had an urge to turn it to face the wall. The dome of glass made her feel confined. The silence somehow seemed very loud.

She looked around, thinking about what Tristyan had said. At first, she couldn't see how this storm-tower was different from a lighthouse. But as she stepped closer to the glass and looked properly, she could see the joins where the panes of glass met each other had fine, silvery-white wires running through them. There were also what looked like electrical cables running from the edge of the glass and downwards through the gaps in the floorboards, before converging together and going upwards along the sides of a sort of pedestal in the middle of the room. There was nothing except a brass ring fastened on to the top of that, about as large as a bicycle tyre. It looked a little like the sort of attachment you screwed a lightbulb into, except that it was much bigger, and had exposed, naked wires reaching into the empty space.

'Are you all right?'

Flick jumped.

'Sorry.' Tristyan's upper body emerged from the hole. 'You were being awfully quiet up here.'

'I was looking at that,' Flick said, pointing at the pedestal. 'Where it looks like a bulb should go.'

'Yes,' Tristyan said, frowning. 'I wonder what was there. Perhaps whatever was being powered by the tower. It looks as though something was forcibly removed.'

There was nothing else to see and so they headed back down the stairs together. 'I feel daft thinking it was a lighthouse, now,' Flick said, as she followed him.

'You'd never seen a storm-tower before, you weren't to know.'

Jonathan was waiting at the bottom. All of Clara's papers and books had been packed in the tote bag they'd brought with them. The only thing left on the desk was the walnut box Flick had knocked to the floor on a previous visit.

'Aren't you taking that?' she asked Tristyan.

'Actually, I'm going to use it to try and let her know we've been here.' Tristyan touched the box with a hand. 'Hopefully, she still has the key with her.' He brought a bead of magical glass out from his pocket and broke it carefully right on to the lock. 'The magic searches for two halves, you see. It wants to connect them,' he explained. 'The lock, whether it's in use or not, needs a key. The key will feel the pull of the lock, and the person who owns it will become aware of it.'

'How?' Jonathan asked.

'It varies, but usually the object becomes hot or cold to touch.' Tristyan took his hand away from the box and stood back. 'Unfortunately, there would be no point in trying to send Clara a magical note. It would only end up in your hands, Felicity.'

Flick blinked. Of course. Blood-magic notes searched for the addressee or the addressee's closest relative – closest in terms of distance. It went to whoever it could reach first. And Flick was Clara's niece. Though that felt extremely strange to think about. To try and push the thought away, she took out the brass magnifying glass and looked through it. As expected, magic swarmed through the air plentifully, though less thickly around Clara's papers and books. The walnut box, however, freshly invigorated through Tristyan's spell, was glowing white.

Flick lowered the glass. 'Why do you think Clara came here?' she wondered.

'And why did she leave?' Jonathan added. He frowned, thinking. 'My dad came here too. We know because he left his notebook. Do you think they knew each other?'

'It's possible,' Tristyan said. 'Clara was studying magic. Perhaps their disappearances are connected.'

Flick glanced up, thinking of the empty brass ring at the top of the tower. 'I keep coming back to this place,' she said. 'Over and over. I broke in here when it was meant to be locked. I saved the pirates and the mer-queen by sending them here. And now . . .' She trailed off, wondering. 'It's like . . . the multiverse *wants* me to be here. Like there's a clue I keep missing.'

'Like fate?' Jonathan asked, sceptically. 'I'm not sure I believe in that sort of thing.'

'But believing in magic is totally normal?' Flick looked up again. 'What could have been taken from that fixture?'

Tristyan shook his head. 'It didn't look to me like something had been taken. More as though something had exploded.' He shook his head. 'I think something went wrong here. Very, very wrong.'

CHAPTER SIX

With no new breakthroughs or finds, the mission to pull suitcases back through into Strangeworlds became almost monotonous. And since no one they met had seen anything unusual, Flick started to relax. The Seren began to feel more like a fairy tale than a threat.

But then they received a message from Overseer Cutpurse that Greysen and Darilyn Quickspark had reappeared in the city of Five Lights, and Flick was reminded just how real the Seren were. Flick and Jonathan quickly went through to Five Lights to hear the Quicksparks' story.

'We didn't know who or what they were,' Darilyn said, sipping at a glass of water that Overseer Cutpurse had given her. 'But we knew they were trouble as soon as we saw they had a magnifying glass and were watching the schism. Given what had happened with Glean and her gang, we decided not to wait for them to find us.'

Greysen and Darilyn had then spent the next few weeks in hiding, having piled all their suitcases into one that was easy to carry. They had travelled through to a quiet world where magic was nothing more than a story, and waited until they felt it might be safe to return to the city. When they did, they had seen the devastation, and had felt both guilty and relieved at their narrow escape.

'Leaving was a wise move,' Jonathan reassured them. 'From what we've heard, you had a narrow escape.'

'The cases we have are all in here,' Greysen said, handing over a battered brown suitcase. 'Pull them through to wherever you'd like.'

'You're very welcome to come back with us as well,' Jonathan said. 'If you don't feel safe.'

'I don't think the Seren will be interested in us without our suitcases,' Darilyn said. 'If there comes a time when it's safe for us to take care of the cases again, we will gladly do so. But until then, they will go back with you.'

Flick felt rather conflicted about leaving the

Quicksparks behind in Five Lights, but that was their home world, and there was nothing else to be done.

She stepped back through the pink and gold Five Lights case with Jonathan and landed back in Strangeworlds with her head fuzzy with worry and thoughts.

Jonathan thumped the suitcase down on the desk and cricked his back. 'Another bunch to search through and sort.' His eyes flickered over to the clocks on the mantelpiece, and his mouth thinned a little.

'What are you thinking?' Flick asked. 'Are you worried about time? I still have a while before I need to get home.'

'No, I'm wondering about something,' he said vaguely.

'No secrets.' Flick held up a finger in warning. 'Remember the agreement.'

'It's not a secret,' Jonathan said hurriedly. 'It's just . . .' He bit his lower lip for a moment. Then he went over to the suitcase wall and pulled down a heavy green-leather and wood-trim affair. It was stained brown in places, and the leather had been delicately carved in places with a leafy pattern.

'I like it,' Flick said, as Jonathan handed it to her. It

was large, so she had to balance it on her lap. 'It looks like a forest.'

'It is,' he said. 'Foresta Major.'

'Oh, there's a clock for this world,' she said, nodding at the mantelpiece. 'Is that what you were looking at?'

'The clock reminded me about it, yes, but I've been thinking about it for a while. You see, this world . . .' He took hold of the catches that were facing him and tried them. They held fast.

'It's locked?' Flick guessed.

'Like the Lighthouse world was. Only this is a much older lock than that one. This one has been locked for about ninety years.'

Flick stared down at the green leather suitcase on her knee, thinking. She had broken the lock that held the Lighthouse suitcase closed, broken into a locked world without even meaning to. Was she being asked to do so again? She felt very uneasy about it.

Tristyan chose that moment to come down from upstairs where he'd been taking one of the brief naps he had instead of nightly sleeps. He paused in the doorway between the kitchen and the shop and, seeing the suitcase perched in Flick's lap, and the solemn faces of the two younger people in the room, all his sleepiness seemed to evaporate. 'What's wrong?'

'Nothing's *wrong*,' Jonathan said. 'I've just thought of somewhere we haven't checked yet. An outpost.'

Tristyan walked over and peered at the suitcase in Flick's lap more closely. 'Somewhere we can travel to?'

'I think so, if Felicity can work her magic on the suitcase.' He stood and vaulted over the desk to get to the bookcase. 'See, there's a world called Foresta Major. One of the first outposts The Strangeworlds Society ever established. It was abandoned. No,' he paused, pulling out a tattered guidebook from the shelves. 'No, actually that's not quite accurate. The Society left the world because they were *asked* to, by the people who live there.' He flipped through the pages to find the correct passage.

'Another outpost?' Flick asked, putting the suitcase down. 'But we checked all the ones on the list.'

Jonathan nodded as he turned pages. 'I think we can safely assume the page mentioning it was removed from all of the copies of the *Study of Particulars*, due to the circumstances . . . ah, this is what I was looking for.' He put the battered-looking book down, open on the desk.

Flick leaned over the desk to see a handwritten account of the story.

. . . and so, we have been asked to take our leave of this world by the people whose home it is. I must admit that many of the Society members were initially opposed to leaving this place behind, but I reminded them of our Society oath, and their hearts were swiftly put back in the right place. After all, as our own *Study of Particulars* says: we are not, as some have assumed, the rightful lord of new lands – we are merely travellers, seeking peace and understanding.

'And they just left?' Flick asked.
'Keep going,' Jonathan said, turning the page.

Elara Mercator oversaw the emptying of the Great Glasshouse, and the return of the suitcases that had been stored there to the travel agency. She forbade anyone to enter the Glasshouse whilst she spoke at length with the leaders of the people of Foresta and emptied the building of its suitcases. Then she officially accepted their orders to leave.

This is a record to show that all suitcases have been removed from the world of ~~Foresta Major,~~ Pendularbor and that The Strangeworlds Society is never again to enter into that world without *dire necessity. This is an agreed treaty, and here ends the account and guidebook for this world.*

The writing stopped there and the rest of the ancient notebook was empty pages.

'Pen-dul-ar-bor?' Flick sounded out the new word in the book.

'Oh.' Jonathan pushed his glasses up. 'That must be what the people of that world call it. Foresta Major was what the Society called it. Rather colonialist. I think we should call it Pendularbor from now on.'

Flick nodded, then reread the page. 'The Great Glasshouse? I wonder what that is. And why Elara didn't let anyone else inside whilst she was emptying it. Maybe she kept it private for a reason.'

'The suitcase,' Tristyan said. 'It would have been the perfect place to hide it.'

'Precisely what I was thinking,' Jonathan agreed. 'She may have arranged to leave a suitcase or two behind.' Jonathan raised his eyebrows pointedly. 'It's the last remaining outpost that we haven't tried, and the only locked suitcase here. Worth a visit?'

'Definitely,' Flick said. 'Should we ask any other Society members to come with us?'

'I think the fewer the better,' Jonathan said. 'The

Strangeworlders were asked to leave and never return, after all. We don't want to look like we're expecting a fight.'

'It wouldn't come to that, would it?' Flick asked nervously.

'We have to hope it won't. We've nothing to fight with, anyway.'

Tristyan shrugged. 'There's a bag full of magic upstairs that could easily become a weapon in the right hands. If we needed it.'

Flick actually gasped. 'You can't use your magic like that, Tristyan! *You* need it to live.'

'I can afford to lose some of it,' he said calmly. 'I've lived a long time as it is. I don't mind using it to keep you and your friend safe, or for the good of the multiverse.'

Flick stared at him. 'But none of us should have to lose anything to make the multiverse safe. I don't want you to.'

He gave her a very level look. 'I shall do my best to avoid it, Flick. I promise.'

Flick wondered if they were doing the right thing. She reached into her pocket to touch the eyepatch once worn by Nyfe Shaban, Pirate Queen of The Break. Running her fingers along it comforted her slightly – underneath the leather patch was a piece of magical magnifying glass, which Flick could use to observe magic while having both of her hands free. Jonathan had the old brass magnifying glass she used to carry. Between the two of them and these tools, she hoped they would be able to find the old Glasshouse outpost, or what was left of it, and see if Elara Mercator really had left anything behind.

*

Their departure to the world of Pendularbor was, however, slightly delayed.

The next day, as Flick was sending a text to her parents lying about a piano exam that would buy her extra time before going home, one of the suitcases in the wall began to move of its own accord. Jonathan, recognising the signs, backed away from it immediately. As the suitcase shoved itself further out of the slot, Flick and Tristyan did the same and not a moment too soon.

The bright yellow suitcase tumbled out of the wall, landing hard on the floor. Dust sprang into the air. A second later, the top flew back and a slightly dishevelled-looking Avery Eldritch clambered out of it, rubbing her head.

'Ow,' she said, by way of a *hello*.

Flick didn't even think twice. She launched herself at Avery like a javelin, wrapping her into a tight hug that was, thankfully, returned. 'Where have you been?' Flick demanded, as she let go.

'Nice to see you as well.' Avery sighed, cricking her neck. 'My parents went completely bananas after the last time. Two days I was gone for, and they were climbing the walls. We ended up falling out about all this in a major way, and they said I wasn't allowed to—' She stopped as she caught sight of Tristyan.

'Avery, this is Tristyan,' Flick said. 'He's – he's my – my, er . . .'

Avery frowned as she held out a hand to shake Tristyan's. 'You're Flick's . . . uncle? Cousin? You've got the same nose, so you must be someone.'

'Grandfather, actually,' Tristyan said, smiling as Avery did the smallest of double-takes. 'It's a long story.'

'Tristyan's a friend of the Society, too,' Flick said. 'And he knows who was stealing the magic from The Break.'

'Oh, now *that* I'm interested in,' Avery said, planting herself into one of the armchairs. Her once-spiky short black hair had grown a bit and she had to push it back out of her eyes. 'Some pains in the magical bum called the Seren, right? Jonathan mentioned them in his letter, but he was a bit vague on the details.'

They quickly filled in the blanks for Avery. She took the fact that they were once again on a multiverse-saving mission in her stride. Hearing that Flick was going to break into a locked suitcase, she shot her an approving glance, which made Flick feel like she'd swallowed a bagful of cotton wool.

'Well, I'm in,' Avery said, getting to her feet again as the story ended. 'I think you're going to need all the help you can get. And besides, you need someone with charisma on the team.'

Despite Avery's attempt at a joke there was an air of tension, because things felt serious now. The four of them were heading somewhere The Strangeworlds Society had been banned from ever entering again. And they were searching for the most dangerous suitcase in the multiverse.

CHAPTER SEVEN

There were three suns, all blazing brightly in a line, against a lilac sky. There were so many trees and plants around, Flick felt as though she was walking through a colossal greenhouse. She'd never been to the Eden Project, but she'd seen it on TV, and this felt just like that looked. Despite the triple suns, the air was moderately cool, like early autumn. Flick zipped her jacket up a little.

For all the beauty of the world around her, Flick felt nervous. Unlocking the suitcase to get there had been difficult, requiring so much concentration that Flick had a headache by the time the catches finally released. Her nerves weren't helped by the fact that Tristyan had decided to bring his magic-bottle-slung belt with him, buckling it over his old brown apron, Daniel Mercator's waterproof jacket on top.

'Why the apron?' Flick had asked, trying to think about that rather than why her grandfather had brought a beltful of potential weapons with him.

'Aprons are useful,' he replied. 'Big pockets, for one. And they protect your clothes. Never underestimate the value of a good apron.' He smiled the same smile Flick's dad gave when he was teasing her, and Flick felt a little better.

'Be careful where you step,' Jonathan said, flipping his guidebook open as Avery pulled the suitcase through into the lush green world. 'The plants here are alive.'

'All plants are alive, Jonathan,' Flick pointed out.

'The plants here are *sentient*,' he said, with an eye-roll. 'They have feelings. They can communicate.' He passed the handbook over. 'Plants back home don't have much social structure.'

Flick read out loud:

World: ~~Foresta Major~~ Pendularbor
  People: Tree-folk. Refer to themselves as 'the people'. Although the people in Foresta appear humanoid, they are actually plants rather than

animals, and appreciate being referred to as such. Their life-cycle is complex and detailed overleaf.

Points to note: All plant-life in this world is capable of communicating. Some leaves change colour, some flowers make noises. Vines are capable of grasping hold of anything and anyone they take a dislike to. Make yourselves known to the people on arrival. Beware of anything with thorns and prickles – the plants here see attack as the best form of defence and will actively reach out to try and scratch you. Assume everything you see is venomous, and do not eat any of the vegetation.

Flick winced at the thought of being dragged into the looming trees by some vines that had decided she wasn't supposed to be there. 'This place just got a lot more frightening. Thanks for that.'

'Yeah . . .' Avery looked around uncomfortably. 'Love to be walking through a forest where everything is either poisonous or venomous.'

'Nothing wrong with a healthy dose of fear,' Jonathan said, though he glanced nervously at a squat bush covered in white berries beside him as though it might be getting ideas. 'Perhaps we should stick to the path, such as it is.' He indicated a thin trail of dirt cutting through the grasses and ferns. 'It should reduce our likelihood of stepping on anything, at least.'

They set off slowly, all four of them watching their step. Avery dropped back to walk beside Tristyan, and Flick and Jonathan took the lead. The trail they were following was so thin there were moments when it disappeared altogether.

Flick was trying to skim through the guidebook to Pendularbor as they walked. 'Where are the people?' She turned a page. 'Is there a village? A settlement?'

'I'm not sure.' Jonathan pushed his glasses up his nose. 'Perhaps *they* will find *us*.'

'You're not helping the creep factor, you know,' Avery said.

As they walked, the feel of the forest around them began to change. Flick remembered reading a book once that showed how life in the oceans got bigger and bigger the deeper you went – there had been a wonderfully detailed picture of a colossal squid gripping a submarine to go with this idea. And it seemed to her that Pendularbor was the same. The further they walked into the forest, the taller the trees began to grow. At first, they had been as tall as regular birch trees on Earth. Then, as tall as a house. Then, higher than a church spire. Then, too tall to see the top of . . .

'This is weird,' Flick said softly. She didn't know why she was whispering. The presence of such large, and clearly ancient, trees seemed to demand that she lower her voice. It wasn't that she was worried about frightening them; she was almost hoping that they wouldn't notice *her*. She stopped walking, and looked up at the leaves and the sky, green on dark green, the light like stained glass in the air.

Tristyan stopped beside her, gazing up too. He looked very uncertain, his mouth tight and arms rigid, hands tucked into his pockets.

'You think these trees can hear us?' Flick asked softly.

'I wouldn't like to say,' Tristyan replied, in the sort of quiet voice you usually save for libraries. 'I'm quite sure they won't bother us if we don't bother them.' He looked back at Flick. 'But I get the feeling we're unwelcome.'

Flick nodded. 'I hope the people, wherever they are, are OK with us being here.'

The wind blew then, as if on cue, and made the leaves of the trees looming overhead slap together. Flick wondered how big each leaf was – they looked enormous from the ground – and what would happen if one of them fell. She imagined it would be like being hit with a deflated bouncy castle.

As they walked on, the great trees became spaced further apart, though the gaps between were filled with thick, rubbery-looking vines that reminded Flick horribly of coiled snakes. Some shafts of sunlight cut through the boughs to the ground. Here and there were patches of flowers and smaller plants that seemed grateful just to have a little bit of forest floor to themselves.

'Flowers,' Flick noted, 'but no bees that I can see.'

'There might not be bees, here. Other insects, maybe. Or perhaps creatures that come at night.' Jonathan hunched down in front of one of the plants and took a pencil from his waistcoat pocket. He quickly sketched the flower in one of the margins of his handbook, and measured it, using the pencil as a guide. 'For all we know, the flowers might not even be flowers. We can't assume we know what it is just because it looks a bit like something at home.'

Avery had her arms wrapped around herself much like the vines on the trees. 'You'd think someone would have heard us, by now.' She chewed at her bottom lip.

'I know,' Flick said. 'I can't think of a time we've arrived in a world and gone so long without being noticed. People usually can't miss us.'

'Especially Avery,' Jonathan said, without looking up.

'Hey!'

Flick laughed, and so did Tristyan, making Avery stick her tongue out at them both. But then she grinned at Flick, who smiled back and felt her nerves soften, just a little bit.

Jonathan gave the plant a gentle stroke with the pink eraser-end of the pencil, and then stood back up. 'Perhaps we should shout, or something?'

No one seemed keen on the idea, and if anything their surroundings seemed even quieter after the suggestion.

'I wonder how long the days are here,' Flick said. It seemed important to keep talking, as though conversation might work as a shield against danger.

'The years must be immense,' Jonathan said. 'There's three suns to go around, after all.'

'Are they clustered together in space?' Avery asked. 'Like grapes?'

'I'm not sure. They might be.'

Flick frowned. She remembered something about

stars, and gravity. 'Why don't they all pull together and . . . burst?'

'There must be enough of a pull from elsewhere to balance it out.' Jonathan shrugged. 'I don't know. I'm not Brian Cox.'

'Fine,' Flick said. Then looked around. 'We should keep going. We've got to find someone, eventually.'

It didn't take much longer. Soon, the trees changed again, and this time it was like the plants were blurring, changing from thick straight trunks of smooth grey-brown to twisted, vine-covered, flaking barks that were dappled with green and white. The trees were smaller now, too – only as tall as a house – with branches that reached down, raining thick ropes of leaves and snaking branches. They created dragging curtains of greenery that the travellers had to push aside to move through.

Bulb-shaped growths hung down from the thicker branches. The bulbs, or pods, were of various sizes. Some of them were the size of a guinea pig, but others were so big Flick could have climbed inside one, if it had been hollowed out.

'Is this a fruit?' she asked, lightly touching the outside of one of the smaller ones. It was pitted but smooth, and felt like the outside of an orange.

'I suppose it must be. I wonder how big they get . . .' Jonathan gently touched the one that was as big as Flick. 'It feels heavy. I wonder what the inside is like.'

Avery cupped one of the smallest ones in two hands. 'It's warm.'

'It's not in the sun,' Flick said.

Tristyan frowned. He was the only one of them not touching the fleshy bulbs. 'Are you sure you ought to be touching those? It seems a bit unwise to start touching everything you see, particularly when your book warned about poisons.'

'Mm.' Jonathan took his hand away. 'Good point. Anywhere else, I might suggest taking one down, and cutting it open, but . . . not here. It might hurt the tree. And I do not want to be on the bad side of anything here.'

Despite what Tristyan had said about poisons, Flick couldn't resist running her hands over the fruit, or whatever it was, once more. 'It's got a thick skin. It doesn't even give when you touch it—'

'Stop! Stop touching her!' A sharp cry cut through the air.

Flick snatched her hands away.

A woman – or someone who looked like a woman, at least – was barrelling towards them.

'I'm sorry.' Flick stepped back, her hands raised.

The woman ignored all of them and went over to the fruit, looking at it carefully and whispering to it, as she stroked her hands over the peel. She seemed to be wearing ragged sheets of green and grey moss. Her skin was calloused and thick, her arms deep brown, covered with scab-like patches. She was tall, and her hair was knotted into what Flick thought at first glance were thick plaits, but actually looked more like the vines and branches of the trees around them.

'Who are you?' The woman turned to them. Flick could now see that her face had the same dry skin as her arms, and her voice had a creak to it, like someone bending wood. Her eyes were the amber shade of an egg yolk. 'What are you doing here? Speak.'

'I'm Flick,' Flick said quickly. 'And this is Jonathan, Avery and Tristyan. We're from The Strangeworlds Society.'

There was a pause, and Flick felt as if she was waiting for an axe to fall.

The woman looked between them. When she spoke again, Flick could see the skin splinter around the hole of her mouth, as though she was a china doll who had been dropped face-down on the floor. 'I do not know this society you speak of. Where are you from? Why is your bark so smooth?'

'We, er, aren't from around here,' Jonathan said. 'We're from another world.'

The woman looked even less sure than before, but she didn't back away. 'Another world?'

'Yes,' Flick said. 'We need to speak to you. We're looking for something. Something . . . our people left behind here, a long time ago.'

'How long ago?'

'Perhaps ninety years – well, our years, anyway. Maybe more . . .' Jonathan said, trailing off.

The woman looked between the four of them again, and then finally nodded her head. There was an audible creak. 'I'm Kayda. There is one amongst us who remembers that far back. I'll take you to the Old Mother.' But she hesitated. It seemed as though she was still worried about something. 'What were you doing with the offspring?'

'The what?' Flick blinked.

'The babies,' Kayda said, putting a bark-covered hand to the bulbous fruit.

'Babies?' Flick frowned, but she could see a penny had dropped for Jonathan, whose mouth had dropped open.

'Oh.' Tristyan seemed to understand as well. He was looking up at the branches. 'Of course.'

'Of course, *what*?' Flick asked.

'The fruit seeds,' Jonathan said. 'They're baby trees, if you think about it. The seeds from fruit grow into trees eventually, don't they?' He took out the guidebook again, thumbing through the pages. 'I'm so sorry, Kayda, we didn't realise.'

'Oh.' Flick blushed. 'Babies. Huh.' She smiled.

But Avery was puzzled. 'How come they're so big?'

Kayda looked blankly at her. 'Because . . . that is how big we are?'

Avery still looked confused. 'But babies are small?'

There was a pause. 'Perhaps we ought to go and see the Old Mother,' Kayda said at last.

'Of course,' Tristyan said graciously, stepping aside for Kayda. She creaked and cracked past him, leading them all away from the baby-pods.

Kayda immediately took them off the path they'd been following until then. Her bare feet, calloused and brittle as the rest of her, swept over the grasses and fallen leaves like they were a red carpet. She walked quickly, almost skimming over the ground, so Flick and everyone else had to jog to keep up with her.

Flick tried to see as much of the forest as she could

as they almost ran through it. There were more of the baby-pod trees, other low bushes, draping vines with curling fingers. She was staring up at a particularly long, thick vine that seemed to be covered in poisonous-looking pustules, when she nearly bumped into someone ahead of her.

'Oh,' she said, 'I'm sorry. I didn't . . .' Flick looked at the face of the person. And felt her blood run cold.

It wasn't a person at all – it was a sort of statue in the loose shape of a person, but with a face as featureless and textured as the trunk of a tree. There was only a slight ridge in the face area that gave, if you were squinting, the impression of a nose. The statue, or whatever it was, had arms and legs, and hands and fingers, all visibly sticking out of the main body, which seemed to be made from a tree trunk. Branches with leaves were growing here and there along it. It was completely unnerving.

'Creepier and creepier,' Avery breathed, coming up behind her to look at it. 'I don't like it. Is it half-finished do you think, or did they make it that way on purpose?'

Flick shuddered. 'It looks like a person somehow melded with a tree.'

'Are you all right?' Jonathan had turned back for

them, glancing warily at the wooden figure. Ahead, Kayda had stopped and was watching them with blank curiosity. It was a moment before she came over to join them.

'Is there a problem?' she asked.

'I was just surprised by this statue,' Flick said. 'I thought it was a person!'

'It *is* a person,' Kayda said. She patted the statue's shoulder and smiled. 'She stood still a few months back. I miss her voice, but . . .' She shrugged.

Flick realised she was gawping again. 'That's . . . a person? A person like you?' The creepy feeling was back, this time running over Flick's skin like a swarm of insects. The figure's blank face seemed to be staring straight at her. Avery's mouth was wide open, and Tristyan and Jonathan were both staring in silent horror.

But Kayda was smiling as though this was all perfectly normal. 'Yes. It's unusual for someone to take to standing whilst so young, but Acacia was always very forward. She couldn't wait to grow up and put roots down.'

'Oh.' Jonathan's eyebrows had gone up, as had the pitch of his voice. 'Really.'

But Tristyan was nodding slowly. 'That explains the size of the babies.'

'Does it?' Flick asked. She kept her eyes on the statue-like person. She had a horrible feeling that if she looked away, it might move.

'Kayda,' Tristyan said, turning to their guide, 'your people metamorphose. Change? From one form to another?'

'Yes, there are three stages to our life,' Kayda said, walking on again. 'There is the seedling-stage, that's the pod which you saw, the child-stage like myself, and then the adult. You saw the pods growing beneath the adult tree. The larger ones will hatch soon, and the children will come out.'

'And when you grow up, you turn into trees.' Jonathan had a little smile growing on his face.

'We do not *turn into* trees. We *are* trees,' Kayda said firmly. 'We move about before putting down roots but we are still trees. We are trees from the moment our pods bud on the branches of our parents, and we are trees whilst we move around on the land. We simply have some growing up to do. Over time, our outer bark hardens, our roots seek out the soil, and the leaves we grow demand more height and sunlight. The Old Mother is the oldest of us who can still speak with a voice, though she has the appearance of a great adult tree. But even she will quieten down, eventually.' Kayda glanced back at the frozen wooden person. 'Acacia lost her face and voice before she even put down roots. We all grow at different paces, no two trees are alike. Our change is not something anything, or anyone, can predict.'

The trees, Kayda explained, collectively referred to themselves as a forest. They could communicate with all the other plants on the planet, which were also part of their 'forest'. It was rather confusing. But also amazing.

'On our world,' Flick said, 'people and trees are separate things.'

'But the trees on your world are alive, yes?'

'Yes,' Flick admitted.

'Then how are they not people?'

Flick didn't really know how to answer that without causing offence. 'Things are different on our world,' she said. 'The trees don't move about. Not even when they're young. They grow straight out of the ground from seeds, and stay where they are.'

Rather than looking confused or upset, Kayda looked delighted to hear of such a concept. 'Oh!' She pressed her wooden hands together. 'To have that connection with the land from the start! Not that we feel unconnected when we walk upon it, we are aware of the impact we have . . . but to put down roots as soon as you germinate? Wonderful.'

Flick smiled. Kayda was so completely happy with her own existence, it was refreshing.

'How do you communicate once you lose your voices?' Jonathan asked. 'Can you, even?'

Kayda sighed. 'We still communicate, young man. However, it is much slower. More refined. More considered. What might be a simple audible conversation would take several of our months to express once we lose our voices. That is why we are grateful that the Old Mother still speaks. She is passing on as much as she knows to as many of us as she can, so that we might do the same before we become voiceless. Since the process is unpredictable, it is important to spread information as widely as possible. Sadly, this does mean that sometimes the older tales are lost.'

'We are grateful to you for taking the time to take us to the Old Mother,' Tristyan said.

Kayda turned her head, though it moved rather stiffly. 'You are strange beings,' she said. 'You are like the smooth grubs that feast on the roots of young plants, though bigger. But you seem sincere, and we are a welcoming people.'

'I'm not a grub,' Avery muttered as Kayda

gestured to them to stop, pulling a disapproving face at the flattened vegetation the group had left in their wake.

'We could remove our shoes,' said Tristyan. 'That might help.'

They sat down on the grass to do so. Flick tied her laces together in a loop and hung them off her backpack as she had done on the pirate ships of The Break not so long ago. Jonathan did the same, stuffing his blue, white and pink-striped socks into his shoes.

The grass beneath Flick's feet felt thicker than the stuff in the back garden at home. It resisted the tread of her feet, refusing to move, as though she was stepping on to a carpet of old bicycle tyres instead of blades of grass. She saw Avery rock up on to her tiptoes and back down again.

'I guess this grass has never had to tolerate humans stomping around before,' Flick said.

'This grass covers most of our planet,' Kayda said. 'It is one enormous plant, and has been here since before my people.'

She led them on, and the forest suddenly opened up into a clearing. They had come to a forest of another kind – a kind where the trees walked about on legs and looked up in surprise as the visitors walked into the clearing.

Kayda ignored the stares and led the four of them over to what Flick thought at first was simply an enormous tree. It was as wide as a car was long at the base and the foliage above umbrella-ed out to cover so much of the sky that there was a noticeable drop in temperature once you stepped into its shadow.

What Flick wasn't expecting to see was what looked like the top half of a human body protruding from the tree's trunk, as though it was trying to climb out of it and escape. The torso itself was held in place by thick ropes of climbing vines, and one of its wooden arms seemed to be immobilized in the trunk itself. At first glance, the whole set-up seemed utterly horrifying, as if a person had been eaten by the tree.

But the soft rustling of the leaves and branches above was peaceful, and the person growing from the tree looked to be tranquilly asleep. Her eyes were closed, and her hair, Flick could now see clearly, was growing fast with the rest of the tree, holding her in place.

'Mother?' Kayda said gently, touching the sleeping face. 'Mother, we have visitors. They come from another world.'

CHAPTER EIGHT

The woman in the tree stretched, and a creaking noise filled the forest – like the sound made when you swing on a dry branch and it starts to give way. Dust and flakes of bark drifted into the air. She looked straight at Flick with amber eyes that felt very unsettling.

'Your people,' the woman rasped, 'were banished from this place.'

'I know. We would never have come if we didn't absolutely have to,' Flick said, taking a step forward. She felt incredibly nervous, but this was important. 'But we're looking for something. Something dangerous. And we think it might be here.'

The woman stretched again, and this time leaned further out of the tree as if she was going to climb out of it altogether. Her lined face looked wary. 'When your leader agreed to leave this place,' she said, 'she made an agreement with me and the other Old Ones. She would lock access to this world and never return, so long as she could leave some property behind.' She glared. 'And she did. Two things, in fact. One, a building. Two, a box. We agreed they could remain here, locked away safely. Have you come to seek these things?'

Flick nodded. 'I think so. Can you tell us where they are? We'll leave, as soon as we can, we promise.'

The Old Mother didn't reply for nearly a whole minute. She just stared at Flick, as if reading her mind. It was the least comfortable minute Flick could remember having waited through. When the Old Mother spoke again at last, she no longer sounded as brusque as before. 'Do you realise what the box contains?' she asked.

Flick could feel her friends shifting nervously behind her. 'I think so. Something . . . bad.'

The Old Mother shook her head. 'No, little one. You have *begun* in the right place, but you have far to go to find the Ending. For it is not the Ending that we have hidden here, merely the way to it. You will need to journey from here, to the place called the Glasshouse. And from there, using your magic, to the next place.

And there will be the final doorway leading to the end of all things.'

'That is a really well-hidden suitcase,' Avery said.

'Indeed.' The Old Mother gave her a cracked smile. 'Your leader hid it well on purpose. She said that if the time ever came when someone might consider using it, she wanted to give them plenty of time to think about what they were doing before they got there.'

'We aren't going to *use* it,' Flick said. 'I don't want to end the multiverse – I live in it. We just want to keep it safe . . . from the Seren.'

'Ah, the Seren,' the Old Mother mused. 'A group that were little more than a whispered rumour before Elara Mercator explained their nature and the threat they posed. We have often feared them discovering this world.'

Jonathan stepped forward. 'Because they might consume the magic here?'

The Old Mother nodded. 'The magic here is produced in immense quantities. I understand that the centre of the multiverse is the City of Five Lights – but *this* world, my world, is the greatest producer of pure magic in the entire multiverse.'

'Because of the plant life?' Tristyan clarified.

'Correct.'

Flick, curious, took her eyepatch from her pocket,

and pulled it over her head. She flipped up the fabric patch to look through the glass, and almost immediately had to shut her eye again.

The brightness was overwhelming. The world they stood in was positively bathed in golden light. Sparkles and glittering particles washed around every single inch of the place. It looked as though everyone was drenched in golden paint that was somehow moving over them like the liquid in a lava-lamp.

'This is extraordinary,' Jonathan breathed. He was looking through the little brass magnifying glass. 'I can barely see anyone, the air is so golden.' He looked at Flick. 'I can't even begin to imagine what this looks like for you.'

'Like swimming in glitter soup,' Flick said, pulling the eyepatch off. 'It's almost too bright to look at.' She turned back to the Old Mother. 'This is why you asked The Strangeworlds Society to leave, isn't it?'

'Correct. Such magic would be temptation even for those sworn to protect it.'

Flick saw Jonathan glance at the magnifying glass he held.

Tristyan looked as if he might faint. 'If the Seren ever got here . . . They would tear this place apart. How have you gone undetected for so long?'

'Elara Mercator locked our world tight,' the Old Mother said. 'Until you opened the way back in, we were hidden away completely.'

'And the Seren will be able to find you, now?' Avery asked, eyes wide.

Flick felt horror seize hold of her. If they'd put this world in danger just by coming here . . .

But the Old Mother shook her head. 'The Seren need a great deal of magic to cut their way into this world, and I don't think they have that capability, do they?'

Everyone shifted uncomfortably.

'They cut their way into Five Lights,' Flick said. 'They must have got enough magic from somewhere.'

The Old Mother's expression hardened. 'I see,' she said. 'Then you must act fast. The place you must journey to, the Glasshouse, is on the opposite side of this world.'

'Oh no, I hate walking,' Avery wailed.

'Fear not,' the Old Mother said. 'I know a shortcut.'

*

'A suitcase? Really?' Flick laughed as Kayda handed her a battered and moss-covered suitcase. 'What world does this go to?'

'It stays in this one,' Kayda said. 'It opens beyond the forest of our settlement, close to the Glasshouse left behind by your ancestor.'

'I've never come across a suitcase that opens within the same world before,' Flick said.

'It makes sense,' Jonathan said. 'Rather than keep a suitcase at Strangeworlds that could lead the Seren directly to the Glasshouse, Elara locked the suitcase away within Pendularbor itself. Another hurdle to jump.'

The people of Pendularbor insisted on giving the travellers a ceremony to wish them luck before they left. Flick hadn't known what to expect – music and dancing, perhaps – but the people simply held hands with one another and stood, stock-still and silent, in a circle. It was beautiful at first, but quickly felt rather awkward, like watching someone sleep.

'How do we know when they're done?' Flick whispered after about ten minutes. 'We're supposed to be going as quick as we can.'

'I'm wondering how rude it would be to just leave them to it,' Tristyan said. 'They're clearly not waiting for us to join in.'

Flick shifted on the dry fallen log they were sitting on, then yelped. 'Ouch!' She raised her hand up to see a sizeable splinter sticking out of her palm. 'I've been skewered,' she said, holding it out for Tristyan to see.

Tristyan peered at her hand. 'I didn't bring any tweezers with me, but . . .' He suddenly moved, quicker than blinking, and had pulled the splinter out before Flick could say anything about it. A droplet of blood welled in its place.

'Mega-ow,' Flick said, cradling her hand. 'This feels worse than before.'

'Let me see again?' He held his own hand out, and Flick plapped hers into it. 'It certainly was a large splinter.'

'You don't have to baby me,' Flick said. 'I'm OK with blood and stuff.'

He gave a small snort, not a million miles away from the snort Flick's dad gave when he didn't believe something. 'I should have thought to bring a first-aid kit with me. It's been so long since I did any real adventuring that I've forgotten how dangerous it can be.'

'It was only a splinter,' Flick said, embarrassed.

'Today, yes, but who knows what else might happen?' He examined the bloody puncture on Flick's palm, then gently blew on it like he was blowing away a feather.

Instantly, the blood vanished and Flick's skin healed over. 'Tristyan!' she gasped.

He sat back, a satisfied look on his face as she examined her hand.

'You healed it.' She gaped at him. 'I did something like that for Avery once, when she cut her face, using the magic in the air. You can't use these people's magic, though – we're meant to be protecting it!'

'It's all right, I didn't take it from this world,' he said. 'It was mine.'

She blinked. 'Your magic?' A hot feeling suddenly burned in her face. 'Tristyan, it was only a tiny cut! You can't give up bits of your own life for me like that.'

'Why wouldn't I?' He cocked his head to one side as if genuinely curious. 'Why wouldn't I help you, in any way I could?'

Flick inhaled, trying to think of an argument that wouldn't come.

Tristyan gave a small smile. 'You're my family, Felicity. I spent a long time on my own, after Aspen died and Clara left home. I want to use my remaining life as wisely as I can.'

'In that case it's not very wise to give some of it away,' Flick insisted.

He shrugged. 'My life has been stretched out and

worn thin enough. I want to use what's left of it to do good, in small ways and big ones. That's all I think we can ask of anyone.'

Flick looked across at the circle of tree-people, who had finally let go of one another's hands. Didn't Tristyan realise it wasn't just about him any more, that it would have an impact on *her* if he gave all his life away? 'Even when we've saved the worlds, again, that doesn't mean we have to pretend we don't know each other,' she said awkwardly, trying to explain. 'I mean, it's nice having friends . . . and relatives . . . in other worlds.'

'I think so, too.'

They all got to their feet as the tree-people came over.

'Your journey will include peril,' Kayda said. 'But you are brave. We hope you find what it is you seek. For all our sakes.'

'Thank you,' Jonathan said. 'We'll be back. Soon, I hope.' He knelt down and undid the suitcase, which groaned as the lid was lifted for the first time in a century. 'Are we ready?' He looked at everyone. 'Then let's go.'

CHAPTER NINE

They stepped out of the suitcase in front of a massive glass and metal building. It looked like an enormous Victorian greenhouse – a huge curved-top façade that rose several storeys high – with wooden front gates built into it. There were sweeping, wide glass corridors that ran outwards left and right from the central building. At the top of the main structure, right in the centre, the glass and metal twisted together and upwards into a tower that looked a bit like an oversized unicorn horn. At each end of the long corridors there was another pointed tower. They gave the place a weird look – like a church with crooked spires.

'So this is the Glasshouse,' Flick said softly, looking up at it as Jonathan pulled the case through after them.

The building loomed. It was no back-garden greenhouse. This was big enough to have swallowed Flick's house ten times over. Within the glass corridors, there were a great many plants. Some of them spilled through cracks in the glass, though lots near the ground were brown and dead. The vines and leaves and branches were so densely packed that very little light shafted down through them. That accounted for the dead plants at the bottom, Flick thought. They probably didn't get enough light. The inside appeared very gloomy.

As if reading her thoughts, Tristyan fished around in his apron pocket and took out what looked like half a dozen blue-white rubber balls. 'Here.' He handed them out. 'They're light-balls. Squeeze them, and they give you a few hours of light.'

Jonathan pocketed two. 'How do we get in?' he asked. It was a good question. The timber front doors were fastened tight by thick vines twisted together like chains. 'I don't suppose anyone thought to bring a saw?'

Avery patted her pockets. 'You know, I think I've forgotten to bring mine today, what a clown I am.'

Tristyan considered the vines, each one as thick as his arm. 'They're dead, I think. Hard, but brittle.' He took hold of a wooden branch and pulled hard. It snapped, breaking away from the doors ... only to reveal yet more twisting wood beneath it. 'Well, that's inconvenient,' Tristyan said, dropping the branch.

'Over here,' called Avery.

She had found a smashed window on the left-side corridor of the building. Branches were reaching out of it, but there just was enough room to wriggle past them and get inside, even if Tristyan struggled slightly.

'Urgh,' Avery wrinkled her nose in distaste at the stink of rotting plant matter. It was inescapable: there seemed to be more smell than air in the place. 'This is foul. It's like we've climbed into a bin. No thanks.'

Flick had a go at breathing through her mouth, but then she just felt like she was chewing on the thick smell, which made her gag.

'It is rather pungent,' Jonathan said, pinching his nose delicately.

The floor beneath their shoes was tiled in a thick terracotta, cracked in places so that plants and weeds and thorns grew upwards and out of it. There were branches and rope-like vines, squat bushes covered in luminous berries, vegetables that looked like blue aubergines, and desiccated fruits that had been left to rot and had turned into prune-like shrivels of all shapes and sizes.

But where the reaching arm of the Glasshouse connected to the main body of the building, they came to a door that was clearly plant-proof. It was painted thickly with a mural of yet more plants, made of metal and cold to the touch. A few plants had had a go at twisting themselves into it, but the most they had managed was poking at the hinges. There were no obvious handles. They all pushed it, but it wouldn't budge.

'Maybe it's like the door in *The Lord of the Rings*,' Flick said. 'Maybe there's a password.'

'Oh, please,' Jonathan said, rolling his eyes. 'That sort of nonsense only happens in books. No, I'm sure there's more likely to be a mechanism or a handle or something that we can't see for all these plants.'

Flick started to lift plants up to try and see beneath as Jonathan did the same. The leaves and branches felt slimy and gross. Tristyan, however, was examining the door with an interested look on his face. 'I wonder . . .'

'Wonder what?' Flick asked, watching as he ran a hand over the metal surface. 'Can you see something?'

In answer, Tristyan put a single finger to the gap,

and pressed as lightly as if he were trying to pick a speck of dust from a piece of delicate crystal.

The door swung ever so slowly outward at his touch, moving at a slug's pace. It groaned noisily, stopping halfway open as brown dust rose into the air, making all of them cough.

'*How* did you do that?' Flick choked out, hand over her nose and mouth.

'Sometimes, less force is needed than you think,' Tristyan said, wafting his hand in front of his face. The dust had settled over him like cocoa powder. He coughed. 'It's a rudimentary burglar-deterrent. Can't make a quick getaway, you see?' He led the way into the main body of the building, where the number of plants was replaced by a great silence, and a coldness that went right to Flick's bones.

Tristyan took a bead of glass from his pocket and crushed it between his palms. The white magic wafted upwards, but before it could disperse, Tristyan caught it and sort of twisted it in the air. It shone suddenly blue, and flickered like fire. A torch of blue flames, wrapped around his hand.

'You have *got* to show me how that's done,' Avery said, clearly impressed.

He smiled. 'It isn't necessarily a skill that can be

taught, Avery. It is something you can either do or not. You need to be born with it.' He hesitated, then held the flames at arm's length. A gust of hot air suddenly blew over the flames and right at Tristyan, blasting the dust off his clothes in an instant.

'Convenient,' Jonathan said, brushing at his own coat.

Flick pulled the magnifying eyepatch from her pocket and fitted it over her head. Looking through it, she saw that the place sparkled with the same abundance of magic as the rest of the world, but there was no scored jagged line of a schism shining within the thick swirls of gold. She pushed the glass up to her forehead. 'No schisms here in this room, at least.'

Tristyan held his flames up, so the light cast ahead, making the room appear grey and cold. The front door they hadn't been able to open stood to their left, opposite an enormous sweeping staircase. Flick realised that, despite its appearance, the Glasshouse wasn't actually all glass. Inside, the building was more like an old manor house, with an elaborate landing at the top of the staircase, and doors that led off it in either direction, presumably running alongside the long glass frontage. But it was dark and cold. The whole place felt as dusty and dead as the Lighthouse world that still haunted Flick.

Jonathan looked around. 'No one has been here for a long time.'

'I hope you're right.' Flick shivered. The stone and grey light had a distinct 'haunted house' feeling about it. There was dirt and dust on the wooden floors, and one of the carved bannister-ends was broken, the shattered wood reaching up like fingers in the shadows. Besides Tristyan's torch, the only light came from the plant-filled windows surrounding the front door. The words the Old Mother had said to them echoed in Flick's head as she looked around.

You will need to journey from here, to the place called the Glasshouse. And from there, using your magic, to the next place. And there will be the final doorway leading to the end of all things.

'The Old Mother said we needed to travel from here, *using our magic*, to the next place. She must have meant using another suitcase, right?' Flick looked round at her companions, who nodded. 'So that's what we need to look for now, another suitcase?'

'I wonder if this next suitcase will take us to The House on the Horizon,' Jonathan pondered. 'We already guessed that Elara might have hidden the final suitcase there, and the next place contains the *final doorway*, according to the Old Mother. It would make sense.'

Flick looked up at the staircase again, and the two corridors leading off it. 'If Tristyan and me take the top left passage, you guys check the right?' she suggested.

Avery and Jonathan nodded, and they all headed up the staircase together.

Flick couldn't help noticing how Tristyan walked up the stairs with the same sort of stride as her dad, and wondered if her brother, Freddy, would walk like that when he was grown up. At the top of the staircase, they paused uneasily.

'Meet back here in an hour, if not before,' Jonathan said, taking his keyring torch out to light his and Avery's way. His eyes looked overly large in the weird light.

With a worried smile, Flick turned left and went through the door, Tristyan following. They entered into a long, dark passageway with multiple doors along it. The building obviously went back a lot further than Flick had assumed. They would need to check in each room.

'Can you teach me to do that?' she asked, nodding at Tristyan's handful of flames.

He looked surprised, but pleased that she had asked. 'I would love to. As I said to Avery, it isn't something everyone can do, so you mustn't be disappointed if you can't. I've never known anyone from your world who could use magic like this. But when this is all over, we can try.'

'Were there any people from my world in the Seren?' Flick asked, as they walked down the corridor. She'd been thinking about it for a while, and now Jonathan and Avery weren't there, it seemed like a good time to ask.

Tristyan hummed in confirmation. 'Not at first,' he said. 'Your world is incredibly vast, and though rich in magic, its enormous size means that the magic is thinly spread. The Seren were not interested in the place because it would have taken so much effort to harvest from.' He paused. 'Until Elara Mercator.'

Flick thought of the one fuzzy photograph she had seen of Elara, on the wall in Strangeworlds, serious in her dark dress and institutional-looking bun. 'How did the Seren find her?'

He sighed. 'The Seren were aware of a series of magical disturbances happening on the planet Earth during the nineteenth century. That was in part due to your industrial revolution, and the resulting unprecedented disturbance of the natural world. The disturbances caused a number of things to happen. Firstly, it tore a natural schism between your world and the world the Seren were then occupying. And secondly, it made more magically gifted children be born.'

'Like Elara.'

'Yes,' Tristyan said. 'Elara was born then, and she was *incredibly* magically talented. However, it took the Seren a while to track her down. By the time they found her, she was ten years old.'

Flick's mind filled with the horrors of imagined kidnappings. 'Did they take her away from her family?'

'She was already an orphan, living in a children's home. They offered to take her away from that, and she went with them gladly.'

Flick frowned. 'But . . . did she know what they were?'

'I doubt she did at first. She would have learned quickly enough. The Seren had established a sort of school, where they taught Elara and other magically gifted children how to draw energy from schisms, how to use magnifying glasses, how to bottle and use magic. They ran it like a training academy. No . . . more like a cult. They only told the children the real nature of their new family once they had shown enough potential, climbed high enough in the social hierarchy of the Seren.' For the first time since Flick had met him, Tristyan's placid expression had changed to one of old anger, and it made her realise what it must have been like for him to come to terms with the nature of what he had once called his family.

'So when Elara was first brought to them, could she trap schisms in suitcases?'

Tristyan's mouth went thin. 'No, she couldn't. The Seren did not have the ability to trap schisms, either – they could travel through them, but that was all.'

'But then, how did she learn?'

'She just . . . did it. Much as you tore your way through a world. We always knew she was especially gifted. But no one anticipated that ability. The first schism she trapped, she caught in a box. And she couldn't explain how. She was only eighteen at the time.'

Flick remembered the feeling of tearing into Five Lights, and of expanding the schism that let the pirates of The Break escape. Trying to describe how she did it was almost impossible – it couldn't be explained with words, only with feelings. It had felt natural, but eerie and wrong at the same time. What would Elara have felt when she first trapped a schism? Afraid of what she had done? Or proud of her power?

She looked up at Tristyan, who appeared tired and guilty. 'So, what did you want with her?'

For a moment she thought he would deny having been involved, but to Flick's surprise, he didn't remove himself from the story at all. 'We saw, in her, a way out of our nomadic existence. Her trapped schisms would have allowed us to travel from world to world to harvest magic and yet return to one base, or home.'

Flick pulled a sour face. 'And you were just OK with that? With everything they did until you . . . erm, fell in love and ran away?' Flick knew she sounded disbelieving, but she couldn't help it.

He laughed. 'Something like that.' He held the flames higher as they approached the first door. 'Actually, to be truthful, Aspen was an assignment.'

'An assignment?'

'Yes . . .' He tried the door handle. It swung open, into an empty room that smelled sharply of cold and dust. The window was boarded up. 'I was supposed to kill her.'

CHAPTER TEN

'What?' Flick stopped dead in the doorway. 'You – what?'

'I was a different person back then.' He turned, the blue flames illuminating his face. 'I believed that, as one of the Seren, it was my duty to remove anything and anyone who might prevent us from accessing magic. So that we might survive. And The Strangeworlds Society was one of those obstacles. I had been told to capture any members of the Society I could, to interrogate them. If they couldn't be convinced to join us, then . . . I was to dispose of them.'

Flick stared at him. In his brownish apron and worn-out clothes, Tristyan looked absolutely nothing like an assassin. But she knew Tristyan would never have made something like that up.

He saw her worried face, and held his hands up, one of them still ablaze. 'Felicity. Flick, I don't do that any more. I have changed, I swear. Aspen changed me. Though, in fairness to myself, I think I had already begun to see the error of my ways before I met her. She just gave me the push I needed.'

'You *killed* people,' Flick said, the words heavy and bitter. 'For the Seren.'

He nodded. 'I am not proud of it. And I am not asking you to forgive me, because I don't deserve that.'

She swallowed. 'So, that was your job in the Seren. Did you do . . . that when Elara Mercator was one of you?'

'Yes,' he said. 'We thought we were unstoppable, that no one would ever dream of leaving us. Elara proved us wrong. I think that was the first time I realised there was something else out there for me. But it took me another hundred years to actually work up the courage to run away.'

Somehow, it made Flick feel better that Tristyan hadn't tried to soften the truth. People could change, she knew, and that meant sometimes there were regrets. She couldn't erase what had happened to Tristyan before she met him, and really, the Seren were the ones to blame – they had stolen his freedom to choose any other life.

They shut the door and walked further down the corridor. Flick had a million more questions, but chose the one she was most interested in. 'How old *are* you, Tristyan?'

He gave a surprised laugh. 'Why?'

'Because if you knew Elara then you're at least a hundred and fifty.'

'Of your years, yes. Time doesn't move the same everywhere, you know. I think, in your years, I would be close to five hundred. Maybe a little more, it is difficult to say.'

'Five hundred?' Flick gawped.

'My people live longer than yours, anyway.' He smiled. 'But, like all Seren, my life was extended and controlled by magic.'

'Will you have to eat magic for ever?' she asked. 'Couldn't you . . . just age naturally, now?'

'No,' he said. 'I don't have enough magic in my body to age at the rate I should. I would die before I gained the appearance of the old man I should be.'

'So you're stuck like this?'

'Not quite. I have been rationing magic for a long time,' Tristyan said. 'When I left the Seren, I stole a great deal of it. I consumed it slowly. Allowed myself to age a little' – he pointed at his greying hair – 'and tried to live as normal a life as I could. Aspen could have done the same – become like me, reliant on magic to survive and in exchange given herself a longer life than the one she had – but she refused. I didn't have a choice. Like all Seren, it was forced upon me.' His jaw moved as if he was biting his tongue. 'The problem is, once you start living like this, you can never stop. If you run out of magic, you don't just age and die like anyone else . . . you are consumed by the multiverse, into nothingness. It is reportedly very painful.'

Flick felt a great sorrow well in her chest. Tristyan had been taken from a family he couldn't remember, raised and forced into stealing magic, then left all that behind for a love that ended too soon. It was a wonder he could put one foot in front of the other.

'Aren't you sad?' she asked, suddenly.

To her surprise, Tristyan burst out laughing. He stopped, hand ablaze in blue flames, chuckling loudly for a moment. 'I'm sorry,' he said, wiping his eyes. 'But for some reason that seemed hilarious. Of course I'm sad,' he said. 'I have been for a very long time. After a while, it becomes a new sort of normal.'

They opened several more doors, each revealing

only empty chambers or rooms with a few pieces of broken furniture, until they came to the very last at the end of the long corridor. Flick pushed it open, and this time the air seemed to crackle with tension. Unlike the earlier rooms they had checked, this one was full to bursting with what looked like old junk. Flick moved Nyfe's eyepatch down over her face, and peeped through it. In this room, the air swarmed with magic – even more than elsewhere in this world, though Flick hadn't thought that was possible. The air seemed to be made of solid gold.

'This is it,' she breathed. 'It's got to be in here, somewhere.'

Tristyan didn't ask her if she was sure. He just walked into the room, his flames casting their eerie light, his shadow splintering into weird shapes on the dusty floorboards.

Flick stepped in after him, and then froze. There, in the dust, she could see scuffs and footprints, where neither she nor Tristyan had yet stepped. A cold feeling – colder than the air they stood in – dripped down over her skin. Not wanting to make a sound, she waved to get Tristyan's attention, and then pointed.

He nodded, put a finger first to his lips, then pointed at the stacked-up furniture and junk in the room. He was right – they still needed to search, no matter who might have been here.

But goosebumps rose up on Flick's arms as Tristyan went towards the broken furniture. Someone had been here, disturbed the dust. Who? The suitcase that led to this place had been hidden away, in the forest. She wanted to speak, to point out that they were probably in danger, but she seemed to be rooted to the spot as her mind worked overtime drawing up terrible scenarios.

Tristyan flicked his hand, and the blue flames moved out of his grip and hovered in the air beside him. He lifted a chair with three legs out of the way and dragged a dust sheet off to reveal another pile of furniture and shelves. There were boxes and folded bits of cardboard as well, and thick ropey cobwebs that made Flick think of hairy legs and things with too many eyes.

Flick knew she ought to help, but she was too frightened to move. The emptiness of the corridor behind them seemed to be creeping up on her, and she wanted to both look back and keep her eyes forwards at the same time, because what if there was something there?

'Tris . . .' Her voice sounded too loud in the emptiness.

He held a hand up to quieten her as he moved more wooden things out of the way. 'What can you see through the glass?' he asked softly.

Flick tried to pull herself together. She squinted through the glassy eyepatch. 'There's even more magic now you've moved the sheet,' she said, marvelling. 'Maybe it's under there, somewhere.'

'It may not even be a suitcase,' Tristyan said, examining a damp cardboard box. 'Though given the state of this place, I hope it's something robust.'

Flick took a tiny step closer. 'Shall I call for Jonathan and Avery?'

'No,' Tristyan said. He straightened up, holding something oblong in his hands. 'I've found it.' He turned, and Flick clearly saw a battered leather suitcase. It was filthy and damp and dusty, but there was no doubt it was what they were looking for.

'Oh.' She let out a breath. 'Thank goodness.'

Tristyan swept some of the dust from the top, and read what was carved into the leather. **THE HOUSE ON THE HORIZON**. 'The next step in the journey. We found it.' He looked up at her, smiling, and then his expression changed to one of shock.

'What is it—'

'Flick *get down*!'

Flick dropped to the floor.

A bright something flew like a comet right through the space where her head had been a second ago. It shot towards Tristyan, who dived to the floor. The comet collided with the wall with a smash like breaking china.

Flick, the eyepatch still over her eye, rolled on to her back in time to see a man as pale and thin as smoke striding towards her. He was smashing a glass bottle between his palms, and magic was condensing in his hands as he raised them –

– but something bright gold and glittering crashed into him, travelling from Tristyan's side of the room. It coiled around the man like a white-gold snake, wrestling him to the ground as the magic in his hands skittered into the air and vanished. He fell on to his face, arms trapped, snarling as he fought his bonds.

Tristyan grabbed Flick by the jacket and hauled her into his arms. He ran past the pale man tangled in golden magic, and down the corridor, carrying her and the suitcase.

'What was that?' Flick panted.

'One of them. The Seren. They knew we would come. It was a trap.' Tristyan glanced over his shoulder as he rounded the corner and hurried down the staircase to the main entrance hall. Flick didn't even try to complain at being manhandled; she was clinging to Tristyan's apron strap like it was a seatbelt.

'Jonathan!' Tristyan bellowed as they reached the ground floor. 'Avery!'

There was a BANG from above, and a scream.

Flick struggled out of Tristyan's arms, but he grabbed her backpack and held her back. 'Felicity, your friends have the suitcase that leads back to Strangeworlds. They're in a better position than we are, try not to panic.'

'Too late for that,' Flick breathed, her heart hammering so much she could feel her ribs throbbing. There were thundering footsteps overhead, and then the door to the right-side corridor crashed open.

Avery ran out, followed by Jonathan. They pelted down the stairs as another Seren stormed through the doorway after them, pausing at the sight of Flick and Tristyan over the landing balcony.

'You!' she shouted, pointing straight at Tristyan. At that moment, the man Tristyan had trapped appeared on the opposite side of the landing, clearly free and looking furious.

Tristyan made a noise in the back of his throat, like a snarl. He handed Flick the suitcase to the House on the Horizon and moved his hands to his belt.

Flick held the suitcase tight. Jonathan and Avery joined them, looking terrified. There was no way out. The main doors, held fast by the thick coils of plants, were behind them. To the right and left were the glasshouse areas, where it would be all but impossible to run. The Seren were halfway down the staircase already. To open the suitcase back to Strangeworlds would be like inviting the Seren home with them.

They were trapped.

CHAPTER ELEVEN

The two Seren walked leisurely down the staircase, as though they were two vipers relishing the journey down to their prey.

'Of all the worlds, I never thought we'd find you in this one,' the female Seren said as she reached the bottom step. Her loose-fitting clothing billowed like dry ice, moving gently as if in a breeze, or underwater. Like the man, she was very pale, and, though more robustly built, she had a wispy quality about her, as though she was walking through fog even when standing still. Her lank hair could have been any colour from blonde to red to brown, but she looked so washed over with grey that it was difficult to tell. Flick was reminded of Overseer Glean and her gang of Thieves, though even they hadn't looked as ghostlike as this. 'And who are the little ones? Are they yours?' The words were innocent but there was pure menace in her tone.

'These children are not important, Sephie,' Tristyan said, moving to stand in front of Flick and her friends.

'Oh, but they could be very important to *us*,' the Seren named Sephie said with a sneer.

'Take your threats elsewhere,' Tristyan replied.

Sephie's eyes narrowed. 'A traitor deserves threats, and worse.'

Tristyan stayed where he was, his arms out slightly, as if shielding the children behind him. 'It isn't traitorous to choose the multiverse over yourself.'

The taller male Seren stepped forward. His skin reminded Flick of papier-mâché. His eyes were so cast-over and foggy that Flick wondered if he could see out of them at all. Indeed, he seemed to be struggling as he craned his neck forward and squinted in her direction. 'The children . . .' he rasped, in a voice like the crackle of dry leaves under a boot. 'They have the gift.'

Sephie's grey eyes drifted over to Flick. 'Azarus can always tell who has magical skill. If the traitor is forcing you to work for him, children, we can help you.'

'Tristyan isn't making us do anything,' Flick said. She could practically feel the suitcase vibrating in her hand. 'We're not doing anything you say. We're not scared of you.' She saw Avery raise her eyebrows a bit. 'We know what you are.'

Sephie raised her empty hands. 'Child, we are not your enemies. We know what it is like to be burdened with magic, to be born with innate skills you do not understand. We know what it is like to discover things about yourself that make you different. The Seren are not kidnappers or evil witches. We are a family. We help one another to learn how to handle gifts that can be such burdens.' She looked at Tristyan. 'I can imagine the sorts of things this man has been telling you. This man used to kill people without a murmur. And he would have you trust him over us – the ones who can help you.'

Flick didn't want to listen. But something in the way the woman spoke made her pay attention.

'That man,' Sephie said, 'trapped us and left us to die. He cut us off from magic we had carefully collected, forcing us to turn on one another. That man broke our family apart. Why would you trust someone who would do a thing like that?'

Tristyan's hands were shaking with what Flick thought to be barely contained anger, but he said nothing, staying where he was, in front of Flick and her friends.

Azarus was looking from side to side in a reptilian manner, reminding Flick of a snake as his neck stretched out. 'The magic within them is strong,' he said to Sephie. He raised a hand with fingers as thin as wire.

Flick and Avery backed away quickly, Jonathan copying Tristyan by putting an arm out for them to retreat behind as though he was magic-proof.

Azarus bared his papery, pointy teeth in a dry hiss.

'Interrogate me if you must, but let them go,' Tristyan said. 'They are just children.' His hand slipped discreetly to rest at his belt.

Sephie smiled. '*Just* children? Have you forgotten that we see talent in everyone? Besides, I recognise those badges they wear. These children are from The Strangeworlds Society.'

Flick glanced at the old patch on her jacket sleeve. It felt suddenly like a brand. The magic-filled air around her fizzed with potential, and it was just a matter of time before there was a fight, she knew it. What could they do? What could *she* do? The suitcase in her hand felt like a deadweight.

Avery's shaking fingers closed over her wrist.

The Seren pair inched forwards. 'Tristyan, you may have succeeded in binding us to a single world for decades, but you should have finished us off whilst you had the chance,' Sephie hissed. 'The order Elara Mercator established is almost ended – your wicked plans have come to nothing.'

Flick's heart thumped. There was no time to think. Nowhere to run. 'How did you get here?' she asked, trying to stall for time.

Azarus grinned – or at least bared his teeth widely. 'Coming here was not our doing,' he said. 'This world, though rich in magic, is well-protected. However . . .' His eyes glittered. 'A pathway was made for us. We simply followed it.'

'Made for you?' Flick asked. 'By who?'

Azarus only laughed softly.

'Our orders are to take you alive, Tristyan,' Sephie said, stepping forward. 'But I think The Commonwealth will settle for your corpse.'

Azarus slowly raised his hands.

Flick felt the rush of magic in the air. Time seemed to slow to a crawl as she sensed the crackle of magic being stolen from the world around her. It was coming for them.

She grabbed Avery and Jonathan by the backs of their coats, dragging them down to the floor with her half a second before Azarus threw jagged splinters of magic straight at them. The shards sliced through the air and vanished as they hit the double doors behind them.

Tristyan was already moving. He smashed a glass bulb from his belt between his palms, pulling the magic inside it apart like hot glass. He slashed it upwards as Sephie darted forward, so she was knocked to the floor by the bolt of whip-like magic lashing at her face. It vanished almost instantly, and Tristyan pulled two more glass bulbs out of his belt.

'Get out of here, all of you!' he shouted. Flick, Jonathan and Avery scrambled to their feet, dodging out of the way as Tristyan's magic twisted into two shorter whips that drove Sephie and Azarus further back, before again dissolving into mist.

Azarus twisted his hands, pulled a shaft of ice-blue magic out of thin air and hurled it like a javelin. It missed Flick by a centimetre, splintering into dust behind her. The suitcase to the House on the Horizon clattered from her hands to the floor, and she dived after it.

Tristyan smashed two of his biggest vials of magic between his palms. This time, a great wall of bright, gold-white light flashed out in front of him like a sheet of glitter-filled ice shielding him completely from head to toe.

Both of the Seren held their hands up to protect their eyes from the magical glow of the barrier. The light was blinding. Tristyan, a dark shape against it, was hunched over with the effort of holding it up. 'Go!' he roared.

Flick staggered backwards. Jonathan fumbled with the catches of the suitcase that would transport them to the other side of Pendularbor. The lid sprang open, and Avery made to shove Flick inside but –

but Tristyan was still –

'We can't leave him!' Flick turned to see jagged cracks already appearing in Tristyan's shield. It was smaller now, half the size it had been, covering only the width of his body and shrinking fast. 'Tristyan! Come on!'

He turned his head to look at her.

'Come with us!' she screamed.

But it was too late.

Tristyan's shield vanished as if it had never been there at all. His hands were up in a useless surrendering gesture, and Azarus raised his head again with a snarl.

'Oh, no,' Tristyan breathed.

'Felicity!' Jonathan grabbed her wrist. 'Felicity, we have to go, now!' Flick ignored him. She needed to go to Tristyan, to help him. He was reaching for another glass bottle at his belt. His fingers were so close to it . . .

But then Azarus, a glowing magical field covering him like armour, slammed into Tristyan's chest, knocking him to the floor as though he weighed nothing. The two of them struggled on the floor, fighting hard. The glass bottles on Tristyan's belt crunched and smashed. A pale white mist rose up from the shards. There was the flash of the sharp edge of a blade between the two fighting figures.

Flick had no real plan; she was acting on pure instinct. She shoved Jonathan away, darted over to Tristyan and snatched at the air. She grasped the escaping magic in her fist, feeling the bite of it against her skin.

'Hey,' she spat. 'Seren?'

Azarus turned his head.

Flick raised the mist to her mouth, and blew.

The magical energy transformed into light and heat – into *fire*, that caught Azarus in the chest. His clothes ignited instantly. He shrieked and threw himself off Tristyan in a panic, batting at himself, stumbling into Sephie who had no choice but to shift her efforts to avoid catching alight herself. Sephie slashed at something in the air, and the two screaming, smoking

Seren vanished from sight as if they had never been there at all.

Flick didn't wait to see if they were gone for good. She pulled Tristyan to his feet, almost buckling under the weight of him. Jonathan caught him under his other arm and the three of them threw themselves in the direction of the suitcase.

They fell through it hard, landing painfully on the grassy forest floor of the area of Pendularbor they had left behind only hours before. Flick leapt up and grabbed the suitcase handle from the inside, pulling it through with them, sealing the Glasshouse on the other side. She flopped backwards, shaking. The bone-tired feeling she always got when manipulating magic had hit her hard, and she could only stare at the suitcase, trying to get her breath back.

The Seren had been there, searching for Elara's suitcase at the same time they had been. They'd come so close to losing it. And now the Seren knew they had it.

Tristyan groaned, from where he was still face-down on the grass.

Flick turned her head to watch as Jonathan managed to roll Tristyan over on to his back. He moaned brokenly again, his hands clamped over the front of his apron. His face was damp with sweat.

Jonathan lifted his hands off him quickly. 'Oh, god.'

Flick opened her mouth to ask what was wrong.

Just as the dark stain began to blossom through the material of Tristyan's clothes.

And everything seemed to suddenly come to a stop.

CHAPTER TWELVE

Flick couldn't hear anything except her own heartbeat in her ears. Her hands were shaking.

No, she thought clearly, and calmly. *No, this isn't happening. It can't be happening. It isn't happening. This sort of thing doesn't happen to me. It happens to other people, but not to me. Not in my story.*

'We need to stop the bleeding. We need a compress.' Jonathan wrestled his arms out of his frock coat and balled it up in his hands. 'Oh, god. He's not human, we can't take him to hospital back on Earth. What do we do?'

'I don't know,' Avery said, her voice high and hysterical. 'Flick, what should we do? Flick?'

Flick couldn't answer. Tristyan's eyes were wide, his breathing heavy and quick like he'd run a marathon.

He looked terrified, and when Jonathan pressed the bunched-up coat on to his middle he doubled up in pain, moaning in words Flick didn't understand.

Jonathan backed away in horror, as Avery's hands flew to her mouth. 'He's not going to die, is he?' she whispered.

Tristyan caught control of his breathing, his entire body shaking with the effort. Flick tried to think of something she could do, something she could say, but she seemed to be made of stone. The pressure was making her crumble inside.

What do I do? What do I do? What do I do?

Tristyan's limbs relaxed slightly, as he turned his head to look at her. His skin was shining with sweat. 'Felicity . . . it's all right.'

No, it isn't. She wished she could speak.

Tristyan moved one of his hands away from his middle. His palm and fingers were streaked with pale brown-red blood. He held it out.

Flick knew what he wanted. But she couldn't move. If she stayed very still, if she didn't give the multiverse a chance to start spinning again, then maybe this wouldn't be happening. Maybe none of this would be real, if she just stayed still and didn't give it chance to really happen . . .

Tristyan's eyes shone, and his jaw tensed. 'Felic . . .'

Avery knelt down, took hold of Flick's wrist, and made her put her hand firmly into Tristyan's. 'Wake up, Flick. Just do what he wants. You can't lose it, now, you need to wake up.'

And Flick did wake up. Though the nightmare did not change.

The touch of her grandfather's hand in hers was like hot electricity. It burned her skin with inevitability, with a fierce sense of home, of the unfairness of it all, and of family. She gripped tight, waking up to the sensation of skin on dying skin. The wetness of Tristyan's palm, the soft loose flesh on the back of his hand that was one of the few things that betrayed his age, the hard press of a ring worn on a single finger.

'You used magic to heal my face, Flick,' Avery whispered. 'Can you heal him? Like you did my face?'

Flick shook her head. This was more than just a cut. She didn't need to look through a magnifier to know that.

Tristyan's breathing sounded wet.

Jonathan and Avery drew back. Flick looked at Tristyan's face. She could feel herself starting to panic. 'I'm sorry I didn't—' She stopped, her heart on fire.

'I didn't ask you more about – about Aspen, or my dad, or . . .'

Tristyan squeezed her hand. 'Doesn't matter. What matters is that we had time . . . together.' He grimaced then, tensing horribly as his free hand clamped tighter over his stomach. He held on to Flick's hand so hard she felt her bones creak. Then he shuddered, his face suddenly rigid with fear. 'Don't tell him,' he said, his voice breaking. 'Don't tell Isaac. What I did for the Seren. I couldn't bear it if he had to know . . .'

'I won't,' Flick said, her throat made of knives. 'I won't tell him. I promise.'

'He won't understand.'

'It's OK.' Flick nodded, tears running down her face now. 'It's OK.'

Tristyan gripped her hand hard again. 'I love you, Felicity. If . . . more time, I wanted to . . . I'm sorry . . .'

'Don't be sorry,' Flick shook her head. 'It's OK.'

Tristyan gave a nod. Then smiled, just a little. 'You look so much like your grandmother,' he whispered, his voice barely more than breath. 'You can stop the Seren, Felicity. I know you can. And – and I'll be with you. Always.' Then he tensed. 'Oh, no,' he breathed. 'No, I – I don't want to . . .'

Flick grasped his hand tight with both of hers. The

air between them seemed to electrify with magic, the energy of Tristyan's life-force struggling to keep going, spluttering like a candle at the end of its wick. There was a sharp jolt where their hands joined, and Flick felt the familiar rush of moving magical energy.

Tristyan's eyes went wide with the effort to stay alive,

and, with a final frightened, shuddering sigh, he died.

Flick felt the hand in hers tingle with the loss of its magic and slowly relax. It became a deadweight, and then fell out of her grip on to the grass.

The sheer silence around them was crushing.

Flick put a hand on Tristyan's unmoving chest. It was warm. She splayed her fingers out like a star, covering as much of Tristyan as she could with her hand. She could feel something building inside her like an explosion, something powerful and dangerous. Her eyes and nose were burning but she ignored their streaming.

Then, Tristyan's body felt less solid beneath her hand.

Flick raised her head. She quickly pulled the magnifying eyepatch back down over her eye, gasping as the glass showed a soft gold-white light surrounding Tristyan's body. It glowed for a few heartbeats, as if lighting him up from the inside, ever brighter with every moment, and then . . . the light, and Tristyan's body, glittered away into nothingness, until it was little more than shine on the breeze, racing into the air and disappearing amongst the other golden flakes of magic.

CHAPTER THIRTEEN

It wasn't just Tristyan that had died. Any opportunity Flick might have had to ask him about her family, her grandmother, even her aunt . . . was now gone. Now, there would never be a 'later'. There was never going to be another chance.

Flick couldn't have described how she felt. It was an emptiness and a regret and a guilt so deep and so dark that it seemed to go on forever. One moment she had him, the next he was gone for ever. The suddenness and finality of Tristyan's death seemed impossible, unreal, something that should not have happened. And yet, it had.

Jonathan, his face white and drawn, had insisted they go back to Strangeworlds, and Avery had helped an unresisting Flick back into the suitcase.

Back in Strangeworlds, the silence and familiarity of the place somehow made Flick feel worse. It all seemed so normal, like nothing had happened, like Tristyan could come out of the kitchen holding another failed baking experiment at any minute, his expression full of hope. Flick shook her head to get rid of the thought. She had planted herself in one of the armchairs and didn't really know how she was going to stand up again.

Flick had stopped crying, but the painful strangling feeling in her throat was still there. 'I never called him "Grandad",' she whispered. 'He wanted me to, but I never . . .' She curled up, twisted and hunched over against the crush of grief, and pressed her face into her hands.

Avery was looking at Flick in pure misery. Jonathan couldn't stand still – he knew how Flick was feeling, and he knew there was nothing he could say to make the hurt go away, so he wandered around Strangeworlds in a sort of daze, making cups of tea that sat, untouched, on the desk. Flick felt Avery squash herself on to the arm of the chair and put her arms around her. But she didn't care. Right now, she didn't want Avery. She wanted Tristyan. And she wanted her dad, too.

'I need to go home,' she said. 'I really need to go home.'

'I know. I'll get your things together.' Avery looked at Jonathan. 'What are *you* going to do? Do you think it's safe to stay here? The Seren know we got away.'

Jonathan pulled a *who knows* face. 'It looked to me as though one of them – Sephie – cut her way out of the place. I don't know exactly where she cut to, but clearly they have enough magic to travel freely again. We'll need to warn Kayda's people. All I can think is that Pendularbor might be their next target. Remember what the Old Mother said about how much magic there is there? It will be irresistible to the Seren. And wherever that suitcase leads' – he looked at the black suitcase Tristyan had found – 'we owe it to Tristyan to follow it. To get Elara's end-of-everything suitcase back here, so Felicity can try to destroy it.'

Flick was barely listening. She couldn't stop thinking about all the things Tristyan had left behind. There was his apothecary shop, with all his potions and trinkets and leftovers of his family life. It was sitting in another world, waiting for him to come back, not knowing that he never would. There were even signs of him having lived at Strangeworlds – the photographs he had pinned on to the cork board in the kitchen, the neatly raked garden waiting for seeds that would never be planted, a half-eaten jar of honey on the counter, and his fingerprints in the soap. His presence lingered in the evidence he had left behind.

Avery helped Flick up. 'Right,' she said. 'Let's get your face washed and I'll walk you home. The fresh air will help—'

Suddenly, the dirty and damp suitcase they had rescued from the Glasshouse burst open. Dust, sand and hot air billowed into The Strangeworlds Travel Agency, along with a smell of cigarettes. The air filled with dry dirt like fog.

Jonathan grabbed his cricket bat from behind the desk as Flick and Avery dived for cover behind the armchair.

There was a hacking cough, and some snorting, and then a man stepped out of the suitcase and into the cloud of dust. He was below average height, but there was a wide-brimmed hat on his head that reached up another few inches. His other clothes were travel-worn, his dark denim jeans were pale at the knees and threadbare where they met his boots, and his leather jacket was cracked and split on the pockets and cuffs. He had a dirty and unwashed look about him, and a greasy black-and-grey moustache that ended at the corners of his mouth.

He also had a long, thin rifle tucked under one arm.

Flick squeaked in terror.

The man paused as he stepped into the travel agency. He looked slightly confused, and waved a hand in front of his face to clear the dust. 'Anyone at home?' he called. Then he noticed Jonathan behind him, holding the cricket bat up like a lightsaber. He raised an eyebrow. 'Something wrong there, sir?'

'I have had an *extremely* trying day,' Jonathan snapped, 'and you're the last thing I need. Tell me who the devil you are, or so help me . . .' He drew the bat back as if he was going to smack the man with it.

'Easy.' The man raised his hands, keeping the gun tucked under one arm. 'Look.' He grasped the gun by the barrel and put it neatly on to the desk, pointed at himself. 'That help you any?'

Flick and Avery peered around the armchair.

Jonathan's eyes flicked from the gun to the man. 'I suppose that helps a little. A name might help, too.'

'Yikes. If I knew things were this bad I'd have tried harder to get to you earlier.' The man took a cigarette from behind his ear and stuck it, unlit, in the corner of his mouth. 'The name's Thess,' he drawled. 'Danser

Thess. I'm the Strangeworlds Custodian at the House on the Horizon.'

*

Danser Thess wasn't a big man, but he seemed to take up a lot of room in Strangeworlds. He sat in one of the armchairs and listened silently and respectfully to Flick and Jonathan's story about the Seren, Tristyan, schisms and Five Lights. It was clear he had his own story to tell, but he was in no rush to make himself heard. When their story was over, he took the foul damp and chewed cigarette out of his mouth, and sat back in the armchair thoughtfully.

'Seems like we come close to crossing paths a few times,' he said, with an accent that made Flick think of somewhere at the bottom of a map of America. 'But kept on missing each other.'

'The suitcase you came out of,' Flick began, 'does that lead to—'

'Yes, it goes to the House on the Horizon,' he said, snorting noisily. 'But it's always been pretty useless to tell you the truth, because it connected to the Glasshouse, and as you've learned, the Society was banned from Pendularbor. I didn't want to get on their nerves. But likewise, I didn't want to yank the case through with me in case it was needed, one day. I figured the safest thing to do was lock it against anyone but a Strangeworlder.'

'How would a suitcase know we were in the Society?' Avery asked, sceptically. Flick had been wondering this as well, and was grateful Avery had asked.

Thess snorted. 'Swore an oath, didn't you? Words are magical, young lady. Anyway, when I heard Daniel had disappeared, I knew it would have something to do with the Seren, and I knew that I better start hunting for him and for them.'

'Do you know where my father is?' Jonathan asked, cutting to the chase. 'You've been seen, all over the multiverse. In Tam's forest, in Five Lights, everywhere. Have you heard any news about him at all?'

'Sadly not,' Thess said, flicking his soggy cigarette into the fireplace. 'If you ask me, he either doesn't want to be found or else he's beyond our reach. And I've got long arms, despite my size. I don't mean he's dead, neither,' he added quickly. 'I mean he'll be somewhere you can't get to through suitcase nor schism.'

'And where's that?' Avery sniffed.

'Hell, I don't know for sure, but there's always been

rumours. About a place *outside* the worlds. Some sorta region that's holding the whole multiverse together. The place we can't get to.'

'The Inbetween,' Flick said, without thinking.

'That's right,' Thess said, in surprise. 'You know something about it?'

Flick fidgeted. 'I don't. Not really. I just . . . became aware of it, once.'

Thess gave her a level look. 'Can you wrangle magic, young lady? For instance, could you do this?' He snapped his fingers and a tiny flame leapt up at the pad of his thumb. Avery sat up, impressed, and he grinned at her. 'Comes in useful when you run out of matches.'

'I think maybe I could do it, if someone taught me,' Flick said. 'I wanted Tristyan to teach me how. He was going to.' There was a silence, in which everyone felt awful. Flick cleared her throat loudly, and carried on. 'Back in the Glasshouse . . . I did do something *like* that. Changed magic into fire, without even thinking about it. It felt really weird.'

Thess nodded. 'Mmhmm. Makes you aware of what there *isn't*, doesn't it? Nothing holdin' the worlds together but a bit of magic. S'why I don't like doing it unless I have to. Folks who consume magic find it easier, of course, because they've already become closer to pure magic by extending their lives with it. Those of us who are still human have to learn to manipulate it the hard way.'

Flick stared at him. 'Are you like me, then?'

'In what way?'

'Can you . . . change schisms?' Flick asked, nervously. Avery put a hand on her arm.

Thess waved a hand. 'No one can alter schisms, that's imposs—' He paused. 'Wait. You're saying you can?'

'I have,' she said.

Thess sat up, cigarettes falling out of his pockets. 'You can change schisms?' He frowned, the dirt in the creases on his face emphasising his expression. 'Can you trap one?'

'Like in a suitcase? No.' Flick suddenly felt exhausted. 'But I've made them bigger. That's when I first realised the Inbetween existed.' She remembered the pure nothingness she had sensed on the other side of the schism, when evacuating the citizens of The Break to the Lighthouse world, and she shuddered. 'You really think Daniel Mercator could be there?'

Thess sat back and shrugged. 'There's no way of getting there to check. But it's happened before.'

'Before?' Flick asked.

Thess nodded in the direction of the front door. 'You ever wondered how that brass sign outside got all scraped up? Not long after I took over the House on the Horizon, there was a to-do with the Strangeworlds Society. Reports aren't clear, since it happened off-world, but from the sounds of things, a bunch of them tried to create their own schisms using some sort of machine. Didn't work, obviously. A good dozen members of the Society got pulled into the Inbetween and vanished, never to return.'

'Why in the worlds were they doing that?' Jonathan gawped.

'I'm not sure, but the multiverse did *not* like it.' Thess wiped the back of his hand over his moustache. 'Elara was an old lady by then and I think the shock of it nearly killed her. The Society members who hadn't been involved wanted nothing to do with the ones who'd gone against their code so blatantly. One of them scratched up the plaque outside.'

'The record-keeping starts to decline at that point in time,' Jonathan said softly, thinking.

'The ones left had lost their taste for it. Some kept on travelling and record-keeping, of course. The Thatcher twins joined up in the eighties and worked hard. But the Society had lost its edge. It's been declining ever since. All because of some fools trying to break the rules. Well. I hope they enjoyed themselves in the Inbetween.'

'You just said my dad might be there,' Jonathan said. 'Are you implying he's been breaking the rules, too?'

Thess shook his head. 'No. I know the man and he aint the sort to deliberately break those sorts of rules. I'd say if Daniel ended up there, it was some sort of accident. But s'the only place I can think of where he wouldn't be found. The only place the Seren couldn't find him neither.'

They were silent for a while. Flick thought about it. Could Daniel really be outside the multiverse? In which case . . . could he still be alive? Flick looked at the clock. She was pushing it for time. 'Jonathan,' she said. 'I need to go.'

'I'll walk you,' Avery said. 'I need some fresh air, anyway.'

Thess gave Flick a solemn nod. 'I am sorry about Thatcher,' he said. 'He was a good man. Should've gotten to die asleep in his own bed after the life he had. Damn shame.'

Flick couldn't respond. She felt as if the day had lasted a hundred years. She said goodbye to Jonathan, promised to be back the next day, and took Avery's hand, allowing herself to be led out of the shop.

*

'Are you all right, Felicity?' her mum asked over dinner.

Flick had been stirring whatever they were eating around her plate for a good five minutes. 'Yeah,' she lied. 'I'm OK.'

Her parents exchanged looks. They clearly didn't believe her.

Flick's mum picked up Freddy to go and hose him down after dinner, leaving Flick and her dad to tidy up. Flick could barely look at him – every time she did, she saw Tristyan.

'What's up, bug?' her dad asked, after another long silence. 'Someone been mean to you at school?'

'No, nothing like that,' said Flick, with a sigh. She forced herself to look at her dad's concerned face. 'It's just . . . someone I know has died.' Her eyes immediately started streaming like she'd turned a tap on.

Her dad looked shocked. 'Oh my god, it wasn't a kid, was it?'

'No,' she said quickly, fumbling for a bit of tissue.

'No, it was a – a teacher. A temporary teacher.' That wasn't a total lie. 'I liked him a lot.'

'Oh, sweetheart.' Her dad gathered her up in a hug. She started crying properly then, huge sobs, gulping for air. 'You don't have to explain it to me, it's all right.'

Flick clung to him, like she used to when she was little. She wanted to blurt it all out – that the dead man had been part of their *family*. That she had only just been getting to know him when they'd been parted. She wanted to say sorry, that she should have convinced him to come and meet them all, that she knew he would have loved her dad, just as much as she did, that he would have been so proud of him. She wanted to say that she should have tried harder to save him. But her throat was gripped in a vice of sadness, and all she could do was let herself be hugged tight.

CHAPTER FOURTEEN

'I know what you're after,' Thess said, when Flick returned the next day. 'I just wonder if *you* know.'

'We can't let the Seren get to the Doomsday Case,' Flick said. 'It would be disastrous for the multiverse. We swore to take care of it.'

'I hear you. But why move it from the House on the Horizon? It's been safe there for years.'

'So, it *is* there?' Jonathan confirmed.

Thess ignored him, and stroked his greasy moustache between finger and thumb. He reminded Flick of Overseer Glean, back in the City of Five Lights. Considering, calculating, wondering how much to tell and how much to trust.

Flick wondered what had become of that frightened and greed-stricken woman, banished to another world.

All of a sudden, the Thief's chilling words rose up in Flick's memory.

'*The schisms in the fabric of the multiverse, don't you know where they came from? Don't you know what they will unleash? If you knew what we were all up against, you would destroy those suitcases in a heartbeat.*'

Flick understood now. Glean had been scared of the Seren. All the Thieves had been. They had wanted to run. Flick wished she could go back in time and shake herself. Or possibly shake Glean, to see if she would drop some more information.

Thess sniffed, and wiped his nose up his sleeve, making Jonathan dry heave behind him. 'You gonna tell me what your plan is? Trust goes both ways, you know.'

Flick's stomach twisted. 'We destroy it. I mean, *I'll* try to destroy it. I've done that before: broken suitcases so they don't work any more. I can try to do it again.'

Thess nodded. 'What if they come after you before you can destroy it?' he asked. 'You going to fight them off?'

'They won't get that far,' Flick said positively, though without much self-confidence.

'It's a fine plan, to be sure,' Thess said. 'But who's to say they won't just rip another schism open? They're capable of that.'

'Only if they have enough magic, and Tristyan said they didn't have much left. Maybe their trip to the Glasshouse after Five Lights took it out of them. They disappeared back through a schism after I . . . set one of them on fire.' Flick shuffled awkwardly.

'Maybe not right now they don't have much, but who's to say they won't get more?' Thess sighed. Then looked at Flick, shrewdly. 'Tell me this, kiddo – do you really think you could destroy this suitcase?'

Flick hesitated. 'I don't know,' she said. 'I don't know what might happen if it went wrong. I'm not trained or anything. All the things I've done before have been accidents, or – or guessing. I don't really know what I'm doing. But I have to try, right?'

He was still staring at her. 'I think you're holding back on us, missy. You've done a lot of big things. You might just be the most powerful magical being to have walked through the multiverse since Elara Mercator, and yet you don't think you are. You don't have a lot of confidence in yourself. What is it, modesty? I don't think so. Maybe it's fear.'

'Hey,' Avery said, standing up. 'She's not a coward.'

'I never said she was,' Thess said, holding his hands up. 'But it's normal to be afraid of what you don't understand. You've just got to see it as something fine. Something good. It's your talent, you don't need to be afraid of it.'

Flick stared at him. 'I was going to learn about it with Tristyan,' she said. 'And now I can't. So can you not talk at me like that?'

His eyes glittered. 'Like what?'

'Like you know me.' Flick stood up. 'It's not something I want to be able to do, and I don't like being the only one who can do it, OK?' A pins-and-needles crackle ran over her hands, and she flexed them, glancing down in surprise.

Thess gave her a brief smirk. Then cricked his neck. 'I think you're capable of even more than you've already done. You just haven't figured it all out yet. There's still time, though.'

Flick blinked. She still felt out of sorts, but not cross any more.

Avery caught her eye and gave her a smile, and the aching sorrow in Flick's chest lessened, just the tiniest bit.

Thess sniffed again, and tapped the dirty old suitcase that led to the House on the Horizon with his boot. 'Come on through, then. If you want this nasty old suitcase so much, let's be having you.'

*

Danser Thess' house was as lean as the man himself. Bare wooden boards made up the floor and walls, and there was no decoration whatsoever. Not so much as a picture or a rug. There was a large wooden table against one wall, and four chairs pushed beneath it. A fireplace sat, empty and cold, within a stone setting on the farthest wall. Besides that, the room was empty.

Out of the windows, the landscape seemed to blur in and out of focus, the sand and rocks and dead-looking trees wobbling as though they were underwater. It made Flick feel as if she had motion sickness. Ordinarily, she would have been excited and thrilled to be in another world, but everything felt spoiled now. Flick was so tired she felt as if her eyeballs had dried up and were rattling painfully around her skull. Avery too looked as if she hadn't slept, and Jonathan had developed a twitch in one eye.

The sooner they got hold of Elara's suitcase and took it back to Strangeworlds, the better. With all the suitcases in the travel agency pulled through, being there would be like being surrounded by doorways to which only the Society had the keys. And then Flick could try to destroy the Doomsday Case and rid the multiverse of it for good. They were so close to achieving what they'd set out to do.

Flick pulled Nyfe's magnifier eyepatch down over her eye and squinted through it to take a look around the House. There was barely any magic floating through the air, which made Flick feel even more uneasy. There was almost always a noticeable mist of the stuff drifting about, but the only magic in Thess' house seemed to be a few tiny flecks floating sadly through the air. It made the place feel emptier than the sparse furnishings did.

'There's no magic here,' she said, pushing the eyepatch up.

Avery and Jonathan looked surprised, but Thess nodded. 'Mm, there won't be. This is as detached as you can get from the rest of the multiverse. Hanging on to it by a few threads, I should think. These here being the threads.' He patted the suitcase they had stepped through. 'The House on the Horizon is so far removed from the rest of the multiverse that normal rules don't apply here. Like the horizon itself. You know how you can't get into this building from the outside?'

'Yes. We've landed in the desert before, actually,' said Jonathan. 'We figured out that you can only get inside here by travelling through a suitcase.'

Thess nodded, his moustache flapping. 'And that's not all. There's no time, here.'

'Woah.' Avery put her hands up. 'No *time*? What do you mean?'

'I mean that if you stepped back into that there suitcase, no time at all would have passed between you leaving Strangeworlds and returning to it.' He folded his arms. 'Comes in handy, I can tell you. I've lived here for nigh on a century by your time, and I've not aged a day.'

'But . . .' Jonathan screwed his face up in confusion, lifting his glasses to rub at his eyes. 'But you can't live in a world you're not born into.'

'That's what you've been told, for sure, and it's a good rule to go by, but if the multiverse has taught me anything it's that the darn thing is full of exceptions to the rule. You want to live in a world you ain't been born into? Well, you can, *depending* how much magic that world needs to keep going.' Thess smirked, the dirt on his face creasing into his laughter-lines. 'This one, at the very edge of the multiverse, barely any magic in it at all? The magic I make by being alive here is just overspill, and I can use it to keep on living. I've been here this long and still got my good looks.'

Flick decided not to comment on that. 'It said in the *Study of Particulars* that Elara Mercator found this place.'

'That's true. She knew it was somewhere special, of course, but didn't want to stay here and run it by herself. Wanted to stay with her family, and who could blame her? I volunteered.'

'You knew Elara?' Jonathan asked.

Thess nodded. 'She were an old lady by the time I met her. I'd come to England to claim an inheritance, and got to talking to an old chap in a bar. He asked where I was from, and what I was planning to do with myself in England. Told me he was studying the universe. Well, that sort of thing tickles your interest when you're a young man, so I said I'd head to his shop the next day and cast an eye over what he was doing.'

Jonathan cocked his head to one side. 'Let me guess – when you got there he gave you a magnifying glass and asked you to look through it?'

'Got it in one.' Thess grinned, showing browning teeth. 'And then, o' course, it all comes out. Suitcases, schisms, the multiverse, everything. They offered me the chance to stay, become part of the Society. Well, an offer like that is attractive enough if you've got no strings to cut, but I had a whole life over in the States. And that's a lot to give up. It took me another ten years, and then, having no family of my own left, I moved away permanently, and I been here ever since.'

'Where's Elara's suitcase?' Flick asked, too tired to be polite about it.

Thess smoothed his moustache. 'I know I asked before, but I just wanna make sure. Do you know what you're getting into?' he asked. 'Do you really want this suitcase – the one that could end it all – in your hands?'

'No, I don't,' Flick said. 'But I've got to try to destroy it. We don't have any other choice.'

That seemed to satisfy him. He crossed the room to the bare wall opposite the table and ran a hand over the wood. The wall seemed to shiver; the wooden boards trembled and shifted against one another as if testing the strength of the nails that held them in place. Then they faded from sight and revealed a wall of suitcases, not unlike the one at The Strangeworlds Travel Agency. This wall, however, was not stacked to bursting. It was empty save for a handful of filled slots. And right in the very middle was one very beautiful single case.

It was bright-polished cherry-red, with brown straps and gold finishes. It looked to be in incredibly good condition for a Strangeworlds suitcase. It was small, too, about the size of a cereal box.

Danser Thess pulled the suitcase out reverently, as though it were made of glass. He held it out to Flick, who took it carefully, as though she was cradling a bomb. In a way, she was. It felt heavy and fragile at the same time, full of potential and yet completely unremarkable.

'There y'are.' Danser stood back, his hands on his skinny hips.

Avery and Jonathan started taking down the other suitcases from the wall and dropping them through, back to Strangeworlds.

Flick couldn't stop looking at the bright red case on her lap. She put a hand to the leather, feeling the grain beneath her fingers. Then, reached up and pulled the glass patch back down over her eye, steeling herself before looking at the suitcase.

A part of her had expected it to be glowing white with magical energy, but that wasn't how suitcases worked – they didn't show how much magic was within them from the outside. It obviously hadn't been used, so through Flick's eyeglass, it looked boring and completely ordinary. Clearly it hadn't been used. It was a little bit disappointing.

To cover how she felt, she went quickly over to the Strangeworlds suitcase they had come through and put the Doomsday suitcase through, back into the travel agency, making sure it landed on the desk with a soft *clunk* before she stood up again. Out of the corner of her eye, she saw Avery and Jonathan relax, just a little. Flick understood how they felt. The travel agency was the safest place in the multiverse after all.

When Avery and Jonathan had finished dropping through the other suitcases, Thess snorted, and spat a glob of something into his empty fireplace. 'Now what? The Seren won't stop a-hunting for that just because you've moved it. They've been without magic a long time. Their lives are on the line. That sort of thing makes you desperate.'

'We need to go back to Pendularbor before we destroy the suitcase,' Flick said. 'I want to know how the Seren got there.' She scrubbed at her hair. 'Azarus said something about following a path . . .'

'Mm-hm.' Thess nodded. 'I'd like to know what path they followed to get there, too.' He rubbed his nose with his thumb. 'Maybe we'll get the chance to ask, if we ever get up close.'

'Will you come back with us to Strangeworlds?' Jonathan asked him. 'We could use your help.'

Thess shrugged, good-naturedly. 'I guess so. I just got one other suitcase here, now, in the spare room. Let me grab it and I'll . . .'

But Flick was no longer listening. An electric prickle had raced over her skin, leaving a burning feeling after it. She felt a disturbance. As though a gust of wind had blown through the place, though nothing had moved.

She pulled Nyfe's eyepatch back over her eye, and squinted through it at the interior of the House. Still no magic. The seconds ticked by as if in slow motion. Flick felt the same sort of creeping unease that she'd had when she and Tristyan had uncovered the suitcase hidden away in the Glasshouse.

Something was going to happen.

'Guys . . .' she said softly.

Thess paused with his hand on the door handle. The suitcase that led to Strangeworlds was still open on the floor.

'What's wrong?' Avery asked from the opposite side of the room.

Flick shook her head. 'I don't know. But something is going to—'

There was the sound of a *SCRAPE*, like rocks on

metal. Flick spun around, the patch over her eye showing her the impossible – a huge, gold-white line scratched from head-height to the floor, throbbing and pulsing with magic, and then . . .

Flick gasped as Azarus, the Seren with papery-thin skin and smoke-like hair, stepped right out of the schism and into the House on the Horizon.

CHAPTER FIFTEEN

Avery, Jonathan and Thess might not have seen the schism, but they certainly couldn't miss Azarus stepping into the House.

Thess lunged for his rifle, but Azarus pulled a handful of magic from inside his robes and flicked it towards Thess before he could snatch up the weapon. Thess was knocked back against the wall as though he'd been hit by an invisible wrecking ball, thumping to the floor painfully.

Avery screamed. Jonathan grabbed her by the arms and pulled her backwards towards the suitcase that led to Strangeworlds.

Azarus let out a hiss as he looked around, neck twisting this way and that, as though he was trying to smell the others out rather than see them. Flick's eyes moved to Avery and Jonathan, standing by the wall of suitcase storage. The Strangeworlds suitcase was right next to them. All they had to do was step into the case and pull it through after themselves.

But Thess was on the floor by the back door, groaning, and Flick was on the opposite side of the room from Jonathan and Avery, with Azarus in the middle.

The Seren bared his teeth in a fanged smile. 'Now,' he breathed, his voice the colour of mist. 'Let no one here do anything rash. It has cost me a great deal to reach this place, and I do not plan to leave it empty-handed.' He twisted his neck around again, looking from Flick to Avery to Jonathan and back again. 'Waiting in that ruin of a glasshouse for you to discover a suitcase was hardly the most thrilling of missions, and I do not wish for this to come to a fight when we ought to be on the same side.' He raised his empty hands. 'I am simply asking you to listen. I know what you will have been told about us.'

Thess moaned from the floor again, and Azarus' milky eyes flicked over to him briefly, before continuing. 'We are not the villains you would have us be. We value magic, a great deal more than your pitiful Society does. I wish to take responsibility for the

Doomsday Case I know you now possess. Not to destroy it, but to harness it for the good of all magical people. Human beings are a naturally destructive species. Sephie and I could have drained the magic from the world of Pendularbor as soon as we gained access to it, but we did not. We waited, patiently, for a Strangeworlder who could open the way to the House on the Horizon for us. Until you snatched it away, and forced me to resort to' – he paused – 'cruder methods of travel. The Seren treasure every drop of magic, and we nurture children with enchanted gifts. Gifts the three of you are endowed with.'

'He's a liar.' Thess managed to lift his bloodied head up to snarl. 'Don't listen—'

'Of course he would say that,' Azarus snapped. He kept his hands held up. 'But the power of magic is a wonderful thing.' His eyes moved to Flick, and his arms lowered. 'I know you have contemplated it, wondered about the potential of your own powers, Felicity Hudson.'

'How do you know my name?' Flick blurted. Out of the corner of her eye, she saw Avery stretch out her hand for the suitcase back to Strangeworlds.

Azarus gave his fanged smile again. 'Your name was written on the heart of the man calling himself

Tristyan Thatcher, and when my magic pierced it, I read your name and I knew what and who you were.'

Flick suddenly felt herself vibrating with anger. How *dare* he talk about Tristyan? How dare he say his name? If there had been more magic in the House, Flick knew she might have done something terrible. This man had killed the only link she had to her family's past, and he was standing there grinning toothily about it, as though he had done her a favour. Her fingers itched to grab hold of a rope of magic and wrap it around his neck. 'You don't deserve to even *speak* about him!' she said, her voice trembling.

A look of mirth flitted across Azarus' face. 'I did what I had to do to survive. Survival of the most magically gifted is all that matters. Do you think I wanted to kill Sephie, too?'

Flick breathed in sharply and she saw Avery pause in reaching for the suitcase. 'You killed Sephie? But she was on your side!'

'You forced me to do that,' Azarus snarled. 'You set me ablaze. You snatched the suitcase. I had no choice but to use her life magic to keep myself alive. Sephie died because of *your* actions.'

'That's not true!' Flick shouted, glaring at Azarus.

But a movement over his shoulder caught her eye, and she saw Thess inch towards where his gun had fallen.

Azarus laughed. 'We who survive are the ones chosen by magic. We can and we will rebuild the Seren, for as our powers grow, so do our opportunities. We have suffered so much – so many members of our family have turned against us. Elara Mercator. Tristyan Thatcher. The Gang of Six Thieves. But we remain driven. We are a people chosen by the multiverse to lead, to honour and cherish magic. We are the chosen ones, Felicity.' He cast a hand about at the sparse and dismal space of the House as if showing off just how poor a place it was. 'We are the ones who can turn you from a tool of The Strangeworlds Society into a queen.'

'I don't want anything to do with you,' Flick snapped, keeping her gaze on Azarus as Avery's fingers closed on the suitcase handle, and Thess crept closer towards his rifle. 'I want to *stop* you. You're draining worlds of magic when they've done nothing to you!'

'Sacrifices must be made for the greater good.' Azarus sighed. 'And *we* are the greater good, Felicity. We – you and I – are the ones who can see and manipulate magic. The multiverse has chosen us, and we must join together. Do you not see that?'

'I'll tell you what I see,' Thess interrupted. He was

holding his gun and squinting through the sight. 'I see a target.'

And then everything happened very fast and all at once.

Azarus reached into his robes. Flick dived along the floor towards the Strangeworlds suitcase. Thess pulled his trigger with a *BANG*.

But Azarus moved too fast. He dodged the bullet and lunged after Flick, his scraping ghost-claw hands reaching towards her. Avery already had one leg in the suitcase as Azarus' nails scraped down the fabric of Flick's jeans, his closeness making Avery jump backwards away from the suitcase in alarm.

Flick didn't even think. There wasn't *time* to think. She kicked Azarus' hand off her and grabbed the suitcase handle, lifting the case off the floor. She felt the tiny scraps of magic in the world around her cling to her like a film. Azarus had recovered from the kick and was lunging for her again. If he followed them back through to the travel agency, if he got hold of the Doomsday Case, they were done for.

Something sparked within her.

A darkness – a strange inky magic that flowed from somewhere within and around her – seemed to roll up in front of Flick's eyes. It was the same sensation as when she had held the enormous schism open in the world of The Break, except a hundred times darker, and closer, and stronger. For a moment, she felt frighteningly powerful, as though everyone else in the room were nothing more than insects.

The feeling faded almost instantly, and was replaced with a buzz of magic under Flick's skin. She felt detached from the multiverse and yet everywhere in it, aware of that close darkness that was between worlds, and—

There was another *BANG* as Thess fired a second time, and this time Azarus shrieked and twisted away.

In that moment, Flick lifted the case, pulling it up and over Avery like a sheet, and then she kept on pulling, over Jonathan, and over herself. But the ground rushing up to meet her – to meet all three of them, as Azarus' frustrated screeches filled their ears – wasn't the varnished floorboards of The Strangeworlds Travel Agency.

It barely seemed to be ground at all.

It was as black as night, as soft as velvet and as deep as the deepest ocean trench. It covered them all in a fold of darkness, closing them off completely from Azarus, from Danser Thess, and from the House on the Horizon.

There was no hard landing on to the ground. They landed as softly as if they had fallen into a heap of feathers, rolling over strangely slowly, before catching themselves, and sitting up in the thick darkness.

It was utterly and completely pitch-black. There was a panicked moment where they all scrambled to reach for each other, to find hands and voices they recognised in the dark. Flick opened her eyes wide, searching for a speck of light somewhere, but there was nothing. In her hand, the suitcase she had pulled over them sat like a deadweight.

'Where are we?' Avery asked. Her voice had no echo at all, and sounded flat and close.

'I don't know,' Jonathan replied. He huffed, and it sounded as if he was getting up. 'Felicity, what happened?'

'He was going to follow us through,' Flick said. 'Azarus. He would have gotten into Strangeworlds with us. I had to stop him from following us.'

There was a pause.

'Felicity,' Jonathan asked, his voice calm as a lake might be right before a monster burst out of it. 'What have you done? Where have you sent us?'

'I think . . .' Flick looked around at the all-darkness. 'No, I don't think. I *know*,' she went on, the truth of the matter crushing over her all of a sudden. 'This is the place I saw when I was trying to get all the ships out of The Break. Do you remember? I saw . . . the nothingness that's between worlds. The darkness that's between and around them all.'

'So that's where we are?' Avery spluttered. 'We're not even in a world?'

'We're outside of the worlds,' Flick said. 'We're not even in the multiverse. We're in the Inbetween.'

CHAPTER SIXTEEN

Flick's eyes strained against the darkness. She could still make nothing out. The unseen ground beneath her shoes felt stable enough, but even with her arms outstretched, she felt the need to shuffle forward in case she walked into something.

'Can't we do something about the dark?' Avery hissed. Flick didn't blame her for whispering. The darkness felt as though it could be concealing any number of things, and Flick felt she'd rather not draw attention to herself.

'We've still got the light-balls Tristyan gave us,' Flick said, checking her pocket. 'But I don't know how long they might last. We should keep going in the dark, for a while.'

'Going where, exactly?' Jonathan asked from her left, the question dripping with acid. 'This is the Inbetween. It's *nowhere*. The exact opposite of *somewhere*. There's only us.'

'If there's us, there could be something else,' Flick said, flinching as her hand brushed against something, then realising it was only Avery on her right. 'We can't go back to the House because Azarus is waiting. So we just need to keep walking.'

'Poor Danser,' Avery said. 'He's there by himself against Azarus.'

Flick couldn't stand to think about it. She could only hope that he had somehow managed to get away. 'I think he will have escaped, somehow,' she lied. 'He seemed quite . . . crafty. Or he might have managed to hurt Azarus. The Seren are physically weak, after all.'

There was a silence. 'How long are we going to keep walking when we don't know where we're going?' Avery said. 'We can't even tell how big this place is. If we can even call it a place.'

Jonathan muttered to himself. 'I don't think we *can* call it a place. Felicity's right. This is the Inbetween. There's nothing here. No magic, no worlds, no time. This isn't anywhere anyone should ever be.'

As they walked on, Flick was able to make out the

shapes of her friends on either side of her. There was still no light to see by. It was merely that their bodies were condensed darkness that moved, as opposed to the static dark that was as still as frozen air. Flick wondered what they were breathing, what it was exactly that they were walking on, what they were moving through. The sheer *nothingness* of it all was saddening, and empty. And yet, it was difficult to be frightened of it, somehow. It was as though their emotions were being scrubbed out by the darkness all around them.

No one said very much. The nothingness seemed even to be stealing away the urge to speak.

'Let's stop a minute,' Flick said at last.

They sat down together. Flick drummed her fingers on the suitcase, trying to get her brain to work, whilst Jonathan handed out biscuits from his backpack. Avery didn't say much at all. It was strange how the place wasn't cold or warm, wasn't uncomfortable or safe, wasn't frightening or pleasant. It just *was*. Flick felt as if she was sitting in a bowl of tepid soup.

'I don't know how to get out of here,' she said.

'We're going to have to use the suitcase, aren't we?' Avery said.

'I think so.' A prickling feeling of unease crept

down Flick's legs. 'We can't wander around here for ever. There's nothing here, in every sense of the word.'

'If we go back, we'll get caught,' Jonathan said. 'Azarus will be sitting in the House waiting for us to return. He wants you, Felicity.'

Flick sighed, grim realisation nesting in her chest. It was the heavy feeling she'd carried around since Tristyan's death. She couldn't find any drive to try and save herself. If Azarus wanted her, so be it. 'If it's me he wants then at least you two will be all right,' she said.

Avery snorted. 'Oh, OK, we'll just hand you over and run off, shall we?' She gave Flick a small push. 'Don't talk wet.'

But Flick ploughed on. 'I mean it. Just run. Azarus won't bother chasing you if he can have me. You heard him.'

'You're being ridiculous,' Jonathan said. 'Besides, where would we run *to*? That case in your hand takes us back to the House. All the other suitcases we dropped back into Strangeworlds, which is now inaccessible.'

'I *hope* that this suitcase will work properly again once you're back at the House,' Flick said. 'This suitcase still connects between Strangeworlds and the House on the Horizon – we just got here by accident.

Going back into the main multiverse would . . . sort of re-set it, I think. I can distract Azarus, and you two can hop it back to Strangeworlds. That's how it'll have to be.'

'And just forget about you?' Avery asked, incredulously. 'Are you for real?'

Flick didn't know what to say. 'I don't see how we can all make it home, this time. One of us has to either fight or distract the Seren, and the other two get away. And we know Azarus wants me. It's all right,' she added, 'it's all right, if it keeps you both safe.'

Avery and Jonathan both made loud noises of disbelief and annoyance, and Flick let them lecture her without arguing back. Anything to avoid thinking about Azarus, waiting for her on the other side.

It wasn't just the knowledge of what he could do, or what he had done. His very appearance sent revulsion shuddering through her. She hated his grey, half-dead face, his eyes dull and sunken back in the sockets, and the cold touch of his hands. Flick shuddered. The Seren claimed to be using magic to keep themselves alive, but from the looks of things they had been doing it for too long. They looked dead already.

Azarus' words were slithering around inside her head like worms.

'*We are a people chosen by the multiverse to lead, to honour and cherish magic. We are the chosen ones, Felicity . . . I know you have contemplated it, wondered about the potential of your own powers . . .*'

Flick stood abruptly, as if by doing so she could escape the memory. The worst thing was, there was some truth to his words. She *had* wondered what she was capable of. If she had not seen what the Seren could do, what they had done, what they had already taken from her, then Azarus' words might have been as tempting as sweets. As it was, they sank into her like poison.

Avery tugged on the leg of Flick's jeans. 'I think we should walk a bit further,' she said, clearly making the decision for everyone. And Flick was grateful for it.

'OK. But let's have some light, this time.' Flick took one of the glass bulbs from her pocket, and squeezed it hard. The rubbery ball brightened to an orange light in her palm, so it looked as though she was holding a small glowing satsuma. It wasn't nearly as impressive as the handful of flames that Tristyan had been able to conjure, but it did the job. The amber light threw Jonathan and Avery's faces into view, and Flick was relieved to see they didn't look angry or upset. No more than usual, at least.

Jonathan took the suitcase from her. 'Lead the way,' he said kindly.

The light didn't penetrate far into the darkness, but its glowing warmth made all three of them relax a little as they walked. They could have been going around in circles, but it didn't seem to matter – the important thing was to keep moving. None of them mentioned opening the suitcase again, though. There had to be another way out.

Flick let her mind wander as they walked. The only way to move between worlds, without using a Strangeworlds suitcase, was to travel via schism. Flick herself had done this – she'd gone through a schism that she'd torn out of nothing, stretched another so that others could travel through it, even closed one up to stop people travelling through. But each time she had, she'd been surrounded by spare magical energy. Without a store of magic to use as fuel, a schism would devour the traveller using it, destroy them. Even if Flick could have made a schism here, to get all of them through it would have taken a colossal amount of extra magic.

There wasn't a scrap of magic in the Inbetween.

Except for the three living people wandering through it. There was plenty of magic living within the three of them. Maybe even enough to—

Flick deftly snapped that thought in half, and tucked it away. That was how the Seren would think, seeing people as sources of magic rather than living things. She wasn't going to be like them.

'There's only one way out, isn't there?' she asked, after what felt like an hour.

They stopped walking.

There was a cold pause.

Flick sniffed, guilt and fear welling over her like she'd been dropped into a huge beaker full of it. 'I'm sorry. I didn't know what I was doing. I couldn't let him follow us into Strangeworlds, and I just – I just panicked.'

'It's not your fault,' Avery said quickly.

'No, it isn't,' Jonathan agreed. 'We would have been followed and Azarus could now be in any world he chose. And worse – that Doomsday Case is just lying on the desk at the travel agency. He could have ended up with that in his clutching hands.'

'But all he has to do now is wait for us to come out!' Flick rubbed between her eyebrows. Avery touched her arm, but Flick pulled away.

Jonathan took a deep breath. 'All right,' he said calmly. 'So, we have to go back. But you've given us some time to think. We're smarter than he is. Aren't we? We need a plan. We'll just have to move too fast for him to catch us. *Any* of us,' he said, giving Flick a severe look. 'We should split up as soon as we get back. Then we can run, distract Azarus from the case while it's closed and re-opened again properly, and then we try to get back to Strangeworlds ... Perhaps if Thess is still there, he can help us, though we can't bank on that.'

Flick tried to hide her scepticism, but Jonathan saw it in her face.

'I know it's not much of a plan, but it's all we've got. Somehow or other, at least one of us will get back to The Strangeworlds Travel Agency.'

'. . . Strangeworlds?' A voice, no louder than an intimate whisper, came from far away.

The three of them froze, nerves ablaze.

'Please tell me one of you is messing about,' Flick whispered.

Avery and Jonathan shook their heads.

'I say . . . I can't find you. I'm . . . Strangeworlds . . .' The voice was minutely louder, now. Closer.

'It's a *person*,' Avery said.

'One of the Seren?' Flick wondered, her senses prickling like mad.

'Could be. We should stay still. Maybe they won't see us.'

'Oh, right, yes, I'm sure this glowing ball – which just so happens to be the only source of light here in the Inbetween – is *completely* unnoticeable, Averina,' Jonathan snapped.

Flick stuffed the ball into her jacket, where it continued to glow through the fabric.

'Thank goodness for your quick thinking,' Jonathan sighed. 'We're invisible now.'

'Shut up.' Flick clamped her hand over the ball, succeeding in only making it glow a deep red.

They stayed still, listening as the voice called again, this time barely audible. Whoever they were, they were now heading away.

'They might be someone who can help us,' Avery said softly. 'Maybe they're a friend.'

'Who happens to reside here in the Inbetween? I'll take my chances without them, thank you very much,' Jonathan scoffed.

Flick badly wanted to take the glowing ball out again to see better, but the thought of the voice belonging to one of the Seren stilled her hand. The idea of the yellowish light illuminating a papery, dead-looking face was horrifying.

'Is anyone there?' The voice made them all jump. It was much closer, now. Avery dug her fingers into

Flick's arm. 'I heard you say "Strangeworlds",' the voice – a man's – went on. It wasn't a hiss like Azarus' voice, it was a strong voice, a living voice. A British accent, clipped and somewhat familiar, though still that of a stranger. 'I'm not here to hurt you. I can see your light.' The voice sounded wary, but soft, like the voice someone would make when approaching a wounded animal. 'Please?'

Jonathan swore under his breath.

'Please.' The man's voice came again. 'If – if you want me to come closer . . . hold your light up?

There was a pause where no one moved or spoke, and then a big sigh. When the voice spoke again, it was low, morose and hopeless-sounding. 'What am I doing? What's the likelihood they even speak English, whoever they are?'

Just when Flick thought he'd given up for good, one more quiet sentence floated through the darkness to them. 'I'm a friend, I promise I mean you no harm.'

'We should check who it is,' Flick whispered. 'He sounds . . . normal.' *And sad*, she thought.

'What if it's one of *them*?' Jonathan hissed back.

'Well, there's three of us. We could—'

'We could *what*? Overpower whoever it is and force them to make the rest of the Seren surrender and stop sucking all the magic out of the multiverse? This isn't a comic book, and I don't think any of us are capable of fighting an ancient magical being.'

Flick gripped the glowing ball. 'Tristyan said they're physically weak, if you can get close enough to them. We could just . . . I don't know, try it. But we need to check. It could be anyone, maybe even someone who needs our help.'

Jonathan was silent for a moment. Then said, 'On your head be it, Felicity.'

Avery didn't say anything. She just pressed herself closer to Flick, like a kitten trying to hide behind its mother.

Flick took the glowing ball from her jacket and raised it. The light immediately illuminated her face, and threw Jonathan and Avery into orangey shadow. The rays of light spread weakly through the darkness, but the silence was now punctuated by approaching footsteps, one after the other, growing closer . . .

. . . until a man came into view.

Flick let him come close enough for the light to throw his features into relief. He was clearly not, she was relieved to see, one of the Seren. He was a tall man, a little on the thin side. His collarless shirt was crumpled, and his wavy hair had probably once been entirely black or dark brown, but was now streaked through with grey. He was handsome in the dad-ish sort of way that Flick's mum tended to like, had a neatly trimmed beard and rectangular glasses, and his face . . .

Flick knew where she had seen that face before.

Jonathan pushed past her, into the light. 'Oh . . .' His mouth dropped open.

The man's expression mirrored Jonathan's: both shocked faces looking eerily like one another. He pushed his glasses up his nose and stepped closer, and Flick could see now just how familiar he looked: the same thick eyebrows, the same short chin, thin nose and sparkling eyes. The same narrow frame that seemed more rapier-like than fragile. It was as though they were two photographs of the same person, taken thirty years apart.

'J . . . Jonathan?'

Flick and Avery turned to look at Jonathan, who had gone whiter than ever.

'Dad?'

'I missed you so much,' Daniel said, pulling his son in for a hug and holding tight.

Jonathan sagged into the contact with full-bodied relief, his hands coming up to grip tight on to the back of his dad's shirt as he thumped his face down on to his shoulder.

Flick and Avery didn't say anything. It felt intrusive to even be there, but the joy radiating from the two Mercators as they clung to one another, stared into each other's faces and laughed at the unlikeliness of their reunion was something you couldn't look away from. Flick brushed at her eyes. Happy tears. There were tears on all sides, in fact. And then, when everyone had calmed down a little, there were introductions, and apologies, and, eventually, explanations.

The group of four sat down where they were, and the long tale of Jonathan and Flick's adventures was told. They told Daniel Mercator about saving Five Lights, and about Flick finding his notebook at the Lighthouse, and what had happened to the crumbling world of The Break. They told him about Tristyan, and Danser Thess, and the growing threat of the Seren.

And there, it was Daniel's turn to pick up the story.

'The Seren were precisely what I was researching,' Daniel said, steepling his fingers just as his son liked to do. 'I'd been noticing mysterious disturbances for a while, in worlds like Five Lights and The Break. I had read about the Seren in the old Strangeworlds guides, but they weren't called the Seren in the books, you see. So, it took a while for me to make the connection.'

'What were they called?' Flick asked.

'The *Unseen*. They seemed to be a myth of sorts, but, as I went on researching, it became clear that they very much existed,' Daniel went on. He pushed his spectacles up his nose, and Flick could see one of the lenses was chipped. 'But the records were quite limited. The records kept by The Strangeworlds Society get rather thin by the 1940s – I had assumed this was because so many members of the Society went to war and did not come back. But it turned out it was because of . . . an accident.'

'Mr Thess told us,' Jonathan said. 'Some Society members were trapped here' – he gestured at the emptiness – 'after trying to create a schism of their own.'

'That's right.'

'Idiots.' Jonathan snorted. 'Who would do something like that?'

Daniel looked suddenly guilty.

'Dad?' Jonathan asked hesitantly.

The friends stared at Daniel. Flick felt her heart skip a beat.

He held his hands up. 'Before you judge me, I wasn't exactly trying to tear a schism of my own. I'd read the story of what happened to the Society. I was hoping to be able to control an existing schism, one contained within a suitcase.'

'What do you mean?' Flick asked.

Daniel pulled a rueful face. 'I was trying to prevent the Unseen coming back to full strength. I knew they had to be getting stronger, that they were travelling again, because of the disturbances in the multiverse. But I didn't really have any leads on where they were or how to stop them. Until I met someone – someone who could use magic – who was also trying to track them down.'

'Who?' Jonathan asked, suspiciously.

'Her name's Clara,' Daniel said. 'She's not a Strangeworlds member, but her father had past dealings with the Seren, and she was able to patch some of the gaps in my knowledge, such as the Unseen's true name, where they were and what exactly it was they did to other worlds.'

'That wouldn't be Clara Thatcher you were working with, would it?' Flick asked, her stomach jumping like she'd swallowed a frog on a pogo stick.

'Do you know her?' Daniel asked in surprise. 'Wait – was she still there, at the storm-tower?'

'No, it was abandoned,' Flick said. 'But we found all her papers and stuff. And we went there with . . .' She stopped, the words she wanted to say about Tristyan getting stuck in her throat.

But Daniel didn't seem to notice. He sagged slightly as if defeated. 'I had hoped Clara might still be there.'

'The tower and the world were there, but the whole world was pretty empty of anything else,' Flick said.

'Lifeless,' Jonathan added.

'What *exactly* were you and Clara doing at the tower, anyway?' Avery asked.

Daniel looked even more miserable. 'An experiment. The one that sent me here.' He pinched the bridge of his nose under his glasses, for a moment, before continuing. 'I don't know what you all know about storm-towers, but the lightning they capture can be used to power things. Machines, usually.'

'But there wasn't a machine at the tower,' Jonathan said.

'There was the empty fixture,' Flick reminded him.

Daniel sighed. 'I suppose that's all that's left of it. We knew the Seren had been trapped in a world—'

'Serentegra,' Flick interjected.

'Yes, that's right. They *had* been trapped there for more than thirty years – but we were aware that they were beginning to break away from whatever had been containing them. They had found at least one way out and were travelling – but clearly were still limited in their abilities, as they kept retreating back to Serentegra. They were acting like scavengers, not invaders. Neither Clara nor I could stand the thought of the Seren reaching full strength again, and travelling freely. Clara has studied magic all her life. She can use it, like the people in Five Lights, to crafts spells and objects. She thought if we attached suitcases to storm-towers in two different worlds, we could use the energy in the connection they shared to close off any exit from Serentegra, and seal the Seren away for ever.'

Flick and her friends exchanged looks. Clearly, Daniel and Clara's plan hadn't worked at all.

Daniel went on. 'We had access to one storm-tower, the one where Clara was studying. We just needed a second, to forge a link and amplify the magical energy before using it to secure Serentegra. I found mention of a storm-tower deep in the Strangeworlds archives. It turned out to be the very storm-tower where the old Society members met their fate. It was located in a forest world.'

'Pendularbor,' Jonathan sighed. 'We've been one step behind you this entire way. But how did you even get there? Felicity had to break in for us.'

'Clara had found a suitcase that led there during her searches,' Daniel said. 'The plan was that she would handle the tower at the beach, and I'd stay in the forest. Since Clara had magical abilities, I trusted her to know how to direct the schisms. We thought it would be easy. We fixed a suitcase into each of the machines, and waited for a storm to hit the towers, to give the schisms trapped inside the suitcase a magical boost. Storms are magical, of course, because schisms are born when lightning flashes—'

'I knew it!' Flick said triumphantly, thinking of that muggy summer's night before her adventure in The Break when the air had felt heavy with static and potential. 'I knew storms weren't just weather!'

'But when lightning struck the storm-tower I was working on...' Daniel shuddered. 'I can't really explain what happened. One moment I was standing watching the lightning crackle through the cables of the machine, the next there was a flash so bright I thought it might blind me. For an instant, I actually saw Clara, working at her own storm-tower, and it seemed as though she could see me. And there was something else. A tearing sound, like someone ripping up paper, and a pale figure, laughing. But then Clara vanished from my sight, and I was falling through the dark, and then... I was here.'

'Sounds like the multiverse didn't want you to be doing that,' Flick said. 'You were lucky to get away at all. All that magic concentrated into one place, all that schism-birthing lightning-powered magic? You did exactly what the Society members attempted in the 1940s! You didn't seal off Serentegra, you ripped a schism open right into it! You made it possible for the Seren to get straight into Pendularbor. You did the exact opposite of what you were trying to do!'

Avery groaned. 'Oh, no. Azarus said a path was made for them. *You* let them into Pendularbor!'

Daniel's expression went from miserable to horrified like the flick of a switch. 'I – I never thought—'

'They were waiting for us,' Flick said, shaking her head as if she could somehow erase what had happened like wiping clean an Etch-A-Sketch. 'They knew we'd come back to look for the case that led to the House on the Horizon. This is . . .'

'This is my fault,' Daniel finished.

No one argued with him.

Jonathan took a deep breath. 'So what happened to Clara? Did she end up here, too?'

Daniel shook his head. 'I don't know what happened to her. I have no idea if she's still alive. I don't even know how long I've been here. Or how to get out.'

There was an unpleasant silence.

'We have this suitcase.' Jonathan held it up. 'It could take us back to the House on the Horizon. But Azarus, one of the Seren, is there. He'll be waiting for us. He'll know we don't have any other way out.'

Daniel nodded. 'I did wonder why you hadn't used it. You're certain the Seren will still be there?'

'No, but there's a good chance he will be.'

'We may well have to take that risk,' Daniel said.

'We already came to that conclusion,' said Jonathan. 'We were trying to work out a plan when we heard you . . .'

Daniel meanwhile, was looking at Flick. 'You said you tore a schism once, when you had to escape the prison world in Five Lights. Could you do that now?'

'It takes magic to do it,' Flick said, shaking her head. 'There's no magic here. The only things giving off any magic at all are the suitcase, and us.'

'So, we're stuck,' Avery said. She put her face in her hands. 'We finally found Daniel Mercator, and we're stuck with him.'

CHAPTER EIGHTEEN

The glowing ball in Flick's hand went dark.

It hardly seemed worth lighting another one. Everyone was tired and anxious enough without having to see each other's worried faces in the eerie pale light. The darkness felt like a comfort, and Flick let her mind wander as she half listened to Jonathan and Daniel talking about the months of time together they had missed. *It must be strange,* she thought, *to think you've lost someone, only to have them come back to you when you least expected it.*

A spark of hope kindled in her chest as she thought of Tristyan. Perhaps . . .

No, she told herself firmly. He was dead. He'd faded back into pure magic – he hadn't even left his body behind. He wasn't coming back. Not ever.

She was grateful for the darkness as she let the tears run silently down her face.

'Hey,' Avery whispered, suddenly beside Flick. Flick could hear her rubbing her hands together nervously. 'You OK?'

'Fine,' Flick whispered back. 'Just thinking.'

Avery sniffed. 'You're crying.'

'Am not.'

'I can smell it!'

Flick paused. 'You can what?'

'I'm not the same sort of human as you, Flick. I can smell your tears. It's OK, I won't say anything.'

Flick felt the lump in her throat swell until it felt like she'd tried to eat a tennis ball. 'I just wish . . .' She couldn't finish.

'He saved us,' Avery said, knowing exactly what she was thinking about.

'He knew he wouldn't make it back with us,' Flick said. 'He conjured up that shield to give us time to run, knowing that it would mean *he* couldn't run. He . . . he sacrificed himself, just to give us a chance.'

Avery was still for a second. Then she moved closer and rose up on to her knees, wrapping her arms around Flick.

Flick's heart bashed against her ribcage. She could

feel Avery's breath against her hair with every exhale. Gradually the tight feeling in her throat softened, and though the sadness didn't go away, it didn't seem so sharp, either.

'Feeling better?' Avery asked.

'Yeah, a bit.' Flick didn't pull away.

But Avery did. 'It's weird,' she said, leaning back. 'After everything that happened at The Break, I sort of didn't want to see you. Not because I don't like you. But because I do.'

Flick sniffed. 'You like me?'

Avery shuffled about a bit. 'Is that OK?'

'Of course it's OK!' Flick almost burst out laughing. 'I – I like you, too.'

Avery gave a small laugh, then sighed. 'What are we going to do?'

Flick shook her head. 'I honestly don't know.'

And they took hold of each other's hands and sat next to each other, squished close together against the vast emptiness of the Inbetween.

*

Flick awoke, surprised to find she had dozed off. She had no idea how long she'd been asleep.

She pulled a second light-ball from her pocket. There seemed little point in saving them. She pressed it firmly, and it blossomed into light, revealing two sleeping cousins on the ground, and Daniel Mercator sitting, looking at Jonathan like he was afraid he would vanish if he took his eyes off him. Jonathan's arm was curled over the suitcase.

Daniel got up and came over to sit beside her. The light seemed to relax him a bit. His shoulders came down, and he exhaled as though he had been holding his breath. She still couldn't quite believe that they had found him – pretty much when they'd stopped looking. In the pale glow of the light-ball, he looked very tired. It was weird meeting him at last, and even weirder to see just how alike he and Jonathan were. It was like a peep into the future. Daniel gave her a nervous smile, and Flick returned it, feeling slightly as though she was sitting with a teacher.

'We're out of options, aren't we?' Daniel said softly, so he wouldn't wake the sleepers.

Flick nodded. 'Going back to the House will mean certain death. We can't get out of here any other way. I don't know what to do.' Admitting it should have made her feel better, but if anything she felt worse.

Daniel gave a sigh, and for a moment he seemed to

be considering what to say next. 'You're a very talented young lady,' he said eventually. 'What you did, for the people of The Break? It's incredible. Thank you. Captains Nyfe and Burnish are some of my oldest friends.'

'What – both of them?' Flick had to grin, thinking of the animosity that had been brewing between the two captains during her time there.

Daniel huffed out a laugh. 'Well, I take your point, there. But yes, they're both people I admire, though for different reasons.'

Flick nodded. 'Yeah, they're nice people. Well. Nyfe can be when she tries, I guess.'

'She's definitely an acquired taste.' He tapped his fingers on his knees. 'I feel like I owe you an explanation. I know what Danser Thess told you about people from Strangeworlds who tried to make a schism before, and I agree they were foolish. But what Clara and I were doing, it wasn't for greedy or selfish reasons. We had good intentions.'

'Hmm,' Flick replied. 'I think people say that a lot.'

'Well, quite.' His finger-tapping became sharper.

Flick shrugged. Whether or not Daniel and Clara had meant well, messing with schisms still sounded like a terrible idea, to her.

After a few minutes, Daniel spoke again. 'Felicity, the way you tore out of the Waiting Room into Five Lights—'

'I know what you're going to ask. And I've already told you, I can't do it here,' Flick said. 'There needs to be spare magic for me to get hold of. And all that's here is us, and these little glowing ball-things. They won't be enough, and I can't exactly use any of us.'

Daniel frowned. 'What do you mean, use any of us?'

'People are full of magic, aren't they?' Flick looked at him. 'Overseer Glean, of the Thieves, threatened to bottle my life-energy if I didn't do what she wanted. And the Seren do it too, don't they? Sap people's lives away. Even each other's. Azarus did, after he was hurt.'

He nodded slowly. 'So – a life *could* be harnessed.'

Flick felt extremely taken aback. 'In theory. But I wouldn't do it. I'm not like the Seren.'

There was a prickly sort of silence. Then Daniel cleared his throat softly. 'But *if* you had a source of magic,' he said carefully, 'you might be able to tear a schism here?'

'I've never done it on purpose,' she replied. 'That time in the Waiting Room, I was . . . full of anger and I was frightened and it just happened.'

'Are you not frightened now?' He sounded amused.

She shrugged. 'Well, yeah, but not in the same way. Back in the Waiting Room it was like fiery fear – it was hot, and it burned. This . . . this is like being under a wet duvet. It's suffocating but not urgent.' She put her chin on her knees.

Beside her, Daniel was thumbing at the bristles on his chin as he thought. 'There is always the possibility,' he said slowly and calmly, 'that we might not *all* make it out of here.'

Flick's heart gave a jolt. She had said the same thing to Avery and Jonathan, but hearing someone else say it felt like an electric shock, and she suddenly realised she must have hurt her friends with her words earlier. 'What do you mean?' she snapped.

'I mean . . . Look, it's really my fault we're all here. I should never have been messing about with schisms and storm-towers.'

'The Seren would have still found a way in to Pendularbor eventually,' Flick said. 'It was just a matter of time.'

'Perhaps. But I'd do anything to get us out of here.'

'But there's nothing you *can* do.' Flick shrugged. 'Our only option is to go back through the suitcase. We'll have to be fast to get the case back open and hope that at least some of us—'

'I would,' Daniel repeated, talking slightly louder over her, 'do *anything*. To save my boy. And his friends.' He met Flick's eyes, and Flick realised, with a sick drop in her chest, what he meant. '*I* don't have to get out of here, just so long as he's safe. So long as all of you are safe.' He lowered his voice. 'You can use my life, use the magic inside me, to get yourselves out of here.'

'I can't do that,' Flick hissed. 'I can't . . . use you like a battery. You'd die.'

'You're here because of me,' he said. 'This is my fault. You—'

'No!' Flick stood up. 'I'm not doing that.'

She marched away, taking the glowing orb with her. She was shaking. How could he ask her to do that? She was a lot of things, but she could never be a murderer, even if it was to save her friends. Even with permission. She felt sick at the very thought of it.

It might work, though, a horrible little voice in her brain whispered. *Living things create an awful lot of magical energy, just by being alive. He could be your ticket out of here.*

Flick mentally stomped on the voice until it was squashed flat. If Jonathan ever found out she'd thought that, even for a second, he'd never speak to her again. Well, maybe he would speak to her again, but not for long and with sharp and painful words that she'd deserve, and that was if he didn't do something worse first.

She stood fuming, the anger rushing through her veins with a familiar tingle that made her aware of just how much of life was fuelled by magic. The thought rolled around her mind, sickening, but true. Life was indeed highly magical, and wonderous. You could do anything, with a life. A life had enough power to tear a schism, that was for certain.

Except . . .

Except, Daniel Mercator's life wasn't the answer, here.

There was another option.

Flick stayed still for a moment. She felt as though she was watching herself from the outside as she thought about what she was worth to the Seren. She knew that they wanted her, her magic, her abilities. But not *only* her. They also wanted Elara's Doomsday Case. Together, she and the suitcase would be the ultimate prize, a prize so appealing that the Seren would never stop hunting for it.

There was a solution to all this, and all it would take would be for her to . . .

Flick shut her eyes, listening to the rush of air in her lungs, feeling the throb of pulse in her tight fist until both rhythms slowed into something sure and peaceful. She took a moment to arrange her face into something innocent, then went back to the group.

Jonathan and Avery had woken up, though both still looked exhausted. Flick knew she needed to tell them. But there was no need to tell them *everything*. 'I think I've had an idea for how to get out of here,' she said. 'But we need to check that the House on the Horizon is definitely out of the question.'

Jonathan put a hand on the suitcase. 'You're certain you want to open it again?'

'No,' Flick admitted. 'But . . . I just want to be sure.' She pulled the case towards her and lay on her stomach to undo the catches. Her fingers paused on the lid, shaking.

'Be quick,' Avery said. 'Like, faster than fast. Like lightning.'

Flick didn't know if she had it in her to be fast, but she could be sneaky. She lifted the suitcase lid the tiniest fraction, and pressed her eye to the gap to see.

There was darkness, and the barely-visible lines of the planks of wood that the house was made of. It was quiet. Pale light on the floor that was probably cast by a moon.

Flick blinked, and relaxed a fraction.

Then there was a *hiss* and a shadow that shot across the moonlight and Flick slammed the suitcase lid down so hard she almost trapped her fingers. She kicked the suitcase away and scrambled backwards, as though Azarus might clamber out of the keyhole.

'It's all right.' Jonathan caught her arm. 'It all right, it's shut. He can't come through.'

Flick brushed at her eyes, which had welled up with frightened tears. 'I know. I know.' She sat up, and Avery put an arm around her.

'You said you had another plan?' Avery asked.

'Yeah.' Flick stood up. 'Yeah, if we can't get back into the House, I've got another idea.'

Avery and Jonathan looked expectant, but Daniel's face creased in confusion, before settling on resolute. Flick refused to look directly at him. It didn't matter if he thought his life was still on the line. Maybe it was better if he continued to think that, actually, otherwise he might try to stop her. Flick spoke to the darkness, rather than looking her friends in the face. 'I'd only get one shot, and that suitcase will probably end up broken if I manage it, but I *think* I can tear us out of here.'

'To where, exactly?' Jonathan asked.

'Back to The Strangeworlds Travel Agency,' Flick said.

Avery narrowed her eyes. 'But you said you'd need magic to do that,' she said. 'Where would you be getting it from?'

Flick wished she was a bit less perceptive.

'I think,' she said slowly, lying, 'that I can use the magical energy in the suitcase itself. Sort of . . . draw it out, and change it. Use it to make a tear in the fabric of this world.'

Jonathan's expression mirrored his cousin's. 'That sounds like an awful lot of guesswork, Felicity.'

'I know,' she said. 'But it's our best option. Isn't it?'

The dubious looks from the others quickly changed to expressions of determination. Flick's heart thumped painfully. Her friends were all so brave. They trusted her so much. She wondered why she wasn't scared. She felt closer to magic in this moment than she ever had before, though she was about to become part of it, and nothing more. Perhaps, this was what she had been meant for, her whole life. Her whole, short, life. Maybe, this was why she had walked into the travel agency that day, *this* was why the multiverse had given her such powers. Because, one day, she would use them to save her friends.

There was no way she would rob Jonathan of his one remaining parent, and no way she would leave any of them here to starve or waste away or however they might come to an end in the Inbetween. Especially not when, out in the multiverse, the Seren were wreaking havoc, unstoppable.

Not all of them were going to make it out of there, it was true. But it wasn't going to be Daniel Mercator who gave his life up for them to escape. It was going to be her.

Flick was going to have to use herself to tear open a schism. It should have scared her to death. But it just felt empty, and final. It was this, or nothing.

Maybe she'd vanish into magical energy, just as Tristyan had. That wouldn't be so bad.

She realised she was shaking.

'Felicity?' Jonathan asked again. 'What's wrong?'

Lie.

'It's – it's going to take a lot of effort,' she forced herself to say. 'And – and it might mean me taking some magic from all of us.'

Avery looked alarmed. 'How much?'

'I don't think much,' Flick lied harder. 'I'm not going to put anyone in danger.'

No one spoke. Daniel Mercator looked resigned –

he thought she was going to use him, and he wasn't uttering a word of protest.

'All right,' Jonathan said, glancing at his dad as if expecting him to say something. 'If that's what it takes. We can't stay here for ever, can we?'

'No.' Daniel put his arm around him. 'No, you can't.'

Flick wanted to tell Daniel her plan, so he wouldn't cling to Jonathan with such finality, but she knew he would try to stop her, if he knew the truth. They all would. That hurt, but in a good way. She knew for certain that her friends wouldn't want her to give herself up for them. She felt very lucky to have known that sort of friendship. Even if it meant she was about to lose it.

'Right,' Flick said, fixing Nyfe's eyepatch over her head. 'Let's do this.'

They all stood in a circle, the closed suitcase sitting in the middle of the four of them. Though at the moment it led through to the House on the Horizon, the friends had also used it to travel *from* Strangeworlds. Flick was planning on using her magic to lead the schism back to the travel agency. And then . . . she just had to feed the schism, to keep it open as her friends escaped, and she . . . didn't.

Oh, god, there was so much she had wanted to do with her life.

There had been so much more she wanted to see.

Was she crying? She couldn't feel her own face any more.

She glanced at Avery, who looked scared and confused. She would probably never see her again. And she couldn't even say goodbye because then she would know, and try to stop her.

Flick closed her eyes. She felt for the magic in the suitcase. A warm familiarity met her mind; she felt the pulse of the trapped schism. It was a condensed bar of magical energy – a stick of dynamite ready to explode. She would be the spark.

The last thing she would do would be to get her friends home. That was OK. That was a good thing. That was the last good thing she would ever do.

Flick took a deep breath, and reached out to the schism with all the magic of her mind.

CHAPTER NINETEEN

The suitcase fell open, the schism inside expanding, searching for magic to feed itself as Flick released it from the case. She stared through Nyfe's eyepatch, watching the schism condense into a line in the air, looking like any other schism she had seen in the wild. It was hungry, and wanted to tear back to the travel agency, and she let it. A small rip in the darkness emerged.

Then Flick stretched it, like she had in the world of The Break, to become a window large enough for someone to just stick a hand through.

Already the aching fatigue was coming for her bones.

Flick could see Avery and Jonathan holding hands tightly, clinging to one another as they stared at the open suitcase. The schism was invisible to them for the moment of course, but as soon as Flick started to feed it, it would grow to be a window-sized gap in the Inbetween.

She could still stop.

She could say she tried.

No. *Grow*, she told the schism. And the schism, already a gateway between the travel agency and the Inbetween, strained to yawn open further.

All it needed was a push of magic.

All it needed was the life of Felicity Esme Hudson.

Her heart ached as she let the swell of magic inside her brim to the surface. It seemed to be coming from a space inside herself – inside her soul – that she hadn't been aware of, before. She could feel it, but not in the way you can feel something beneath your hand. She felt it in her heart, in her bones. Magic was coming from her – from somewhere no scientist could have pointed to, but from somewhere that existed nonetheless.

She had expected it to hurt, to have her magical life-force drained away. But all that she felt was a strange mixture of love and sadness, as if she was saying goodbye to something precious to her. As if she was grieving.

Like she was grieving for Tristyan all over again.

The feeling inside her reminded her so much of him. It reminded her of that terrible cake he had made, of his apothecary shop, of that leather bag still half-full of bottled magic back in the travel agency. It felt like his smile, that familiar kindness she had made room for in her heart just to have it snatched away. It felt like the fizz of magic against her palm as he had gripped her hand tight for the last time and told her *I will always be with you.*

In the same moment that the magic she was controlling pierced through the Inbetween and found The Strangeworlds Travel Agency, a jolt of realisation ran through her. It felt more wonderous than tearing a schism, more frightening than controlling magic, more forbidden than lying to her friends.

She wasn't just remembering Tristyan. He was there, with her.

Tristyan? she thought, as loud as she could. *Is that you?*

No voice answered. But a warmth spread through her – the same as when her dad hugged her. It was a familiar wraparound of love, and Flick couldn't stop the happy tears that welled up in her eyes.

It was him. He was still with her after all, just like he said he would be.

The magic of him lived in her.

Her grandfather, her friend, Tristyan . . . the crackle of magic she had felt when he died hadn't been the end for him, after all. What was left of him – the energy that had powered him in life – was now within Flick, and it was streaming out of her, opening the schism for her, for all of them, to escape to safety.

This was Tristyan's final gift to her. And his final goodbye.

'Flick?' Avery said, her voice weirdly distorted by the rush of magic.

'It's open – quick!' Jonathan pulled at Avery's hand.

'But what is she doing?' asked Avery.

Daniel looked from the schism to Flick, apparently not able to understand why he wasn't dying.

Jonathan was dragging Avery through the schism. 'Dad, come on!'

Daniel snapped out of it, and the three of them rushed through the schism one after the other. As each of them went, Flick felt the pull of the schism as it tried to steal their life-force. But it was held in check by the old magic of Tristyan, and his long, long lifetime, fortified for years on end.

Daniel stepped through the schism last, and Flick was left by herself, alone in the Inbetween.

She was just a step away from the schism, the last of her grandfather's magic holding it open for her to escape.

Are you still alive? she thought.

A sorrowful feeling ran through her. *No*, it seemed to say. Then the same warm wash of love returned, this time more urgently. *Time is running out*, it was saying.

She hesitated at the edge of the window. *After this . . . will you be gone for ever?* she asked. It was one thing to lose someone once, and quite another to get a second chance at a goodbye.

The answer came to her like an idea, like a picture in her mind, like a memory.

Your magic and my magic are one and the same. As long as you remember me, I shall live in your magic, in your heart. You, and Isaac, and Clara, were all written through my heart, and now I am written in yours. It was as though she could remember Tristyan saying those words to her, though he never had. *I will always be with you.*

And Flick realised that Tristyan *had* always been saying those things. Without using words. And now, it was the end.

She gathered up the magical energy around herself

like armour. She felt the edges of the schism close behind her as she stepped through out of the darkness, and back into the world of her friends, her family, and her future.

CHAPTER TWENTY

Flick stumbled into The Strangeworlds Travel Agency as the schism collapsed behind her. She inhaled deeply, letting the smell and air of her own world soak into her lungs, into her skin. There was Elara's red suitcase on the desk – the bright red leather case that they had dropped through moments before Azarus had arrived. The suitcase no one was supposed to open. She couldn't even feel too worried about what they were going to do with it, because she had escaped. She was safe. She was *home*.

She grinned hugely, and almost lost her balance as the room suddenly seemed to sway.

Avery caught her by the arms, holding her steady. 'What – what the heck did you do?' she asked desperately. 'What were you *doing*?'

'It's OK,' Flick said, feeling more wobbly now Avery had hold of her than she had when standing by herself. 'Avery, it's OK, we all made it through—'

'Were you going to stay behind?' Avery shook her arms slightly. '*Were* you? Flick, were you going to let us all get through and leave you behind? Is that what you were doing?'

Jonathan and Daniel gawped at her, identical looks of shock on their bespectacled faces.

Flick couldn't answer.

'For gods' sake!' Avery threw her hands up. 'Flick – you can't just do that!'

Flick's cheeks burned. 'I'm not supposed to try and save my friends?'

'No! Not when it puts yourself at risk, you stupid turnip!'

They glared at each other.

Daniel Mercator raised a hand like he was in school. 'May I ask *how* you found enough magic to expand the schism, Flick?'

Flick's eyes were still on Avery. 'It was Tristyan,' she said, her voice catching like cloth snagging on a branch. 'When he died, I think some of his life magic went into me. That's what I used to make the schism bigger. But I didn't know it was there until I tried.'

Avery's expression was somewhere between furious and admiring. She looked at the ceiling for a moment. 'You can't do things like that,' she said again, looking back at Flick. 'You didn't *know* Tristyan was going to help you. Why didn't you tell us?'

'I knew you'd try to stop me,' Flick said honestly. She glanced away, feeling terrible. 'I couldn't let you know. It was the only plan I had.'

Avery opened her mouth again, as if she was going to say something else, then stormed out to the back of the shop and up the stairs.

Flick's heart sank down to the floor.

Jonathan cleared his throat. 'Well. I, for one, am very grateful we all made it out.' He went over to Flick, and patted her awkwardly on the top of the head. 'Though no more self-sacrifices, please? We are supposed to be a team. We work together. I think we've learned from previous experiences that secrets don't get us anywhere.'

Flick glanced at Daniel Mercator, who was doing a good job of trying to look innocent. She could so easily drop him in it and point out that he had asked her to sacrifice *him*. But she didn't. She nodded, instead. 'Hopefully, it won't come to that again.'

Daniel relaxed slightly, then turned to look at his

son, standing beside the desk in the old travel agency. His face lit up. 'I never thought I'd be here again, or see you like this. You've got no idea what this feels like.'

'I think I have,' Jonathan said. He gave one of his barely-there smiles. 'Really, I know exactly how it feels.'

Flick smiled at them both, watching them look somewhat self-consciously around the place, like they were waiting for instructions. They'd have to figure out what came next by themselves.

She quietly walked out of the room, leaving them to their reunion. She went around the corner of the kitchen and looked up the stairs, where Avery was sitting halfway up, her chin on her hands. 'Hey.'

Avery moved only her eyes. 'Hey.'

'Room for one more?'

She didn't move over, so Flick had to sit on the step below her, Avery's knees beside her head.

They sat quietly for a few minutes, listening to the indistinct words coming from the Mercators in the room beside them. Avery moved one of her hands away from her chin, and let it rest on Flick's shoulder.

'Are you still mad at me?' Flick asked.

Avery snorted. 'Yeah, course I am. I'm going to be mad at you for five years.'

Flick looked up as Avery smirked down at her, and

Flick's heart rose back to its proper place, and then higher, until it felt like it was in her throat. 'Are you really angry with me?'

'Of course I am,' Avery said. 'Because ten minutes ago I thought I was going to say goodbye to you for ever, and it was the worst. I don't want to do that again. Not even a little bit. I don't care if we're friends or – or something else, I just want to know you're only a suitcase away. OK?'

Flick smiled. 'Yeah, that sounds OK.' She reached behind herself for Avery's hand, and took it. 'Sounds pretty good, actually.'

Avery's smirk softened. The look in her eyes made Flick feel warm, and wanted, and accepted.

Maybe it wouldn't be happily ever after; they were only thirteen, after all.

But it would be all right.

Flick leant up as Avery leant down, and they kissed. In secret, on the old stairs, in the back of The Strangeworlds Travel Agency.

*

'I was so stupid to think I could stop the Seren the way I did,' Daniel said. 'If those towers are ever activated again, the Seren could get straight back to Pendularbor without even trying.' He looked more determined than he had in the Inbetween, as if being back in a real world was revitalising him. 'We need to get back there, immediately, and make sure that storm-tower can never be used again. At least, *I* do.' His face creased in a grimace. 'This is my duty, as Head Custodian.'

'If you think I'm letting you out of my sight again, think on,' Jonathan said, as if he was the parent and Daniel was the child. 'Absolutely not. I'm going with you.'

'And me,' Avery said. 'I'm not even a Society member but I'll do what I can.'

'Wait.' Flick held a hand up. 'You're going to destroy the storm-tower?'

'I have to,' Daniel said. 'I need to make sure it can't be used ever again. It's too dangerous. So is the one at the beach.'

Flick rubbed her temples, an idea growing in her mind like a headache. 'No. We shouldn't destroy it – we should activate it. Don't you see? If that tower is switched on again, the Seren will head straight from Serentegra to Pendularbor. Like flies to honey. We can bring them straight to us, and . . .' She trailed off.

'Fight them?' Avery asked. 'You want to invite them

over for a fight? We've only just got away from them. Again.'

'I know, but we don't have any choice. You know they're not going to stop searching for this suitcase,' Flick said, gesturing to the small red case on the desk. 'Even if I destroy it, they'll keep searching for it, for Strangeworlds, and for me. I'm sick of running. We could trick them. Lure them to Pendularbor and then trap them somewhere they can't escape from ever – somewhere with little or even no magic. Maybe in a suitcase only we can access.'

'To trap them we'd need to overpower them first,' Daniel said, tapping his fingers on the desk. 'And none of us can wrangle magic. Even those who *can* use magic are often overpowered by the Seren,' he added, carefully avoiding mentioning Tristyan. 'We wouldn't stand a chance.'

Flick rolled this over in her mind. 'The Seren aren't just our problem, they're everyone's. We need people who can cast spells, make weapons out of magic, *and* are good at fighting. Ask them to help us . . .'

'Oh?' Daniel said. 'Do you have anyone in mind?'

'Yeah,' Flick said thoughtfully. 'I think I do.'

CHAPTER TWENTY-ONE

Flick stepped out of the suitcase and inhaled the smell of sharp saltwater and cold air. There was grey stone beneath her shoes, and a spray of seawater misted over her face. The sky was iron grey too. The whole world looked as though someone had washed water over an ink painting.

The suitcase itself had been a bit like that, too. Found in the Strangeworlds cellar, it had been almost stuck fast with rust and salt corrosion. But Flick was grateful it existed at all – she'd broken the first one, after all.

Flick was about to call out, to ask if anyone was there, when hands grabbed her by the back of her jacket, and shoved her to the ground. She landed hard on the rock and her knuckles skinned painfully on the rough surface as she twisted around, trying to see her attacker.

A face she recognised swam into view. And it was furious.

'I hoped I'd get to set eyes on you again.' Glean, Overseer of the Thieves of Five Lights had hold of both of Flick's wrists in one hand, while one of her knees pressed against Flick's legs to hold her still.

'Hullo, Glean,' Flick rasped, winded by the fall. She couldn't even try to struggle free, she was held so fast. It had been months since she had locked Overseer Glean and her gang away in this remote island world, but here Glean was, alive and fighting, though looking slightly worse for wear.

Glean's blonde hair was lank, and her skin looked mottled and sick, as if it was stretched hard over her bones, but the fire in her eyes was the same. Flick would have shrunk back if she wasn't being held down on the rocks.

'I didn't think I'd get the pleasure of seeing you so soon, but clearly someone up there likes me.' Glean grinned wider, showing off her stinking teeth. She had on the same clothes Flick remembered from when she'd last seen her, and though they looked damp and slightly dirty, they weren't ragged. Flick realised that this must be a world where time moved at a crawl. 'I knew you'd come back for us, as soon as you learnt the truth, as soon as you dug deep enough through the mess of Strangeworlds history,' Glean said delightedly. 'Did you find out about Elara Mercator, girl?'

'We found out about where schisms come from,' Flick said, talking quickly. 'We know Elara was part of the Seren, once, and that you were too—'

Glean cackled with manic laughter. 'You should have done as I asked back in Five Lights. You should have destroyed all those suitcases whilst you had the chance. Well. You've breathed your last, Strange-worlder.' She pulled a jagged blade from the back of her belt.

Flick thrashed in terror, fighting harder to get away.

Glean's wicked eyes ran over her, as if trying to decide where to start. 'I'm going to enjoy this,' she said softly.

There was the sound of a throat being cleared, and the unmistakable *click* of a gun being cocked. 'I wouldn't do that, if I was you.'

Flick and Glean both looked around.

Danser Thess was leaning out of the suitcase, his long-barrelled rifle pointed straight at Glean. He was smirking behind his moustache. 'Now, unless you want folks to be using your skinny old torso as a porthole, put the knife down and get on your feet.'

Flick grinned in relief.

Glean gave Flick a look of pure loathing, then stood up, the knife still in her hand.

'I told you to drop that knife,' Thess said in a bored voice. 'I don't like having to repeat myself.'

Glean rolled her eyes, but tossed the blade away, so it clattered over the rocks. 'Who are you supposed to be?'

Thess stepped out of the case, keeping the rifle aimed right at Glean. 'I'm Danser Thess, ma'am. Lifetime member of The Strangeworlds Society. I'll thank you to stand back whilst the rest of us get outta this thing.'

Flick got to her feet, shaky but grinning in relief as the suitcase let out Jonathan, Avery, and finally Daniel.

Glean gawped in furious disbelief at the crowd. A muscle was twitching in her cheek. 'I see, you've expanded your little band of followers, have you? How did you get here? We were under the impression that the schism leading here was destroyed when *that girl*' – she looked seethingly at Flick – 'did something to the suitcase.'

'There's more than one way to skin a cat. Or get to an island,' Daniel said. 'It took some searching, but we eventually found another suitcase that led here. And an old friend,' he added, nodding at Thess, who was keeping his eyes firmly on Glean.

Flick glanced about. Besides the Strangeworlds Society members and Glean, there was no one else around. The crash of the waves against rock was like white noise, making everything feel close and claustrophobic. 'Where's everyone else? Pinch and Hid and the rest of them?' she asked.

At this question, Glean slumped slightly, her sneer dropping for the first time. She looked younger without it, though still eerie. It was strange, Flick thought, how whilst Glean and the Seren like Azarus looked barely corporeal, Danser Thess looked as real and solid as any other human being. This, Flick supposed, was proof that consuming magic for so long wore people away. She wondered how long before Tristyan would have started to look the same. Perhaps the only difference was that Tristyan had consumed *less* of it – he hadn't schism-jumped, after all, and Flick knew you had to consume huge quantities of magic to survive that.

'The other Thieves *are* still here, aren't they?' Jonathan prompted.

'Oh, yes. They're over the ridge.' Glean gestured behind herself with a thumb. 'I'm not permitted to sit with them any longer. They blamed me for getting trapped here. Said I should have been more cautious, made sure it wasn't a trap. Maybe they were right. Anyway, they ousted me. They've got a new Overseer, now. Overseer Swype. Much good it does to the lot of them. We're all stuck here. Or we were.' She looked hungrily at the suitcase.

Jonathan bent down and picked it up, quickly. 'That's enough of that, thank you. If you're good, and willing to negotiate, we might be able to make a deal.'

'A deal?' Glean repeated, raising a sceptical eyebrow. 'Whatever it is, I refuse.'

'You heard her,' Thess said loudly, pointing with his rifle from Glean to the case in Jonathan's hand. 'Back in the suitcase, everyone, she'd rather stay here.'

'Glean.' Daniel raised his hands, ignoring Thess. 'Please, listen to us. This is bigger than anything else. This is about the Seren. They're coming back. We need to stop them.'

Glean's face twitched into a grimace for a moment, as if she'd smelled something bad, but she quickly regained her composure and stood straight, arms folded. 'That is not my problem,' she said. 'I didn't spend years of my life plotting to get away from them, just to put myself in their firing line again. Do you have any idea what it's like to know you're going to spend the rest of your life running and hiding? For decades the six of us have flitted from world to world, until it seemed like the trail had gone cold, and they were finally leaving us alone.'

'They weren't,' Thess snorted, taking a filthy cigarette from behind his filthy ear and sticking it into the corner of his mouth. 'They didn't give up on you, they were inconvenienced. Unable to travel, y'see?'

Glean's eyes glimmered with interest. 'Unable to travel? What stopped them?'

'Their magic stores were smashed,' Flick said.

'By who?'

'Tristyan Thatcher.'

Glean blinked, then frowned. 'I don't know a *Thatcher*, but if we're thinking of the same Tristyan . . . Tall, dark hair? Different woman on his arm every week?' Glean raised her eyebrows and glanced over the group. 'Well, I don't see him here, for all his heroics.'

'He's dead,' Flick said.

'Didn't get very far, then, did he?' Glean snapped, her words sharp and hurtful. 'Look – the Seren and the Strangeworlders are each as bad as each other. I want nothing to do with either of you.' She gave the suitcase another longing look. 'However, a way off this rock might be worth suspending my morals for, I'll give you that.'

Flick stepped forward. 'What's your other choice? Stay here until you starve?'

'You were happy enough to condemn us to that when you trapped us here,' Glean pointed out. She smirked at the discomfort on Flick's face. 'Oh, yes. Don't like thinking about that, do you? But it's true. You locked us in here, without so much as a moment's thought. You think you're the good guys? The heroes?' She shook her head. 'There's no such thing as heroes or villains.'

'We acted poorly,' Jonathan admitted, 'but it was in defence of all the worlds in the multiverse. Do you blame us for that?'

Glean scoffed.

Jonathan went on. 'You're right. We're not the good guys. We wouldn't have come back for you if we didn't need you. And we *do* need you. We need as many people who can use magic as we can get hold of. We're gathering everyone we can.'

'Are you preparing for a last stand or something?'

Glean drawled. But she didn't sound entirely dismissive.

'Something like that,' Flick said. 'The Seren are coming back, and we know where they're heading. They've got enough magic to travel through schisms again. They stole so much magic from The Break that its inhabitants had to flee to another world. We need to stop them before they take any others.'

'And that's my problem?'

'It is *everyone's* problem,' Jonathan said. 'The multiverse will be nothing but a buffet to them if we don't put an end to it.'

Glean smiled, and for a moment it looked as though she was chewing on a delicious secret. Then she clicked her tongue, and glanced over her shoulder at the ridge. 'Well,' she said, 'I do want to get out of here. But I'll leave you to convince Swype and their friends to join. Good luck with that one.'

CHAPTER TWENTY-TWO

Swype and the other Thieves took a great deal of persuasion, though not for the same reasons as Glean.

'We want assurances,' Swype had said, 'that we will be left alone once this fight is over. I don't want to have to answer to Strangeworlds.' Swype stood protectively in front of the rest of the Thieves, arms folded, a scowl on their face. Unlike Glean, Swype looked relatively clean and presentable, though tired. Their white hair was plaited back and their pale eyes were narrowed in suspicion.

'If we manage to put an end to the Seren, you can do as you please,' Jonathan had said. But Daniel and Danser didn't seem so keen on the idea.

'Remember, they helped drive Five Lights to ruin,'

Daniel pointed out. 'There's no guarantee they won't do the same somewhere else.'

'They did what they did in Five Lights because they were scared that the Seren were coming for them. Take that threat away, and they won't act like that again. Will you?' Jonathan looked at the Thieves, who gave reluctant shrugs and nods.

'We're willing to stake out the world for you,' Swype said. 'Fight too, if necessary. But after this, we want our freedom. It's all we've ever wanted, ever since we escaped their clutches.' They sighed, and glanced over at Glean. 'We'll take her, as well, I suppose. We've come this far together, after all.'

Glean scowled back, but went over to stand by her old friends with an air of relief. Pinch had given her hand a squeeze, and Garner had patted her shoulder.

With the vow that this would be the first and last time they stood together, it was agreed. With a promised armed escort in the shape of Danser, the Thieves dropped through the suitcase to Pendularbor, taking Tristyan's bag of leftover magic with them.

*

Danser's re-appearance in the world of the Thieves had been a huge relief – Flick had been more worried about his fate than she'd admitted, even to herself. She really didn't want to lose anyone else.

'How did you get away?' she had asked. 'We thought Azarus . . .'

Danser had snorted, and when he snorted it sounded like a disaster in a snot factory. 'Managed to clip him on the second shot. Right in the shoulder. They're weak, you remember? Could barely get hisself off the ground, which gave me time to get into my last suitcase and high-tail it out of there and back to the travel agency. You can tell things are disturbed in the multiverse for sure . . . the time difference between my House and Strangeworlds shouldn't have existed at all.'

'So Azarus is still in the House?' Flick had asked. 'When we were in the Inbetween, I checked in the suitcase and I thought I saw him.'

'I couldn't tell you, and I don't fancy going back to check, neither. But he got in, so he may well be able to get out, even wounded as he was.'

It was both a comfort and a worry, but their conversation had to be paused as Daniel and the Thieves began organising their journey to Pendularbor.

Avery had gone back to her own world for a brief visit to her own family, and Jonathan was helping his dad.

Flick had taken herself to the back garden to get away from the commotion in the travel agency. She was thinking so hard there was an ache between her eyebrows. She had a plan, but it had holes in it. It was all well and good trying to confine the Seren somewhere, but it would have been so much easier if she could trap schisms like Elara, or if she'd had a chance to let Tristyan teach her how to use magic properly. He'd been taken from her, and she needed him more than ever, now.

The other thing she needed was time. She had run out of excuses for her parents about where she was, and was at risk of having to hurt and disappoint them. Fortunately, with there being no time at all in the House on the Horizon and very little in the Inbetween, she hadn't been gone long enough for them to worry too much – yet. But maybe time wouldn't always work in her favour like that. They'd soon start to ask questions.

Her thoughts were interrupted when Danser came outside, spitting and grunting as usual, lighting up as soon as the fresh air hit his face.

'Danny says I can't smoke in there,' he said, before puffing out purple smoke. The smell wasn't nearly as bad as Flick had expected, nothing like regular cigarettes. This was almost like a scented candle, but so thick in the air it stole your breath. Danser leaned against the wall, his moustache fluttering as he gripped the cigarette between his lips. Finally, he removed it with his grubby fingers, and tapped the ash off the end. 'Difficult, I imagine,' he said, 'trying to come up with a plan to stop these villains. Particularly when the man who was supposed to be teaching you how to get a handle on your magic ain't here no more.'

Flick looked at her shoes.

She saw Tristyan, holding up a magical shield that was getting smaller and smaller, covering only half his body and shrinking fast.

She saw jagged cracks appearing.

And then the shield was gone, as if had never been there. Tristyan's hands were raised . . .

Flick couldn't speak. She nodded.

'S'a darn shame.' More purplish smoke filled the cold air. 'I know I'm a poor substitute for your grandad, but I'm not pure useless.' He dropped the cigarette and dragged his boot over it. Flakes of tobacco blew in the wind. 'When we get to Pendul, I'll do what I can. I'll teach you how to wrangle that magic you're so close to. Might just be the difference between a plan and a panic, you know?'

Flick smiled. 'Thank you. I'd like that.'

'It won't be quick,' he said. 'Nor easy. I've had several lifetimes to practise, but then I didn't have your talents. I think between the two of us, we can make a decent start. Maybe even get you moving them schisms into suitcases. Trap the Seren somewhere there's no escape from, like you did with them Thieves.' He sniffed and walked over to the back door. 'I suspect you don't want to think about it, but someone's got to say it: you probably won't be heading home for a while,' he said softly. 'I'm not saying it'll be for ever, but right now we need you more than your schoolwork does. Giving something up to stay here – that's a choice comes to everyone who gets chosen by this Society. You're just having to decide about it younger than most.' And he went back inside.

After a few minutes, Flick followed him. He was right. If The Strangeworlds Society was going to be taking a stand in Pendularbor, she could no longer expect to flit back and forth between school, home and the travel agency. She was going to have to do what she had never wanted to do: leave a part of her life behind, at least, until they defeated the Seren. *If* they defeated the Seren, she corrected herself.

Danser had just disappeared through the Pendular-bor suitcase when she got inside. Avery was back, in clean clothes and carrying a squashy-looking rucksack. She gave Flick a wide smile, but Flick's smile in return was small and brief.

'What's wrong?' Avery asked.

'Not wrong, exactly,' Flick said. 'I've just . . . realised something.'

Avery, Jonathan and Daniel looked at her expectantly, like she had something big to say.

And she did.

Saying it out loud was horrible.

'I can't go home any more,' she said. 'At least, not until this is over. I need to learn to move schisms, and I can only do that in Pendularbor, where there's enough spare magic. Plus, I need to be there when the Seren come. I can't be always coming and going.' She looked at Daniel Mercator. 'Can I?'

'Being part of The Strangeworlds Society,' he began slowly, 'is a job that takes and takes from you. It certainly wouldn't mean leaving your family for ever, but who can say when this crisis might be over? Only you can decide if the benefits outweigh the heartache of being away from the people you love for so long.' He glanced at Jonathan, before turning back to Flick. 'I am never going to say it's something you *have* to do.'

'Flick, you don't need to make the decision now,' Avery interrupted. 'You can still go back and forth for a while. My parents and I are always fighting. All because of these suitcases, this place.' She took Flick's hand in both of hers, the kitchen light dancing off her chipped black nail varnish. 'Don't rush to tell them.'

'It won't be for ever,' Flick said. 'If I can do this full time, just for a while, I can help everyone bring an end to the Seren.'

'You don't know that for sure. This might go on for months. Maybe years!'

'Avery's right,' Jonathan said, joining in. 'I thought I was an orphan. It felt like nothing else I've ever experienced. Don't give up your family willingly, Felicity.'

'What else am I meant to do?' Flick cried. 'You need me to work magic. I'm already having to hide all my family history that's mixed up in this place from my dad.' She took a deep breath. 'It won't be for ever. But I have to leave them. For a bit.'

Even as she said it, she felt a pain in her heart blossom, like a flower just beginning to unfurl.

The three Mercators looked at one another.

Avery let go of Flick's hand, though she squeezed it before she did.

'Do you need someone to come with you?' Jonathan asked.

'No,' Flick shook her head. 'I think it's better if I do this on my own.'

*

Flick almost hoped her parents wouldn't be home when she got in. But they were, of course, and none too pleased about the hour.

'Honestly, Felicity, it's half past eight! This really isn't good enough,' her mum said, tailing her up the stairs. 'You need to be more responsible – I hoped that you'd learned your lesson after the summer . . .'

'Mum.' Flick turned, her cheeks burning. 'I'm sorry. Believe me, it's not going to happen again.' She paused. 'I love you.'

Her mum huffed. 'You can't just say that and think I'm going to roll over and play nice. This cannot keep happening. I know you said you'd been out with a friend, but no friend – or girlfriend – is worth you worrying me and your dad half to death. Understood?'

Flick only nodded before closing her bedroom door. There was nothing else to say or do. She had wanted to tell them, she really had, but now that she was standing there, she knew they would never believe her. She needed to pack some clothes and go. She would have to just run away.

She stuffed clothes into her school rucksack, trying to pack for all weathers. She hadn't seen it rain in Pendularbor, but she guessed the trees didn't grow that big without a shower or two. She packed her copy of the *Study of Particulars*, giving a small smile at Aspen Thatcher's name scribbled inside the front cover. She decided to wear the walking boots she had got for Christmas – they were tough and waterproof, better than trainers. She snuck back down the stairs and through the kitchen into the adjoining garage where everyone's winter clothes were in storage boxes.

The realisation that she was actually running away from home suddenly crashed into her with the force of a train. She leaned forward and pressed her head against the boxes. She was really doing this, then. Leaving her home and her family to go and save the multiverse.

She'd be back.

One day.

Maybe sooner than she thought.

But until then, she would be gone. Beyond the reach of parents or police or anyone else.

How long would they spend searching for her? Her mum and dad would comb the country for her. They'd call the police, cover every wall and lamppost in posters, and ask for help from everywhere they could, looking for a girl who had chosen to never be found. But for how long would they search? Everyone gave up, eventually. Would Freddy forget he had ever had a sister? When would the Hudson family resign itself to being a group of three?

'Flick?'

She looked up guiltily, the fully packed backpack at her feet, boots in her hands, coat already on and zipped up. 'Oh. Hi, Dad.'

He peered at her for a second in the gloom of the garage, then clicked the faint orange light on before coming in, and half shutting the door behind him. 'What are you doing?'

'Nothing,' she lied, putting her boots down and pretending the stuffed backpack was invisible. 'Just looking for something.'

Isaac Hudson's dark eyes rested on the backpack, and his mouth twitched. 'Is this what I think it is?'

'Dad—'

'Because you really don't have to,' he said softly. 'Whatever it is, we can sort it out.'

Flick almost laughed. Her emotions were like bubbles in her chest waiting to explode. 'I really don't think you can. This is . . .' She sighed. 'I can't even talk about it, because you wouldn't believe me. *That*'s what it is. Something I can't even talk about.'

'Not even to your old dad?'

'No.' She shook her head. 'You wouldn't understand. And not because it's something that's in my head. You wouldn't understand because . . . because it's magic. It's magic, and it's real and it's stupid and . . .' She stopped, and looked at him. 'What if I said I'm leaving because I have to go and save the world?'

He gave her a look she couldn't quite define. Then he walked to one of the old cardboard boxes still stacked up from their move last summer. He dug to the bottom of it and pulled out a slim walnut box with a gold catch.

With a dropping, sick sort of feeling, Flick realised she had seen that box before, last summer, when they first moved into the new house.

. . . She pulled the box out. It was heavy. The inside was stuffed with yet more papers and envelopes . . .

But that wasn't all. For she had seen another box exactly like this one, but in another world.

. . . she knocked the chair, and it banged against the desk, sending several books and a slim walnut box with a gold catch straight to the floor . . .

. . . Tristyan came over and lifted the box in his hands. It looked smaller in his spidery grip, and his thumb tapped on the latch as if impatient . . .

She stared at the box in her dad's hands. 'What's going on?' she whispered.

He half sat against a leaning stepladder and flicked the catch up to open the box. 'Have you ever looked in here?'

'I did when we moved in here. It was just full of papers,' Flick said.

He smiled, the same smile she knew he shared with someone else, now gone. 'Yeah, papers. Papers can tell you a lot, though, if you read them. And envelopes can hide a lot of surprises.' He pulled one out, and held it, looking at his daughter. 'I wondered, when we got this house, if you'd be happy. You did seem to be. But then . . . then you started asking me about my parents, which you'd never done before, and . . . I knew. I knew you'd found it, and I knew there was nothing I could do about it.' He put the box down, but held on to the envelope, looking at it with tired eyes.

'What . . . do you think I found?' Flick asked. Her heart was hammering through her body like drumbeats beneath the ocean.

Isaac held out the envelope to her.

Flick took it, and slid something out of it. Something that made her breath catch.

It was a photograph.

Out of the picture smiled Tristyan and Aspen Thatcher, and in their arms were two tiny babies. They were all sitting on a sofa, the adults squashed together, the babies propped up in their arms so their faces could be seen. One of the babies was open-mouthed and yelling, the other looked like Freddy when he was about to eat something he knew he shouldn't.

She looked at her dad, who had taken another envelope from the box, and was looking at her with an expectant and yet sad expression. 'I know who they are.'

He gave a sigh. 'I think it's time we told each other what we know,' he said. 'About our family. And about The Strangeworlds Travel Agency.'

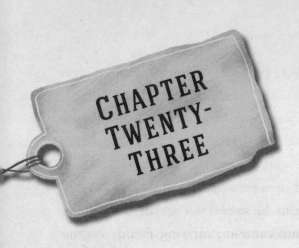

CHAPTER TWENTY-THREE

'The people who found me must have read through everything in here,' he said, handing Flick a letter from the walnut box. It had been softened by time and many readings. 'But they probably thought it was a practical joke. There's no such thing as other worlds . . . is there?'

They were sitting in the living room now. Flick's mind felt like it had been through a washing machine. All this time, her dad had known about Strangeworlds and about where he came from, and he had never said a word.

Flick looked at the letter. The side facing her was addressed to *Isaac Thatcher Hudson*. 'This says *Thatcher* on it,' she said. 'But you don't use that name.'

'No, he said, 'not as a surname, anyway. It gets

used as a middle name on a few forms, but I've never been a fan of it. I. T. Hudson sounds like a computer company.'

Flick ran a thumb over the edge of the paper. 'I don't know if I should read this. Isn't it personal?'

'It is, but I don't mind. It's your history, too.'

'What's going on in here?' Flick and her dad looked up as Flick's mum came in, carrying Freddy on one hip. He was dribbling like mad, his new teeth keeping him awake at night. 'Oh, guilty faces, is it?' Flick's mum asked, putting the baby down. He immediately began to crawl in the direction of the stairs.

Flick thought about hiding the piece of paper behind her back, but what was the point? 'Um.'

'I'm showing Felicity my baby box,' her dad said, saving her. He got up to intercept Freddy. 'I've shown you before, Moira.'

Her face fell slightly. 'Oh, that.' She glanced at her daughter. 'What do you think about it?'

'It's OK, Mum,' Flick said. 'I already know a lot of it.'

Her mum actually took a step backwards. 'What do you mean?'

'I mean, I know about the other worlds. All of that.'

Moira pinched between her eyes. 'Isaac, you can't

go around telling her this is real, she's liable to believe you!'

'But it *is* real,' Flick said. 'I know it's real. I found out about where Dad comes from before he told me anything. I . . .' She swallowed hard. 'I even met my – I met Dad's dad.'

Isaac stopped, frozen, a struggling Freddy in his arms. 'You . . . you met my . . .'

'Yes,' Flick said, her throat on fire. 'But he died. I'm really sorry. He died saving me, and my friends.'

Her parents looked at each other, and then at their daughter. Moira sat down on the sofa as if she had forgotten how to stand. 'I think you ought to explain what you mean, Felicity. All of it.'

Flick took a deep breath.

And told the story. Right from the start.

She began with arriving in Little Wyverns and finding The Strangeworlds Travel Agency. She told the story of meeting Jonathan, of finding out she could see magic, of saving Five Lights. She described every detail about the first time she met Tristyan (though telling that part hurt) and how he seemed so familiar right from the start. She told her parents about The Break, the pirates, and how, at the end of that adventure, she had found out who Tristyan was.

'What was this man's excuse for abandoning his son like he did?' Moira snapped. She'd been flinching with a restrained need to interrupt every ten words or so, but this had apparently been too much to hold in.

'He said he didn't want to. But Dad kept getting sick in their world. Tristyan wanted Aspen – that's Dad's mum – to stay with him here, but she chose . . . not to.' Flick grimaced. There was no way to make what Aspen chose to do sound any less painful or wrong. 'She stayed with Tristyan, and their daughter. Dad's twin.'

Isaac was rocking Freddy absent-mindedly. 'What's her name?' he asked. 'The letter just says *your twin sister*.'

'Clara,' Flick said. 'Clara Thatcher.'

'She's still alive?' Moira asked.

'I don't know,' Flick had to admit. 'I hope so. Daniel Mercator, Jonathan's dad, was working with her.'

She picked up her story again, giving a very potted explanation about the Seren to avoid her parents freaking out completely. She told them how Tristyan joined with herself and her friends to try to save the Strangeworlds suitcases, and how – after an unexpected confrontation – Tristyan had put himself between the children and danger, to take the wrath of the

Seren alone, and had been badly injured and killed in doing so.

'He made a shield to protect us,' Flick said, 'but it didn't last long. Azarus – that's one of the Seren – he was able to get close enough to hurt him. We managed to get him back to the travel agency, but . . .' She suddenly had to give the ceiling a very hard stare. 'We wouldn't have made it out of there without his help. He saved us.'

Isaac was standing now, looking out of the living room window, a dozing Freddy dribbling on to his shoulder. He hadn't spoken the whole time Flick had been telling the story of Tristyan's death, and now his jaw was clenched so tight he looked as if he might never speak again. Flick's mum was ashen in the face, and her hands were clenching fistfuls of cushion.

Flick knew they needed to feel whatever it was they were feeling, so she sat quietly and let the dark mood in the room condense, and then lift as Isaac turned back around, and gave her a small smile.

'Thank you,' he said. 'Thank you for telling me that.'

She smiled back at him.

'So,' her mum said, finally letting go of the cushions. 'This . . . is all real, is it?'

'Very,' Flick said. 'There's other worlds, and magic,

and people and places you could never imagine!' She suddenly beamed – the joy of being about to *talk about* The Strangeworlds Travel Agency was like a tonic after the misery of the Tristyan story. 'There's worlds where the trees are made of glowing crystal, and others where the trees walk about and talk like people for a while. There's cities made of stone and coral where the gravity is so low you can bounce around or float right up into the sky. And . . .' She stopped, aware that she was grinning so widely her face hurt. 'You've got no idea.'

'You've always wanted to travel,' her mum said, fighting back a smile.

'Yeah.' Flick threaded her fingers together. 'It's a dream come true, in some ways. But it's a lot of work, too. Right now, it's quite dangerous.'

'These Seren people are the ones who killed Tristyan?' her dad asked. 'And *you've* got to stop them?' He frowned.

'Yes,' Flick said. 'I have to. It's only me who can see schisms, and it's only me who can control them. It *has* to be me. I can't sit this one out.'

'You're talking like it's your . . . destiny,' her mum said softly.

'Maybe it is.' Flick shrugged. She looked at the packed backpack she had brought into the room with her. 'It's bigger than home or school or anything like that. It's everyone and everything. It's the whole multiverse. I need to go back, and I need to be there. With The Strangeworlds Society. With my friends.'

Her parents looked at one another. Neither of them looked sure of what to do, and Flick knew they couldn't really understand. Not unless they saw it for themselves.

'Come with me,' she said. 'I was supposed to keep the place a secret, but it's too late for that now. And it's sort of a family matter, don't you think?' She looked at her dad. 'Come and see how it's done, come and talk to Daniel, he's an adult.'

Her mum nodded. 'I think that would be a start.'

*

Flick had arrived back at Strangeworlds with her entire family in tow. Jonathan had been horrified at the sight of ordinary people piling into the travel agency, but Daniel looked unsurprised. The Doomsday Case had been neatly slotted into the empty space in the wall of suitcases, standing out a bold scarlet amongst the brown.

Though they already had their daughter's explanation about how the magical travel agency worked, it still took several hours of explaining (and a few suitcase demonstrations) before Flick's mum and dad seemed completely at ease with the idea. Neither wanted to attempt stepping into one themselves.

'Adults,' Jonathan said, scathingly. Flick and he had retreated to the kitchen at the back of the shop, where they were working their way through all the snacks they could find. Jonathan handed her a hot cocoa made with the Coral City confectioners' mix. It was so thick it was like trying to drink cake. 'Their minds are so much more difficult to introduce new ideas to. Won't come to terms with magic even when it's happening right in front of their eyes.'

'Hey, I didn't believe you at first either,' Flick pointed out, stifling a yawn. It was close to midnight.

'No, but you didn't resist for very long. I think you *wanted* it to be real, which helped. They very much do *not* want this to be real. Because, if it is, they're going to lose you. I don't mean for ever. I mean, during this mission. In some ways, you'll become a mystery to them. They'll never understand this. Not completely. Not in the way we do. Even your dad, who has a good genetic chance of being magical himself, has left it too long.'

'I don't think it's just that,' Flick said, watching

Daniel hold up a magnifying glass and explain to her parents how it worked. 'I think some of it's painful for him. This is where he was abandoned by his mother. It's associated with bad things that happened to him in the past, even if he can't remember them properly. Without this travel agency . . .'

'He never would have been born,' Jonathan pointed out. 'I'm not making excuses, and certainly not trying to justify Nicolas Mercator abandoning him, because that was unforgivable. I'm just saying . . . he might make his peace with this place, one day. I hope he does.'

Daniel beckoned them back over, to where Flick's parents were looking mildly less mystified, and rather more concerned. 'Flick,' he said, 'I think we've reached a stalemate here. Your parents are happy to let you keep coming here and travelling, but they don't want you to give up your home life and schooling for it.'

'But if the Seren manage to get hold of this world, there won't *be* a school!' Flick almost yelled. 'This is more important.'

Isaac ignored her, standing and holding his hand out to Daniel Mercator. 'Thank you,' he said. 'I think we need to go home and talk about this as a family.'

They walked home, all four of them, Freddy asleep in the pushchair, and talked about what it would mean. The lies to the school for starters, the uncertainty and the worry. The danger, the secrets, but also the necessity of it, the impossibility of doing nothing.

By the time they got to the front door, after many promises to come home safely, as soon as she possibly could, the decision had been made. And Flick slept in her own bed that night, for what she hoped would not be the last time.

CHAPTER TWENTY-FOUR

Flick had imagined there would be a lot of waiting around, back in Pendularbor. However, the Glasshouse was already buzzing with activity when she arrived. Kayda's people, upon hearing that the Glasshouse and its storm-towers were now a place where the walls of the multiverse were thin, had encouraged plant-life and large vines to grow in a wide perimeter around the building. The Strangeworlds members watched as great wooden arms sprutted from the ground and wove together in a tangle of branches and leaves that stretched tall and wide. It was a wall as much as one built from bricks, and would take more than a single blast to get through. It reminded Flick of the forest of thorns around Sleeping Beauty's castle.

The Thieves had cleared out several of the rooms in the Glasshouse and made themselves at home there. They kept their own magnifying glasses in their hands at all times, and their once-empty belts were now slung heavily with the magic bottles Tristyan had left behind at Strangeworlds. Flick didn't exactly feel great about that, but the Thieves didn't cause trouble – in fact, they were the ones who dug through the wreckage on the right-hand side of the Glasshouse to get to the storm-tower operation room and began the process of cleaning the machine. Daniel explained what had happened the last time.

Unlike the storm-tower by the beach, the machine at the Glasshouse had not one tower but *three*. The tall, glass, unicorn-horn-like towers that stretched upwards into the sky had metal plates and wires wrapped around them in twisted coils that snaked down their lengths until they entered the Glasshouse and came together into what looked like an empty fixture for a huge lightbulb. That was where Daniel had fixed a suitcase, before. All that was left now was a charred mess and some metal buckles on the floor. The entire machine would have to be taken apart and rebuilt – which meant a serious team effort.

Kayda's people showed them where to get fresh

water, and Thieves Garner and Pinch got the plumbing working again, though there was no hot water and certainly no washing machine. The rest of the Glasshouse was cleared out and opened up, fresh air coming in for the first time in years. Hid and Lute hacked their way through the jungles that had overgrown the orangeries either side of the main building, and over the space of a fortnight, the Glasshouse became an almost pleasant space, though Flick still disliked having to pass through the main entrance hall.

The communal-living arrangements took some getting used to. The Thieves were competent cooks, but refused to make meals for anyone not in their inner circle. Jonathan tried to escape to Strangeworlds every hour or so in search of biscuits, tea or clean tea-towels, and had to be bullied into helping strip down the storm-tower machine.

'Manual labour?' he groaned, as he was handed a rag and a pot of grease. 'I'd love to, but unfortunately a court order says I mustn't.' He was ignored, and made to work on loosening some of the tighter bolts. Avery fared better, as she understood more about engineering, and would end each day covered in dirt and oil that didn't entirely budge with soap and water.

Each night, Flick and Avery would lie in their

sleeping bags and watch the lilac sky of Pendularbor dim to a deep blue-purple, slashed by flashes of lightning that stabbed down between the trees every few minutes. The planet was one giant stormforest, illuminated by softly glowing bioluminescent woodland and a small cluster of moons that appeared in different areas of the sky every night. Flick and Avery didn't speak much as they watched the storms, but sometimes their pinky fingers found one another and looped together, as if anchoring themselves against drifting away.

Despite multiple attempts by everyone to get him to stop, Danser continued to smoke like a chimney almost everywhere, except where Kayda's people could see him – it was a dead plant he was smoking his way through, after all. Though he had eventually been persuaded to take a bath and clean his clothes, it seemed to be for naught as he smelled like a cigarette factory two minutes later. 'I'm not giving up now,' he said when confronted, as if he'd been asked to abandon a noble cause. 'I've come this far, I might as well see it through.'

He did, however, make good on his offer to teach Flick how to manipulate magic. Whilst everyone else worked on the storm-tower and the Glasshouse, Flick and Danser spent every minute they had trying to crack the secret of putting a schism into a suitcase. As Danser was forbidden to smoke during these lessons, he became quickly twitchy and irritable, but since Flick was in much the same mood, they at least matched.

Whilst Flick had, after a week or so, learned how to twist magic into the handful of blue flames that she had once admired in Tristyan's hand, she was still left smouldering with frustration every time she tried – and failed – to move a schism. Whenever she thought about doing it, the part of her mind that dealt with magic seemed to insist that such a task would take a great deal of power. She and Danser had promised Kayda and the Old Mother that they would use as little magic as they could get away with during these lessons, but even with the heavy, magic-thick air around her, Flick couldn't seem to channel it in the way she had before. The strange red-hot magic that shot from her when she was angry or frightened was out of reach.

One day, at the end of the second week of 'lessons', Danser was pacing up and down the tree branch they were meant to be standing still on. They were an hour's walk away from the Glasshouse, but still within Kayda's perimeter of thorns, trying to trap one of the small schisms that they'd found there. They'd been trying for more than an hour to get Flick to do *something* with it, and Danser was now chewing noisily on an unlit cigarette, which was dangling damp and disgusting on his lower lip.

Flick tried to ignore him. She shut one of her eyes, looking through the eyepatch with the other. When Flick looked through it, she could see what no one else could – she could see the breaks in the multiverse itself. Schisms.

In the warm gloom of the forest world, the schism she was trying to manipulate shone like a jagged lightning bolt. It glowed a bright yellow-white and went fuzzy at the edges because sparkles of magic were constantly moving into and out of it. Though the broken bolt in the air looked frightening, a schism was no more harmful than a snake in the wild. It wouldn't do you any harm if you ignored it and left it alone. However, what Flick was doing was the equivalent of poking it with a stick.

Even though Flick was becoming very good at using magic and getting it to do what she wanted, she couldn't work out how to trap a schism. She was beginning to wonder if she ever would.

'I can't move it,' she sighed, letting her hands drop for the eighth time that hour. 'It *wants* magic from me, and I don't have any to give it. I can't even seem to give it any from the air.'

Danser moved his vile, wet cigarette to the other side of his mouth. 'None of this seemed to cause you any problems when you stretched that schism for them pirates.'

Flick pouted. It was true. 'That was different,' she said. 'That was already a trapped schism. This one's . . . in the wild.'

Danser snorted, and some of the paper peeled away from his tobacco. 'So what? It need taming or something?'

Flick rolled her eyes. 'I mean that I can't just move it about, like I could if it was in a suitcase. It's not like I can pick it up. It's not . . . solid. It's not even really there. You can't touch it.'

Danser walked over to where the schism was and waved his arm about. 'How 'bout now? Am I touching it?'

Flick looked through the glass. His arm blurred the magic moving around the schism, but didn't go through it. 'You're just stirring it up like a spoon.'

'But I'm not going through it?'

'No.'

'Huh.' He folded his arms. The cigarette gave up

the fight to hang on to his lip and fell to his boot with a soft splat. 'Guess they really do know whether you're going to travel through them or not.' He frowned. 'Makes you wonder, don't it?'

Flick sat down on the ridge of the tree branch. She took the eyepatch off her head and ran her thumb over the smooth glass of it. 'Maybe Elara was meant to be the only one who could do it. Maybe it was her for a reason. She did what she could to keep the Seren from getting hold of magic.' She looked up at Danser. 'That was her whole life. I wonder if she ever wanted to do anything different with it.'

He was quiet for a moment, then adjusted his hat. 'She liked to draw,' he said. 'Especially maps. Even when she was an old lady, she was always there with a pencil or charcoal in her hand. Very talented. I think she might have been an artist, had things been different.'

'I don't like how this place takes over everything. Strangeworlds, I mean, not this forest. It's like . . . the Mercators *have* to do this. They can't do anything else. They were born into it.'

'Not always born,' Danser said. 'Elara adopted her children, Anthony and Nora.'

'But the children were magical?' Flick asked.

'Did she check for that before she adopted them or something?'

Danser laughed, a throaty hack. 'Don't be so slow,' he said when he got his breath back. 'You think magic cares what you're born into? If it's meant to be in you, it'll be in you. If it's meant to be in your family, it'll be in your family. Magic don't care if your family births you or chooses you, you're still family and that means you inherit what you're due.'

Flick liked that idea, in a way. But if that was true, had the multiverse *meant* for her dad to be forced to live in a world away from his twin? 'But shouldn't people be able to choose some things for themselves? My dad couldn't stay with his family. It's not fair that the multiverse made that decision for him.'

'Ah.' Danser raised a finger. 'But if he hadn't ended up where he did, he would never have had you, now, would he?'

Flick's mouth shut. She didn't know what to say to that.

'Look, I don't like the idea of gods or anyone being in charge of any of us,' Danser said, taking out his tobacco tin. 'But if the balance of magic means it needs someone like you to be brought into being to set things right, well . . . I don't have a problem with that.'

Flick turned this around in her mind as Danser rolled four cigarettes in quick succession and tucked them behind his ears and into the band running around his hat. By the time he had put the tin away again, she was ready for another go at moving the schism.

As she pulled on the eyepatch again, she thought about purpose and fate. Maybe she'd never be able to move this schism. Maybe Elara was the one the multiverse had needed at that time, and now it needed Flick to do something different.

If only she knew what it was.

CHAPTER TWENTY-FIVE

The sign outside read *Quality lightning bolts: Buy one, get one free.*

'How do they even get the lightning?' Flick asked.

'They catch it,' Glean said, irritably. 'Don't start asking me for specifics, I'm not a lightning angler. They catch it and store it, and that's all we need to know.'

'What do people use it for?' Avery wondered, looking curiously around Five Lights.

Glean shrugged. 'Spells. To power machinery. Trick effects in theatre shows. All sorts of stuff. Stop asking questions, will you?'

Glean had volunteered to procure the lightning they would need to power the storm-tower and tear a schism right into Serentegra. Though Pendularbor had regular storms, there was no promise that any bolt that hit the tower would be big enough for their purposes. And if you couldn't wait for your own lightning, store-bought would be fine. Flick, Avery and Daniel had come through with her, to help carry their purchases and also to check in with Overseer Cutpurse, Nicc De Vyce, and the other Thieves.

The City of Five Lights had been cleaned up since the last time Flick had been there. Though the streets were still relatively quiet, the broken fountain had been repaired and the shops were open. There were people walking about with their shopping bags, exchanging news with each other, and it looked, to Flick's relief, like the worst was over for the city. A peep through her magnifier told her that the great schism in the sky was a fraction of the size it had been. If the city continued to thrive, she was certain it would eventually close for good.

Daniel had parted ways from them to go to the Watch building, and Flick and the others navigated the narrow streets of the city. It hadn't taken them long to find what they were looking for. They entered the shop, which had a great deal of merchandise: dried herbs and flowers hanging from the ceiling, open barrels of glittering objects, crystals scattered on table-tops, and – covering one wall of the shop – small glass cubes that were full of lightning. The lightning bolts moved inside the glass cubes like trapped snakes, thrashing and crackling against the sides of their little prisons.

Glean went straight up to the counter, where the shop owner was looking nervously at her Thief reds and obvious attitude.

'How much d'you want for the lightning?' Glean asked, jerking her head at the wall.

'Well, we usually ask for one high-quality trinket for two bolts,' he said, tapping his fingers together. 'However, er . . .'

'I want them all,' Glean said.

The owner paled. '*All* of them, madam?'

'All of them. How much?'

His finger-tapping got very fast. 'Well, there are a great many of them there, madam, the expense . . .'

Glean rolled her eyes and pulled two knives from her belt. The shopkeeper flinched, but she laid them on the counter and pushed them towards him.

'Oh,' he said, leaning over them, his face alight with interest. 'Is this handle dragon-bone?'

'Yes. And that's fae-wrought steel,' Glean said,

flicking the metal with a fingernail. 'These good enough for you?'

The man considered. He seemed to want the knives very much, but he kept looking from the lightning bolts to Glean to Flick and Avery as though he couldn't quite bring himself to say yes. 'But what do you want them all *for*?' he cried. 'They're useless as weapons, you know, madam Thief. They're only good for powering things, or for entertainment. I don't understand.'

'It's none of your business,' Glean snapped. 'D'you want the blades or not?' She reached out a hand as if to take them back.

The man quickly picked the knives up and put them under the counter. 'Would you like a bag?' he asked.

*

It took all three of them to drag the bags out of the shop. Glean tutted at Flick and Avery's struggles to lift their single bags of lightning, marching ahead with six bulging bags in her hands.

'I thought you said she was a bad guy?' Avery huffed, lifting her bag, waddling a few steps forward, and then putting it down again.

'She is,' Flick wheezed. 'Or, at least she was. Maybe still is. I don't know, it's complicated. She definitely had me kidnapped and tried to force Jonathan to give her a suitcase. But . . .'

'But?'

'But she was scared,' Flick said. 'I know that's not an excuse, but it explains it, you know? She was scared of the Seren. She wanted to get as far away from them as possible. I don't like what she did, but I understand it.'

'So, she's only helping us now because she thinks it'll help *her*?' Avery said.

'Pretty much. She cares about stopping the Seren, but only because if she doesn't, they'll find her and . . . punish her for leaving them.'

Avery hoisted her bag up again and held it in front of her, walking like a penguin. 'Are you sure this is even going to work?'

'Not really.'

Avery almost let go of the bag entirely. 'What?'

'Well, I keep trying to trap schisms with Danser, but it never seems to work. It's like . . . they don't want to move.'

Avery gave her a shrewd look. '*They* don't want to move? Or *you* don't want to move them?'

'Hey, that's not fair,' Flick said. 'Of course I want to move them. Then I'd know I can do it.'

'Yeah, you'd know you could do it,' Avery said. 'I imagine it'd be pretty scary, knowing something like that. Knowing you can do something that powerful.'

'I'm not scared of it,' Flick lied.

Avery sighed. 'You need to stop being afraid of what you're capable of, Flick. Just do your best – and don't be scared of what that best might be. It might be something terrible and frightening, but maybe that's what we need right now. The Seren are bad and scary. Maybe we need to be badder and scarier.'

'That's not how I want to beat them – by being worse than they are. I want to beat them by being so good that they couldn't even understand it,' Flick said indignantly.

Avery smiled widely, and Flick realised she'd been tricked. Avery nudged her with her shoulder. 'You didn't really think I wanted you to be the bad guy, did you?'

'Kind of,' Flick laughed.

'Ha. You couldn't be bad if you tried,' Avery said.

Flick put her bag down. Ahead of them, Glean had met up with Daniel, who was waiting expectantly near the fountain. 'If I do this,' she said quietly to Avery, who had also stopped. 'If I move the schism . . . I don't know what will happen.'

'We won't hate you if you can't—'

'That's not what I mean,' Flick said, looking into Avery's dark eyes. 'I mean . . . when I did the schism-stretching for the pirates, I collapsed. I felt awful for hours afterwards. Every time Danser tries to make me move a schism I feel like I've been run over. This stuff is dangerous. Messing about with magic, it's not good for me.'

Avery stared. 'What are you saying?'

'I'm saying . . . I don't know what it'll do to me. If I manage to pull this off.'

There was an unpleasant silence. Avery made sure her bag wasn't going to fall over, then took Flick's hand and squeezed it. There was nothing either of them could say to make Flick's words less worrying or less true, so for a moment they just held hands and shared their fear. Because it was shared, it did somehow feel less of a burden.

By the time they dragged themselves and their bags over to Glean and Daniel, the adults had been joined by two more familiar faces.

'Nicc!' Flick dropped her bag with less control than

Glean would have liked, and ran over to her. 'Has everything been all right?'

'Better than it was.' Nicc shrugged, though she was smiling. The bandage was gone from her arm, and she was back in some red Thief robes, though they looked a bit too big for her. 'Cutpurse heard what you're planning to do.' She gestured to the Overseer, who was talking in undertones with Daniel. 'He wants to know if you lot need reinforcements.'

'Reinforcements?' Avery blinked.

Nicc grinned. 'Look, the Seren took our home from us, and we're not the type of people who'll sit by and pass on the chance to get our own back. If you're trying to bring them to an end, we want to help you any way we can.'

Flick threw her arms around her. 'Thank you,' she said after a quick hug. 'Though, I should warn you, Glean and her gang are there as well.'

Nicc shrugged again. 'We've got a common enemy, haven't we? We'll just stay out of each other's way.'

Daniel beckoned them over. 'Did you hear? Overseer Cutpurse is offering some volunteers,' he said. 'I'll stay here and make sure they all get through all right.'

'OK,' Flick said, kicking the suitcase open. 'We'll

let you pull the suitcase through when you're done.'
And she stepped smartly into the suitcase.

Getting back to Pendularbor involved a quick stop-off at Strangeworlds, hopping from one suitcase to another. As Flick was helping Avery and Nicc into the next suitcase, she paused. Something had caught her eye.

In its slot in the wall, behind the desk, was Elara's glossy red suitcase. Perfectly safe in Strangeworlds. For now.

Flick put her bag of lightning bolts down and went over to pull it from the woodwork. Just like before, she was aware of how ordinary it felt in her hand. How small it was, and how light. She often sat marvelling at the potential of the ordinary-looking Strangeworlds suitcases, but this one felt as though it had potential in a completely different way.

She put it on the desk and put her fingers to the catches.

'That suitcase that contains the end of the multiverse . . .'

She thumbed at the gold fastenings. She had planned to destroy this, though now it was here it seemed so harmless, pretty and ornamental. Much like Strangeworlds itself, attention seemed to slide off the red suitcase like oil. And yet it was full of such power . . .

Around Flick, the travel agency creaked as it settled in the afternoon sunlight. The clocks ticked their unique melody of multiversal time. The dust in the air swirled like magic.

And it was some minutes before Flick picked up the red suitcase, along with her bag of lightning, and followed her friends back to the storm-tower at Pendularbor.

CHAPTER TWENTY-SIX

A few days later, Flick managed to create a thin stick out of magic and hold it in her hand.

Danser gave a low whistle of admiration. 'That's more skill than I've got. You've made a solid object. How's it feel?'

'Weird.' Flick moved the white-gold stick to and fro. It felt like holding a handful of bees, it was buzzing and vibrating so. She loosened her grip and the stick vanished into thin air. 'It almost feels like holding my breath? I know magic is all around, but making it stay in one place, or moving it about, is really unnatural.'

Danser screwed up his mouth thoughtfully. 'If you can move bits of magic like that, what's stopping you moving a schism?'

'They're bigger,' Flick replied, concentrating on forming a shape in her hand again. 'It's like . . . moving a house compared to moving a box.' A shape of a sphere began to materialise in her hand. It wasn't as fast or as graceful as when Tristyan had done it, but it was happening. Already she could feel that dark pull at her heart, that awareness of the emptiness between worlds, as if a curtain in her mind was being twitched back. Manipulating magic to do what she wanted made the multiverse feel fragile. How did other people do this without being afraid? She felt tiny and breakable every time she tried it.

A little glowing white ball became solid in her palm.

'Looks good,' Danser said. 'We're getting there. Or rather, you are. Guess my teaching is redundant at this point.'

'Don't say that,' Flick said. 'You helped me a lot.'

'I just gave you a nudge,' he replied, taking out his tobacco tin. 'Magic's in your blood. You were made for this.'

*

Flick demonstrated her new abilities for her friends that evening, conjuring another sharp stick that glowed strangely in the dark room they were using as a dormitory.

Jonathan watched her, warily. 'I've been thinking,' he said.

'Careful,' teased Avery.

He rolled his eyes at her. 'Look, we have a decent gathering here. Strangeworlders and Thieves, not to mention Kayda's people. But I think we could have a few more.'

'Are you worried?' Flick asked, letting her small stick disappear.

'I've been listening to Swype and Glean,' he said. 'Whilst we've been working on the machine in the tower, they've been regaling us with tales of things the Seren are capable of.' He wrung his hands. 'I don't know if we've got enough firepower.'

Flick thought about this. The plan entirely depended on physically overpowering the Seren. They needed to be restrained for long enough for Flick to get hold of a schism . . . though that part of the plan was already changing in her mind. She hadn't said anything to her friends, yet, but there was another secret she had been nursing since her trip to Five Lights.

She glanced at the red Doomsday Case, which was sitting innocently close by.

'I know who else we could invite,' Avery said, interrupting Flick's thoughts. 'Nyfe, and Burnish.'

'The pirates?' Flick blinked. 'They're not magical, though.'

'No, but they are vicious,' Jonathan said, flexing his left hand where a scar shone – a reminder of a sword fight aboard a pirate ship. 'If they had a Thief as a partner to protect them magically, they could easily overpower a physically weak Seren.'

'Plus, imagine how mad they'll be if they ever found out we didn't invite them over for some revenge,' Avery added with a grin.

Flick nodded slowly. 'You're right. Both of you. We should get a message to them.'

Jonathan got to his feet and cricked his neck. 'Never mind a message, I think they deserve a visit, and as soon as possible.'

*

Burnish and Nyfe were waiting for them on the beach. Their ships idled on the water, back where it was deep, though there were four jollyboats scrunched into the sand, and two distinct groups of pirates waiting beside them, muttering amongst themselves.

Burnish came forward and raised a hand. 'Nice to see you're still alive,' he grinned, taking hold of Daniel by the elbow and crushing him into a hug. 'We did wonder.'

'Nice to see you, too,' Daniel said, from somewhere inside Burnish's beard. He managed to extract himself and shook hands with Nyfe. 'You got our message, then?'

'We're ready to fight,' she said. 'I meant what I told your young ones – if I ever get my hands on those who stole my world from me . . .' She cracked her knuckles loudly.

Flick had to grin. The pirates might not have had any magic themselves but they were undoubtedly a force to be reckoned with. She could see Edony, Nyfe's shipmate and wife, covered from head to foot in both tattoos and cutlasses, talking to Captain Bee, who seemed to be wearing a sash hung with tiny clay pots. Flick guessed they were some sort of explosive.

'It's a shame we can't bring a cannon or two,' Burnish said. He whistled at his crew, who followed them all up the beach towards the suitcase. 'We built a forge on one of the islands here, and managed to repair some of the old pistols and get the ships' cannons back in working order. Still, I'd take on these magical villains with my bare hands if I had nothing else.'

Nyfe gave a curt nod. 'They had better be ready for the sailors of The Break. We do not forget, and we do not forgive.'

'And we're very happy to have you,' Flick said.

Burnish chuckled. 'I reckon you'd have Leviatha herself coming to help you if you weren't fighting on dry land. So, the plan is to give them a good hiding, is it?'

'That's the first part of the plan,' Daniel said. 'The second part is that whilst we restrain them, Flick here' – he put a hand on her shoulder – 'will move a schism and trap them inside it. Put them somewhere they can't magic their way out of.'

'The Inbetween,' Flick said. 'There's no way out of there.'

Nyfe narrowed her eye. 'You got out, though?'

'We had a suitcase,' Flick said, 'and besides . . . they can't do what I can do.' She blushed, unused to talking herself up.

Avery smiled, hiding it behind her hand.

'Right, then.' Burnish gave a quick count of heads as his crew gathered close by. 'We're headed into battle. I don't know how many of us will return, or what sort of a fight it'll be. Anyone thinking of turning back, do it now. There's no disgrace in it.' He paused for a moment, but no one moved. 'Are you ready?'

There was a roar of assent from the pirates, and cutlasses and pistols were raised into the air.

'I'd say that's a rather convincing answer,' Jonathan said, his hands over his ears.

One by one, the crews of *The Serpent*, *The Aconite* and *The Onslaught* all clambered through the suitcase into Pendularbor. Flick watched them go, before turning to look at the lighthouse on the edge of the cliff.

Her heart ached.

This was one of the last places she had come to with Tristyan. The place they had hoped Clara Thatcher might return to. But there was still no sign of her.

Daniel came to stand beside her, and let out a sad sigh.

'I hate this place,' Flick said. Though she wasn't sure how much she meant it.

Daniel nodded. 'Me too.' Then he checked his watch. 'We should follow them. Glean and Swype said the storm-tower was almost operational again. This might be our last night of peace.'

Or our last night at all, Flick thought morbidly, as

the reality of what she was going to have to try and do settled over her like the darkest and thickest of fogs.

*

'What's going to happen?' Avery whispered, that night, 'if we invite the Seren through here, but we can't stop them?'

Flick was facing her in the dark, snuggled into her own sleeping bag like it was a cocoon. 'We *will* stop them. The Thieves and pirates are going to battle them until they're weakened, and then I'll get them through a schism into the Inbetween.'

Avery stared at her. 'Have you actually managed to move a schism yet?'

There was no point in lying. 'I will.' She almost told Avery, then. About the *real* plan she was thinking of, about how risky it was, and how it all depended on a lie. But she didn't want to scare her, so Flick stayed quiet. If everyone concentrated on weakening the Seren, Flick could handle the rest.

Avery sighed, and reached out across the space between them. Flick took hold of her hand and squeezed it. 'I don't want you to do anything stupid,' Avery whispered. 'And don't say you won't, because you have done, before. Lots of times. I don't want to lose you.'

'You won't,' Flick said. 'I'll always be with you.'

Avery didn't reply, but her eyes glistened in the dark.

*

The machine was fixed. The lightning was ready. The assembled group of people, magical and non-magical alike, were gathered in the entrance hall of the Glasshouse. Flick stood to one side, trying to ignore the way her stomach was churning like a washing machine. Daniel was standing on the stairs, reminding everyone of what to do, and what to expect.

'We will force open a schism,' Daniel said, 'using the lightning cubes to power the storm-tower's machine. If it works as it did last time, the connection between this world and Serentegra will be widened, and the Seren will have immediate access to Pendularbor. We expect them to pour in instantly, so do not drop your guard for a moment. Anyone who cannot wield magic must stay close to someone who can.

'Our goal is to weaken the Seren enough for Felicity here to tear a schism through to the Inbetween and trap the Seren within it. Remember,' Daniel said, 'the Seren have a lot of magical power, but very little physical. If you can get close enough to them, you should be able to overpower them. We know they are not impervious to gunshot or fire. And . . . Good luck, I suppose.'

There wasn't any applause, but there was a generally positive feeling in the air. 'I don't need luck,' Glean said, tapping the magical bottles at her belt. 'Just aim me in the right direction and I'll give them what they deserve.'

'Fine sentiment.' Captain Nyfe clapped a hand down on her shoulder and Glean's knees buckled.

'We can't promise to take them all out,' Swype said, pushing their sleeves up to their elbows to show off what looked like wrist-to-elbow gauntlets. 'But we can contain them a little. We can conjure ropes to drag them where you need them.' They twisted something at their wrists and three curved blades clinked out from within each of the gauntlets, turning the Thief's arms into weapons. 'What will you do?' They looked at Flick.

'My best,' Flick said. The red suitcase was in her hand.

Swype's eyes moved from it to her face and back. 'You'd better not be thinking of using that thing.'

'Not exactly,' Flick said. 'It's just . . . in case.'

Swype gave her a hard stare. 'There isn't time for *in case*. You've wrought and wrenched magic in this world and others. You did it by reaching into that grim place inside yourself and letting your emotions do the heavy lifting. I know that, because that's what we all do. That's the real Inbetween.'

'What do you mean?' Flick asked, confused.

'I mean that there's a part of you that doesn't want to wield magic because it's nasty and scary and it frightens you,' they said. 'It makes you feel bad, and you're scared. Scared you'll go too far and die. Each time you've had to do it in the past, you've been in a life-or-death situation, and that sort of pressure makes it easier. But your abilities come from a dark place within *you*. The space between your anger and your calm, the gap between your emotions that gets you hot in the face . . . that's how you get your magic, burning under your skin. And you can access it any time you like.' They shrugged. 'It's frightening, yes. It puts you in danger if you do enough of it. But it's powerful. Incredibly powerful.'

Flick didn't know what to say. She glanced behind her to see if anyone was listening, but they were all busy. 'I can't just . . . make myself get angry, or whatever,' she said crossly.

'You don't have to,' Swype said gently, and the smirk that was usually playing at their mouth was gone. 'That dark and fiery bit of yourself is always there. Emotions just make it easier to get to, that's all. But you're always capable of it, Felicity.' Swype twisted their gauntlets again and the blades clicked back inside, out of sight.

Flick stared up at the pale Thief with their barely-there complexion and washed-out eyes. 'You're older than Glean, aren't you?' she asked. 'When did the Seren get you?'

Swype smiled ruefully. 'I was there at the start,' they said. 'One of the first kids stolen to be part of their *family*, as they called it. It took meeting Glean to open my eyes to what was going on.' They looked over at the woman, who was speaking to Daniel. 'She's always been the smart one. Ruthless, though. Guess that's why I like her.'

Flick had to smile as well, just for a second, as Swype stalked off back to the other Thieves. Her smile faded as she looked over at the pile of lightning cubes beside the storm-tower's machine, ready to be fed into it. When the tower was activated, no one was quite sure what would happen. But one thing was for certain – they were in for one heck of a fight.

Jonathan came over. 'Nervous?' he asked. As one of the non-magic users, he was tasked with loading the storm-tower with lightning. 'I wish I was going down to the battlefield with you.'

'No, you don't.' Flick prodded him. 'You'll be nice and safe in here.'

'I don't want to be *safe*,' he said. 'I've spent too long trying to be safe. I wasted my time in that travel agency, not questioning things enough, too wrapped up in myself. I want to *do* something.'

'You were looking for your dad,' Flick said. 'That's hardly self-absorbed.'

'Come on.' He looked at her. 'Let's not forget that I was going to trick you into doing that for me.'

She laughed. 'And now look at us.'

'Indeed.' He adjusted his glasses. 'You will take care out there, won't you?' He looked pointedly at the suitcase in Flick's hand. 'Shall I hold that for you?'

'There's no need,' Flick said. 'I know what I'm doing.' She went up on tip-toe to whisper into his ear. When she dropped back down, Jonathan's eyes were wide.

'You're sure about this?' he asked.

'Sure as sure.' She nodded. 'Tell Avery, it'll be OK. Just watch for my signal. When you see it . . . that's when we all need to be ready.'

For a second, Flick thought he was going to argue, but instead he gave a single nod. 'I trust you,' he said. It was all he needed to say.

And then, it was time. Jonathan pulled her into a hug, and Avery suddenly appeared beside them and joined in, grabbing them both and squeezing hard, before giving Flick a hurried kiss on the eyebrow.

'Be careful,' she warned.

'You too,' said Flick, watching her walk away with her cousin. It was strange – for the first time, she felt sure of herself, rather than frightened. There was still so much to worry about, but whatever happened next . . . she was going to do her best.

Danser nudged her. 'Come on, kiddo, let's get outside. You feeling ready?'

Flick snatched at the air, and electric-blue fire crackled around her hand as she balled it into a fist. 'I'm ready,' she said.

*

Inside the storm-tower, Avery and Jonathan exchanged nervous looks. They were in the machine room with Daniel, with the door bolted, ready to crack open the

301

lightning-cubes and turn the world of Pendularbor into a maelstrom of a stormforest.

Out of the window, they could see the Thieves, Danser, Flick and the others, spacing themselves widely around the perimeter, the forest of thorns behind their backs. Kayda's people had retreated deep into the covering forest, their own magic too slow-growing and flammable to be of use. The Thieves all had magic-filled bottles on their belts, Danser had ammunition slung over his chest, and Flick ... had a small red suitcase and nothing else.

'Here goes nothing,' Daniel said grimly. He opened the breakers in the machine's circuit and aimed the first cube of lightning at the exposed wires.

*

Outside, the ground shook and there was a sound like a giant snapping a tree in half. It was a cracking, wrenching, breaking, tearing noise. The lightning released into the air crackled and flashed noiselessly, and then wrapped itself around the tower. Sparks, visible to everyone's eyes, flew upwards into the sky, joined by more as another lightning bolt was fed into the machine.

The noise got louder, and Flick saw Pinch – one of the smaller Thieves – wince at the volume. The drifting sparks were forming a line, now, like a dotted line on paper showing you where to cut with scissors.

One more bolt would do it. Flick could feel it.

With another lightning cube, the tearing, snapping noise suddenly stopped. The wind picked up instead, rushing past Flick's face in a whirl, whipping her hair every which way. The dotted line in the sky vanished from sight. Flick pulled her eyepatch over her eye, and saw it reappear as a bright glowing white-gold scratch in the air.

A schism.

The line vibrated suddenly, throbbing and moving as though it was a worm of some kind, trying to crawl along the sky.

A very unstable schism. If it wasn't closed quickly, there'd be no telling what it might—

'Look!' Swype shouted, pointing.

They poured out of the schism like ghosts, like foam off water, like fog off dry ice. They floated down to the ground from the world of their imprisonment as though they had parachutes, and Flick was struck by two things. One, how graceful they were. Two, how few of them there were – no more than twenty.

And then, the third thing struck her. Right between the ribs.

'Oof!' She fell flat to the ground, landing painfully on her arms and trying not to drop the suitcase. She rolled away as a Seren – who was shockingly tall and had four eyes to go with their four arms – made to hurl another magical blast at her.

There was no time to think. Flick felt the magic in the air rushing towards her, ready to knock her backwards. She raised a hand and caught the blast as if it was a ball.

The Seren paused, all four hands up, shocked.

Flick grinned. 'Here,' she said. 'Catch.' She hurled the magic back towards them. It hit the Seren like a cannonball, knocking them off their feet and sending them skidding and thumping over the grass until they came to a halt, groaning, eyes fluttering.

Flick gave a tiny fist-pump in the air. This was what had been missing in her lessons with Danser – there had been no real danger. But at this point, it was now or never.

There was a CRACK above her as the schism closed – her friends had turned the machine off. Thank goodness. To her right, Danser looked like he was in a Tin Can Alley fairground game, firing over and over with the occasional whoop in victory as Hid – another of Swype and Glean's Thieves – held up a magical barrier to protect them both.

Flick could see Captain Nyfe slashing hard at a Seren as her metal sword clashed with a magical one, moving too fast for her opponent to grab any magic to throw at her. Pirates Burnish and Bee were back-to-back, throwing blades and small explosives at the Seren as Thief Pinch beat back magical weapons thrown in their direction. The other Five Lights residents, Nicc and Cutpurse, were directing the remaining Thieves to follow them, magical shields raised above their heads as they headed around the edge of the perimeter. Flick took off in the opposite direction. She wanted to find Azarus.

If she was going to fight anyone, she wanted it to be him.

A Seren screeched from behind her, making Flick skid on the grass to avoid a blue javelin-like bolt of magic thrown at her. Flick ran, zigzagging to avoid being hit, but the Seren kept on coming, bolts flashing from her hands, over and over, closer and closer.

Flick looked around desperately. There was a tiny floating schism to her left – one she and Danser had tried in vain to move. She reached for it and grabbed hold of it, as if it were a stick. No, not a stick: a sword.

Flick swung the schism in her hand before the Seren even realised what was happening. It passed through the Seren's body like smoke, and for a moment Flick thought that it hadn't done anything, but then the Seren crumpled to the ground, unconscious. The schism vanished immediately. Flick almost laughed. The schism had used the magical energy in the Seren to close itself.

She ran on. Azarus had to be around here, somewhere.

CHAPTER TWENTY-SEVEN

She didn't have to run far.

Azarus was advancing on two Five Lights Thieves, deflecting their magic as easily as swatting away flies. He wasn't even pausing for breath.

Flick couldn't wait. 'Looking for this?' she yelled, holding the suitcase up.

Azarus' head whipped around in a serpentine fashion, and his eyes went wide. 'How did you . . .'

'Escape the Inbetween?' Flick asked, as the Thieves scurried away, one of them limping and leaning on the other for support. 'That was easy. Anyone could do it.'

Azarus looked impressed. 'Fascinating. You truly belong amongst those who recognise how gifted you are.' He gave her a sly smile, but she thought she saw a little bit of fear behind his eyes.

'I'll never be one of you. But you don't have to do this,' she said. 'Stealing magic just to stay alive. You could live out your life like you're meant to.'

'I am *meant*,' he seethed, 'to rule. That is my purpose. To lead those who have the gift of magic. People like yourself. You clearly have talent – enough to work closely with me, if you had the nerve for it. You could live for ever.'

'No one should do that,' Flick said.

'Not even your grandfather, Felicity? Wouldn't you have loved to keep him by your side for ever?'

Rage rapidly surged up inside Flick like magma, and electric sparks crackled over her fists as she raised her hands, suddenly hating Azarus so much she wanted to blast him off the face of the world.

But he was quicker. His hands flashed, and Flick didn't have time to blink before something hot sliced into her forehead. She staggered back, clamping her hand to her head.

Azarus laughed. 'Not as good as you think, are you? Still, time and training would hone your skills.'

Flick looked at her hand. There was blood on her

palm, and her hairline stung with what felt like a deep cut.

'I don't want to do this. I would much rather have you amongst my family. But I cannot have you opposing me. I have suffered too much to indulge indecision.' He lunged, flinging a handful of magical shards at Flick's face. She threw an arm across herself, the shards splintering on the magic clinging to her skin as if they'd hit a shield. Azarus was coming closer.

Good, Flick thought. *Keep coming. Up close, I'm stronger than you.*

As Azarus raised his hand again, Flick leapt forward like she was on springs. She shoved Azarus to the ground, his magic shooting into the air and vanishing in a golden mist. She was too close to grab any magic, but so was he, the two of them struggling on the ground just as he and Tristyan had before. Flick lifted the red suitcase and hit Azarus hard with it. It made his arms stop scrabbling at her, just long enough for her to get up.

But then Azarus, deep blue blood streaking down one cheek, grabbed her by the backpack and hauled her back down to the ground, his hands like claws.

Flick kicked hard, getting him right in the shoulder, making him let go.

'You're making a mistake!' he shouted, as she scrambled up again. 'If you join us, imagine the freedom you could have. We could create a utopia – a heaven for those who use magic. Your friends would be safe, and so would you, in a multiverse free from persecution and harm.'

'I don't want to live in a utopia just for *me*, or people who can do things like me,' Flick spat. 'I want to do what's right for *everyone*.'

Azarus grinned, his papery face seeming to light up from the inside, and Flick realised the cut on his cheek had already stopped bleeding. He wiped the remaining blue away with the back of his hand. 'What is *right*? Right is a point of view. When bad things are on the horizon, every single living thing in this forsaken multiverse is out for itself. How do you think I survived for so long? On good fortune alone? I am one of the first Seren – a survivor from our time before your world was even a cloud of dust in space. I have survived not through charity or goodness, but through doing what I needed to do.'

'Look where it's got you!' Flick pointed at him. 'You look dead, and you should be. Nothing is meant to live as long as you have.'

Azarus' grin widened, and he got to his feet. His

eyes were shining, and Flick noticed they were no longer white and milky, but dark blue, almost black.

Flick stared. Her heart was hammering so much it felt like there was a huge drum in her chest. 'What *are* you?'

'I might be the oldest living thing in the entire multiverse,' Azarus said. 'And I intend to remain so, even if it does mean wearing this disguise.' He raised a hand to his face, brushing his fingertips over his crepe-like skin.

Flick gasped.

Azarus' appearance blurred for an instant. And then it began to change – no, not *change* – to be revealed for what it actually was. The glamour that made him look ancient and papery fell away, to reveal a healthier-looking complexion. His deep blue eyes were suddenly framed by dark eyebrows, and there were fewer wrinkles and lines cutting through his skin. His body filled out slightly, and his hair – though it remained white – softened from straw-like strands to softer locks. Only his teeth, which were too sharp and too many for him to pass as human, stayed the same.

Flick couldn't bear it. How much magic was Azarus using, just to hide how he looked? How much was he burning through, every moment of every day? 'Why?' she asked.

He smiled, and with his true face it looked almost friendly, though his eyes stayed cold. 'Why hide my face? Because the fools I command would only be envious. They expect me to suffer in the same ways they do. It is a small price to pay to continue my work.'

'Your *work*?' Flick asked.

'My purpose: to rid the multiverse of the magic-less. Non-magical people are a waste,' he said. 'They do nothing with their lives, they are unimportant and prevent the rest of us – people like you and I – from being our true selves. Now you have handed me this place.' Azarus spread a hand out. 'The most richly magical world in the whole multiverse, literally teeming with enough power to sustain my followers and I for decades. And when I get that suitcase from your cold grasp, I shall be able to do what I have always strived for – rid the multiverse of the swathes of worlds that serve no purpose other than to bring me greater power.'

There was a sudden flash of light. Flick threw an arm up to shield her eyes as Azarus did the same, the brightness forcing their eyes shut. As the light faded,

Glean swaggered into view. Flick's heart leapt at the sight of the Thief, her blonde hair plastered to her head on one side, and her face sweaty, but looking every inch determined to carry on fighting. Glean looked at Azarus and curled her lip.

'You were always so full of it,' she drawled. Then she lashed out.

Azarus moved, but not fast enough. Glean's punch, wrapped in a thick armour of magic, connected with his nose and broke it immediately. Midnight-blue blood splattered down his face and clothes. He clamped his hands over his nose and mouth and gave a muffled shout of pain.

'Get out of here!' Glean snapped at Flick. She smashed two of the large glass bottles at her belt and thrashed the magic in mid-air until it twisted into a lasso. She got it over Azarus' middle and pulled, sending him to the ground. 'You're coming with me, you shameless waste of breath.'

Azarus snarled, and twisted himself upright, yanking Glean to the ground, where they both began to struggle, magical weapons forgotten in place of hands and elbows.

Flick wanted to help, but Azarus and Glean were fighting too quickly for Flick to get in a clean shot without risking hitting Glean. She turned back to the field, the suitcase in her hand suddenly feeling like a deadweight. All around her, the fighting was still going on, and the air was thick with flying magic. She shut one eye to see properly through the eyepatch. Spare magic was glittering everywhere, thick as oil in water. To her left, she saw Swype conjure up a net the size of a single bedsheet, and prepare to throw it at two charging Seren.

It's too small, Flick thought. As the net sailed into the air, Flick concentrated on it. She reached a hand out, commanding the magic around her to make the glowing magical net thicker, heavier, stronger, larger. By the time it landed on top of the two Seren, it was four times the size it had been, and as heavy as steel cables. It knocked both of them flat to the ground.

Swype looked surprised, and then saw Flick. 'Thanks,' they said, jogging over. There was a cut on their chin, and they were shaking. 'Looks like your lessons have paid off. We seem to be winning. Cutpurse's Thieves have the others trapped, for now. Where's Glean?'

Flick pointed back where she'd come from, at where the forest of thorns curved away. In the time it had taken Flick to help Swype, Glean and Azarus had rolled farther away and they were now barely visible, in a cloud of magic and dust on the ground.

Swype took a step forward, then stopped. 'She went after Azarus?'

Flick opened her mouth to explain what had happened, when there was an explosion. The noise was so loud that it seemed to have a physical force. The ground shook, and Flick's ears rang. She stumbled and Swype caught her.

There was another bang, though not so loud, and Flick and Swype turned to see Glean running at full-pelt towards them, terror on her face. She tripped and fell hard on the ground. 'Run!' she screamed, as she tried to get up.

But there was no time. Azarus was right behind her, his appearance once again glamoured with age and decay. He was visibly vibrating with rage, and sparks of magic were racing over his skin like ants. He stepped over Glean like she was nothing, and looked straight at Flick. 'You should have joined me by your own free will.' He raised a hand.

The ground shook again, and this time it cracked open like an egg. A sour smell of dirt and rot filled the air as a ghostlike hand the size of a house grew out of the steaming dirt and condensed into a foggy shape, reaching for Flick.

She dived out of the way. The hand knocked Swype to the ground and kept on coming. Flick tried to raise a magical shield, but the hand was moving too fast, coming straight for her—

Azarus screamed, and the hand abruptly vanished.

Glean had stuck one of her enchanted knives right into the back of his leg. She was still on the ground, but she was grinning.

But not for long.

Azarus slapped her, open-handed, sending her backwards. The blade vanished as if it had never been there, and he walked on the injured leg without even a grimace. 'Hand over that suitcase, child,' he snarled, 'and I might consider letting your friends live.'

'Get away from her!' Glean was somehow on her feet again, and throwing herself at Azarus. She knocked him to his knees, but he pushed her away like she was just a doll and continued advancing.

'Get behind me,' Swype said to Flick. 'Don't give him anything. We can hold him off.'

But Flick stayed where she was. All she needed was the right moment; she wasn't going to run away again.

'Last chance.' Azarus pointed, and his grip filled with a long, thin javelin of magic. 'Hand it over.'

Flick gritted her teeth, preparing to fight. She gripped the suitcase tight. She thought about giving Jonathan and Avery her signal – for them to activate the secret part of her plan – but it wasn't time yet. She was so close, but what if . . .

Azarus' nostrils flared. 'Time's up.' He flicked his wrist, and loosed the javelin at Flick.

She wasn't ready.

Glean dived in front of her faster than blinking. The javelin disintegrated into nothingness as it hit her, and for half a second it seemed like she had absorbed it somehow.

But then Glean vanished, as though she had never been there at all. The golden magic of her life scattered into the air in a panic, before drifting away to mingle with the rest of the magic in the world.

Swype screamed, an unholy horror of a sound that seemed to come from somewhere deep inside them.

'You need to run,' said Flick. 'Please. Just run.'

Swype looked at where Glean had stood a moment ago. 'I can't . . .'

'Just *go*!' Flick shoved them.

Azarus suddenly moved, pulling a bright gold ball

of solid magic out of thin air, and raising it like an Olympian shot-putter.

Swype's hands moved to their belt, but Flick knew they would never be fast enough. Azarus released the ball. Flick concentrated all her focus on the condensed ball of magic and told it not to disappear, but to come apart. The ball disintegrated into pure magical particles before it hit Swype, scattering through the air. Swype took this as their cue, and finally did as they were told, running for it.

Azarus roared through his teeth in frustration, this time hurling several darts of sharp magic as he strode forward, heading straight for Flick.

Flick shoved her hands out flat in front of her, like a mime stuck in a box, and felt the magic in the air solidify and harden into a sheet of invisible steel. Azarus' darts smashed against her shield one by one, shattering into silver-gold magic and vanishing. He was close, now. Too close.

It was time.

'Wait!' Flick held the red suitcase up.

Azarus paused.

'Do you know what this is?' Flick asked.

He laughed. 'The end of all things,' he said, eyes dancing with *want*. 'A schism so powerful it could bring about the end of the multiverse itself. But, in the right hands, it is limitless power. It is my eternal lifeline. You should never have been trusted with such a thing.'

'Maybe not.' Flick dropped it on to the grass. 'But you shouldn't open it. It could end everything. Why would you risk that?'

'Because it is my destiny,' Azarus said. 'Elara Mercator fled my clutches and threatened all of us with the end of all things whilst really securing my future. Her pathetic Society has brought this case to me now, and, with it – its doom. For I shall be unstoppable.'

He snatched up the suitcase, put his claw-like fingers to the catches, and opened the lid.

CHAPTER TWENTY-EIGHT

Flick ran a hand over the smooth red leather of the suitcase. Just like before, she was very aware of how ordinary it felt in her hand. How small it was, and how light. She often sat marvelling at the potential of the ordinary-looking Strangeworlds suitcases, but this one felt as though it had power in a completely different way.

She put it on the desk and put her fingers to the catches.

'That suitcase that contains the end of the multiverse . . .'

Around her, the travel agency creaked as it settled in the afternoon sunlight. The clocks ticked their unique melody of multiversal time. The dust in the air swirled like magic.

There was no magic around the suitcase.

Flick pulled her eyepatch down, and looked at it again. There was something very odd about this suitcase. It didn't feel like a Strangeworlds one, at all. There was no warmth under her touch, no fizz of potential. Almost as if . . .

She thumbed at the gold fastenings.

She was certain. She was certain in the same way she was certain that fire was hot, and air was for breathing. She pushed on the catches, lifted the lid of the red suitcase that had caused so much fear and worry . . .

And looked down at a delicate silk lining of white and blue stripes, brown elastic fastenings, and little pockets for socks or keys. In one of the pockets was a folded paper note.

Flick took it and unfolded it carefully. In careful copperplate handwriting was one sentence, written in blue ink.

THERE IS ALWAYS HOPE.
EM

Flick smiled to herself, and put the note into her pocket. Then she picked up the suitcase, and followed Avery and Nicc back to Pendularbor.

*

Azarus howled in frustration and hurled the empty suitcase away. It bounced on the grass and Flick snatched it up, her heart hammering.

'Every day, more betrayals,' Azarus screeched.

'Don't you get it?' Flick laughed. 'This isn't a trick. This is exactly what you needed to see. If anyone ever thought that everything was so terrible that they wanted to wipe it all out, they'd be wrong. There should never be a way to end everything, because not everything needs to come to an end.'

Azarus shook his head, as if he didn't understand. 'A schism of such power could never be just a rumour . . . could it?'

'Of course it could,' Flick said. 'No one should have that sort of power, but Elara knew that it would scare you. You, and others. No one should be able to end things like that.'

'Perhaps.' He grinned. 'But it is irrelevant. In creating a lie about a suitcase so terrifying, Elara forced me to find a way to harness that power. Now magic is completely under my command. No living thing has the skills I do, and you, like the fools before you, invited my warriors and I here. Perhaps the schism I was searching for doesn't exist, but it will not be cause for disappointment for long. We are only a few breaths away from claiming this magic-rich world and fuelling ourselves to *near*-infinite power!'

'I'm sorry,' Flick said. 'That's not going to happen.' And she raised the red suitcase above her head.

*

'If you see me raise the suitcase above my head,' Flick whispered into Jonathan's ear, 'you need to put every single lightning bolt we have into that machine. Give it enough power to cut down as deep as possible, so it can go right down to the Inbetween. And leave the rest to me.'

Jonathan's eyes were wide.

'You're sure about this?' he asked.

'Sure as sure.' She nodded. 'Tell Avery it'll be OK. Just watch for my signal. When you see it . . . that's when we all need to be ready.'

He gave a single nod. 'I trust you,' he said. It was all he needed to say.

*

Instantly, the dark blue sky fizzed with static, and the towers of the Glasshouse lit up with cold, yellow-white light. The metal twisted around the glass towers sparked blue and electric, crackling into life as, inside the Glasshouse, the members of The Strangeworlds Society released the lightning bolts into the machine.

Flick looked up, and she didn't need to use a magnifier to see a bolt of white lightning flash across the sky. But instead of fading away, it stayed there, as though it had been painted on. The sky had been torn asunder, an opening ripped from this world into another. It was a schism, the deepest cutting one Flick had ever known. This schism wasn't devouring, it was waiting. This schism led straight to the darkness of The Inbetween.

It was now or never.

Flick dropped the red suitcase. It lay open on the grass, with its fancy striped lining and straps, looking perfectly harmless. She looked back up at the schism, at the darkness within it.

'*You need to stop being afraid of what you're capable of.*'

She raised her hands, and, through the eyepatch, watched the magic race to cover her skin. The dark power within her rose up, but for once she didn't feel afraid. It was a part of her, the same way that her anger, or her joy, or her love, was a part of her. Yes, it was different, and, yes, her power wasn't like anyone else's, but it was what made her special.

'What are you doing?' Azarus shouted. 'What is this?'

Flick watched the magic coating her hands thicken into rope, into webs and then into a net that reached upwards into the sky towards the schism. The net seemed to have claws that mirrored Flick's own hands, and as she flexed her fingers, the magical ropes lashed themselves around the schism.

It felt monstrous. It felt as though her breath was being stolen, her heart crushed, her bones turned into something more delicate than spun sugar, but there was no other option. She had to stop being afraid.

She was Felicity Esme Hudson. She was a member of The Strangeworlds Society. She was the most intensely magical being in the multiverse.

And she was going to put an end to the Seren.

Flick pulled and the schism fell, compressing and crunching as she clenched her hands in the air. It felt to her almost like crushing a ball of aluminium foil. It was all happening so fast, and yet – just like when she had stretched the schism in The Break – it also seemed to be taking for ever. She could see Azarus running towards her, to stop her, but she already knew he would be too late.

It was easy, really.

All she'd had to do was believe she could do it.

The schism became a white-hot glowing line, and she pushed it down towards the suitcase. It seemed to hesitate for a moment, the same way she had the first time *she* had gone to step into a suitcase. So, she did what Jonathan had done for her – and gave it a small nudge of encouragement.

Azarus had barely taken two steps.

The schism flowed into the case like mixture being poured into a mould. It shone brightly in the glass of Flick's magnifier; a square block of pure magic, the schism settled happily in its new container, waiting for its first traveller. Waiting to send someone to the Inbetween.

Azarus reached out.

Flick turned to him, the magic coating her skin like a glowing golden shell. She grabbed his forearm, noticing how thin and scrawny he was. Maybe that was his glamour, or maybe that was real, or maybe that was Flick's power telling her how different they were, but all of a sudden Azarus was tangled in glittering magical rope, his arms trapped by his sides as something from within the suitcase dragged him inside, like tentacles seizing hold of their prey.

And it wasn't just him.

There were shouts, and suddenly the windows of the Glasshouse smashed open, and the members of the Seren who had been trying to break down the door to get to Jonathan and Avery were dragged out by ropes of magic around their legs and bodies. Faster than Flick could have imagined, they were pulled and dragged from all around the battlefield down to the suitcase, which seemed intent on devouring them. One by one, they vanished inside it, and in the blink of an eye, they were gone, down into the Inbetween.

Only Azarus was managing to resist. He was clawing at the ground, his glamour ripped away from him so his face was now youthful again – and yet scarier and more furious than ever. His white hair was whipped back from his face, and his fanged mouth was open in a shout of rage.

'I won't die!' he cried. 'I will not!'

'No,' Flick said. 'You won't. No one dies in the Inbetween. You can live there, for ever.'

He raised his head to meet her eyes.

She smiled. 'It's what you want, isn't it?'

His hands slipped on the ground. For a second,

Flick thought he would be sucked down into the suitcase with the rest of the Seren.

But as he screwed up his face and grabbed for something – anything – to hang on to, the golden cords of magic around his body tightened, and Azarus went rigid. Then, he screamed. A pure, blood-boiled scream of utter rage, of anger so bitter it seemed to make the magic in the air glow brighter, and brighter, and more stunning until –

– the ropes confining him fell away. Because they were wrapped around nothing but a cloud of glittering magic in the air. Where Azarus had been a moment before, there was now nothing but shimmering white-gold magic, and then a haze of movement, and then . . .

He was gone.

The red suitcase lifted into the air, twisting as though it was trying to crunch itself up like a ball of paper, before folding in on itself, and disintegrating in a whirl of gilded magic.

Flick dropped her arms. The golden glow faded from her skin. She felt light-headed, and faint, as though she'd just had a fright and needed to calm down.

Only . . . she wasn't calming down. Her heart was racing, so fast it felt like a buzzing in her chest. It was too fast, and she was so tired, and she felt a spike of fear in the back of her mind, but she couldn't concentrate on it, or on anything, at all. Her hands were shaking, and she knew her knees were buckling beneath her, and . . .

. . . and then, the ground was rushing up to meet her, and everything went black.

CHAPTER TWENTY-NINE

From Avery's position in the storm-tower, the entire world looked incredibly still. She watched Flick fold up on to the grass like a paper doll and Avery's own heart seemed to come to a complete stop. Flick had collapsed as though someone had switched her off.

'Get up,' Avery murmured. 'Please get up, Flick.'

Jonathan shook her arm. 'We need to get down there. Come on.'

But Avery sat down, unable to tell herself to get up, or to run to her friend. She couldn't tear her eyes away from the limp figure on the grass. Her heart felt as if it had been torn out.

They hadn't even had a chance to say goodbye.

*

Daniel got to Flick first. He turned her on to her back, holding her head in his hands before putting his fingers to her neck.

'Is she all right?' Jonathan asked, reaching them. 'She has to be. She's done so much.' He flapped his hands so frantically he looked in danger of taking off. 'Dad, please?'

Daniel just looked up at him.

*

Avery managed to pick herself off the floor, and made her way down to where the others were sitting, looking at Flick. Daniel and Nicc were standing over Flick, talking rapidly. Off to one side, Danser was smoking two cigarettes at once, his sweaty face flushed. The Thieves were sitting or lying down on the ground, exhausted. Swype was sobbing into their hands, hunched over as another Thief rubbed their back in sympathy. Cutpurse was wrapping a bandage around one of his Thieves' arms. The pirates, who had suffered a handful of casualties, were respectfully placing their fallen crew on to makeshift stretchers.

The air smelled like burning.

Flick was lying on the ground, hair spread out, limbs sprawled. She was very quiet, and very still.

Avery felt her heart drop right out of her chest. 'Is she dead?' she croaked.

'No,' Jonathan said quickly. 'She's definitely alive. But she won't wake up.' He had his fingers laced together, propping his chin up. 'We're going to take her back to the travel agency. Take her to hospital.'

Avery looked from him to Flick, and then to the red suitcase, lying innocently on the ground. 'She saved us.'

'Again,' he said. He lowered his hands. 'What she did . . . it was miraculous.'

Avery knew her cousin wasn't one to mince his words. 'Yeah,' she said. 'It was a miracle.' She looked at Flick. 'What if she doesn't wake up?'

Jonathan gave her a wicked look. 'Have you thought that *you* might be the one to wake her?'

'What do you mean?'

'You know, like Sleeping Beauty.' He smirked, though his eyes weren't in it.

Avery gave him a push. 'Now's not the time to make jokes.'

He sighed. 'I know.' He looked back at Flick. 'But I don't know else what to do.'

They sat quietly for a second, watching Flick breathe.

And then, she turned over.

'She moved!' Avery said, delighted.

'It's a start,' said Jonathan. Flick turned over again. 'Perhaps she wants to wake up, but can't.'

Avery leaned over. 'Come on, Flick. Wake up. We need you back.'

'Indeed.' Jonathan pushed his glasses up his nose. He raised his voice, as if he was shouting down a well. 'Felicity, any time from now will be fine, if you don't mind.'

Flick stirred, but didn't open her eyes.

*

Flick dreamed she was on a beach.

It was a beach she knew, and had walked on many times. Only this time, she wasn't alone. On one of the softly sloping dunes a woman was standing, looking anxiously around, a picnic at her feet. The picnic was nicely laid out, with proper plates and glasses. The woman looked at her watch, and then around again, worriedly.

The image blurred. There was a flash in the sky,

and a rushing sound like a train going past at high speed. Flick saw the lighthouse – no, the storm-tower – in the distance, lighting up until it was glowing white . . . and then the woman was running, and something was chasing her, and Flick wanted to help her but she couldn't because she wasn't real. The woman fell on to the picnic blanket, cutting her hand on one of the glasses. A white ghostly shape – one of the Seren – was trying to drag her down to the water. The woman's hands dug into the sand, scraping lines down towards the sea.

No, Flick thought, raising a hand. *No, this isn't how this ends*.

The storm-tower went dark. The woman fought and fought against the Seren holding her and managed to knock them back. She ran through the water, towards the tower. The Seren followed, screaming silently, but the woman was too fast, too far ahead. She scrambled up the rocks by the cliff and up on to the grass verge, entering the storm-tower and leaving a single bloody handprint on the white paint. There was another flash of lightning, and Flick had the sensation that something magical had happened.

Flick watched as the Seren, snarling with frustration,

cut themselves out of the world. The place went still. The wind dropped. The place once again felt as lifeless as the first time Flick had seen it.

It wasn't a dream. It was a memory. A powerful magical event, so significant that it had been written into the very fabric of magic. Now, as Flick's mind crested on the waves of her own abilities, she was seeing it as if she was there. The storm-tower, the beach, the Seren and . . .

And Flick felt so tired she could have lain down on the sand and gone to sleep, drifting away in a dream or a memory, out of reality for ever. She was so, so tired. Down to her bones and beyond.

She knelt down and touched the soft warm sand, letting it trickle through her fingers.

'Felicity . . . if you don't mind?'

She looked up.

She was *so tired*. But she knew who that was.

'Come on, Flick . . . we need you back.'

Avery and Jonathan. They were waiting for her. Flick sighed, trying to stand, but the exhaustion knocked her back down to the sand. So she crawled. Up the softly shifting sand dunes, up towards the grassy cliff-top, her fingers gripping and feet slipping in the moving sand. It was terribly hard to move. But if she could just get to the top . . .

She skidded back down the slope, the sand biting at her hands and arms. It was too hard.

She closed her eyes. It was all right, she told herself, to just lie down for a while. Her friends would be all right without her.

Wouldn't they?

Would *she* be all right, without them?

Flick raised her head and looked up at the slope again. It was steep. But it was just a climb. She could do that. She would take it slowly. One hand at a time.

She reached up, and dragged herself forwards, towards the top. And this time, it felt easier. In moments she was up on the grass, and she wanted to laugh at how easy it had been. Her legs were itching to run, and so she sprinted towards the storm-tower, sand puffing up in golden clouds from her shoes as they banged on to the grass, and then she was there, at the door of the tower.

She pushed it open.

*

Flick's eyes fluttered, slowly opening to the lilac skies of Pendularbor. She felt more tired than she

336

had ever felt in her life, and her vision was blurry. She reached up and pushed the eyepatch off her head with a groan.

'Take it easy,' a voice said. 'Just lie there and let yourself come to.'

She shut her eyes again, listening to the sighs and mutterings of relief around her. 'Did I do it?' she whispered.

'Yeah,' Avery's voice was close to her ear. 'You did it. They're gone.'

Flick gave a small smile. 'I know what happened to Clara Thatcher. Tell Daniel, I know what happened to her.'

A hand stroked her hair. 'Just rest, Flick. You don't need to talk right now.'

Flick opened her eyes again, seeing more clearly this time. 'Is everyone OK?'

'Almost.' Jonathan leaned over to look at her. He looked rather dishevelled. 'There were losses. Including Glean.'

Though Flick already knew about the Thief, misery washed through her at hearing it said aloud. She sat up slowly, feeling a bit better once she was upright. The forest world seemed colder than it had before, and emptier. She could see the crying Thieves, and the stony-faced pirates, and knew that Glean had not been the only one to fall in the battle.

They had finally trapped the Seren for good, and the multiverse could begin to heal without their interference. Flick just wished she could feel happier about it.

Daniel came over, looking relieved to see her sitting up. 'We were starting to worry,' he said. 'You wouldn't wake up.'

'I didn't want to,' Flick said, thinking about the struggle to clamber up the beach in her dream. 'Daniel, I – I know what happened to Clara. She was at her storm-tower. The Seren came, and she had to run. There was another bolt of lightning, and then . . . she was gone.'

Daniel sagged. 'How do you know?'

'I saw it,' Flick said, rubbing her eyes. 'It was like a memory. I saw it because it was something that hurt the multiverse, like a scar. It needs to heal.' She looked up. 'How are we going to find her?'

'Tristyan left that magical beacon on the lock of the box for Clara,' Avery reminded her. 'Maybe she's already been back.'

Flick struggled to her feet. 'We have to go and find her!'

'Flick, calm down,' Daniel said, trying not to laugh. 'We don't have to rush anywhere.'

'Yes, we do,' Flick said. 'Clara doesn't know things are safe. We need to tell her. We need to tell everyone – the magic of the multiverse is safe at last.'

CHAPTER THIRTY

When Flick had pictured Clara Thatcher in her mind, she had always seen a woman who looked exactly like her dad but with long hair – a ridiculous way to imagine anyone, she knew, but since they were twins it didn't seem like too much of a stretch of the imagination.

But the woman standing staring at them now looked more like Flick than Isaac Hudson. She was shortish and slim and had Flick's twisty, curly brown hair, though hers was sensibly plaited back and wound into a sort of messy bun at the back of her head. She had round glasses on her nose, and she was wearing hiking boots and canvas trousers – and a very cool leather jacket.

Flick and her friends had gone straight to what Flick

would probably always think of as 'the lighthouse', even though it had never been one. The place seemed to have changed. Where before the stillness of the water and the sand had been eerie, now it felt calming and peaceful. There were ships floating on the water, and the grass on the cliff-top was speckled with tiny flowers.

The place felt as if it was coming back to life.

After saying thank yous, goodbyes, and oaths of loyalty to pirate captains Burnish, Nyfe and Bee, Flick had led the way over to the storm-tower. But before they got close to it, the door had banged open, and Clara Thatcher – who at that moment seemed more whirlwind than woman – had run down the grass to meet them, loose strands of escaping hair flying out behind her.

'Daniel?' she gasped.

He was staring back at her like he'd seen a ghost. 'Clara!'

'I thought you were dead!' she shouted, voice breaking in relief.

'I thought *you* were dead.' He stumbled over to meet her and they snatched one another up in a tight hug, clinging to one another's shoulders desperately.

'This is weird,' Flick muttered to Avery. 'That's my aunt.'

'And she has no idea,' Avery whispered back.

'Doesn't get much weirder than . . . oh.' Her eyes popped as Daniel and Clara kissed. 'Wow. I guess it does get weirder.'

Jonathan made a noise like the air being let out of a set of bagpipes.

Flick winced slightly as the adults broke apart, apparently remembering they had an audience. Daniel blushed red, but Clara didn't seem embarrassed at all.

'I felt the beacon call me here,' she said, 'but I was so worried about them being here waiting for me . . .' She trailed off, catching sight of Jonathan, who seemed to have turned into a statue. 'Is that your son?' she asked.

'Yes. Clara, this is Jonathan. Jonathan, Clara.' Daniel squeaked.

Jonathan looked as though he was going to faint for a second, then recovered himself. He walked up to Clara, hand out. 'Charmed,' he said. 'It's nice to meet you.' He threw his father a filthy look.

Daniel went even redder. 'Er . . .'

'And who are these two?' Clara asked, either not noticing the awkwardness or ignoring it as she let go of Jonathan's hand and went over to Flick and Avery. 'Are you Mercators too?'

'I am. Sort of,' Avery said, shaking hands. 'I'm a

cousin who might actually be an aunt a few times removed, you know how it is with multiversal travel. Avery Eldritch.'

'Flick,' Flick said, taking her turn. It was *bizarre* how much Clara looked like her. Flick didn't like it. She wished Clara looked more like her dad or Tristyan because even though that would have been emotional, it wouldn't have been as mind-boggling as this. Behind Clara, Jonathan was staring knives and daggers at his father, who was pointedly avoiding eye-contact with him. Clearly, Jonathan had been in the dark about his father's girlfriend.

'Where have you been?' Flick asked her. 'What happened to you after you escaped the Seren on the beach here?'

Clara peered closely at her, clearly wondering who Flick was, and how she knew what had happened to her. After a pause, she answered. 'I was sent halfway across the multiverse. I ended up in Altreia, which is not the sort of place I'd recommend visiting without access to an easy escape.'

'Meanwhile, I was wandering around the Inbetween,' Daniel said, finding his voice again.

Clara gaped. 'The Inbetween? But how?' She turned and looked up at the storm-tower.

'The lightning made a schism,' Flick said. 'But the wrong kind. You could never have controlled it, you two aren't like that. All you did was invite the Seren in, and Daniel got blasted into the Inbetween.' She put her hands in her pockets. 'But that's a long story.'

'Well,' Clara said, adjusting her glasses, 'I've got plenty of time to listen.'

*

Flick and Avery sat on the edge of the cliff-top, legs dangling down to kick at the chalky rock at their heels. In the distance, the great ships *The Aconite* and *The Serpent* were drifting away in opposite directions across the water.

'The more I think about it, the angrier I get,' Avery said, interrupting the quiet. 'I want to travel the multiverse with you, I want to see and know and learn everything *together*, but it's going to end up costing me in the end. It'll cost us all. Look what happened to Aspen Thatcher. She gave up everything and ended up dying before her time. That's not how I want this to go.'

Flick nodded. 'I don't think either of us should be

like Aspen. Giving up everything for someone else doesn't sound healthy, to me.'

'I know.' Avery put her hands on her knees and looked at the blank sky. 'It keeps bubbling up in my mind. Usually when it's just me and you. We've had adventures and it's been brilliant, but what's going to happen when we grow up? What happens when we're tired of travelling and just want to be boring together?'

'I'd quite like to be boring together,' Flick said.

'But we can't have that.'

Flick felt her cheeks prickle with a blush. She turned to Avery just as Avery did the same. In the approaching sunset, Avery's eyes glowed like embers of old magic. 'Maybe we can't have it in the same way other people do,' Flick said. 'But we don't have to never see each other again, that'd be stupid. We can just . . . visit happiness sometimes, can't we?'

There was a deep, stretching silence. Somewhere in the middle of it, the two girls took one another's hands, and held tight. The sun's colour melted from orange to red, and for a moment it looked as though the sky was on fire.

'I love you,' Avery said, matter-of-factly. 'I wish I didn't. It would make it easier to say goodbye.'

'I do wish you wouldn't keep talking about goodbye,' Flick said, putting on a smile. 'We don't have to do a forever-goodbye. Or a forever-promise. Us loving each other isn't dependent on us seeing each other every day. We can just . . . exist. Like this.' She held up their clasped hands.

Avery smiled back. 'I'd like that.'

'Oh, and . . .' Flick swung her backpack around, and dug inside it. 'I know we can't phone each other when we're in our own worlds, but that doesn't mean we can't talk.' She took out a pair of notebooks, a gift that she'd been given on a previous Strangeworlds adventure, and handed one to Avery. 'You write on one, and the message shows up on the other,' she explained.

Avery smiled widely. 'These are fantastic! Where did you get these?'

'Father Christmas,' Flick said. 'He said they'd come in handy. I guess he knows what he's talking about.'

Avery laughed, and Flick kissed her on the cheek.

The end would come for them both one day, that was inevitable. But the worries they had both been holding on to for so long had been set free and allowed to escape into the air. Where holding on to their feelings had been like crawling uphill, this felt like freewheeling downwards. Their journey would be a lot easier now, and more enjoyable. They might have for ever, or they might have never, but it didn't matter, because they had *now*. They always would.

Flick pulled Avery to her feet. 'Let's go home,' she said.

EPILOGUE

'Now, young Frederick.' Jonathan held the magnifying glass up like it was a lollipop. 'Let's see if you can see anything through this, eh?'

Freddy took the magnifying glass and promptly biffed himself in the eye with it.

'It's Freddy,' Flick said. 'Not Frederick. He doesn't have a Sunday name.'

Jonathan snorted. 'What next? People give their children such *ridiculous names* these days,' he practically yelled over his shoulder into the back of the shop.

'They still want to call it something weird, do they?' Flick asked, trying to steady Freddy's hand.

'Last night they decided they liked *Tamarisk* as a name.' He sighed. 'That's a plant.' He tutted as Freddy

348

lost interest in the magnifying glass and began trying to climb up Jonathan's legs instead. He lifted him up on to his hip. 'You, sir,' he said sternly, 'are getting too big for this sort of treatment.'

Freddy beamed, and stuffed Jonathan's tie into his mouth. It was a mark of how much Jonathan secretly liked him that he didn't scream.

Flick leaned back in the armchair, letting the sun warm her through the window. 'Maybe he's not magical. Lucky him.'

'Doesn't mean he won't be interested in it.' Jonathan offered him the magnifying glass again. Freddy took it and stuck it in his mouth. 'No, no, that's not how we treat our things.' Jonathan extracted the glass, which was now covered in drool, and held it at arm's length. 'Uh. Would you mind?'

Grinning, Flick took the glass and went to wash it in the sink at the back of the shop. In the back garden, Daniel and Clara were watering the plants that had sprung up in the warm weather. Flick was happy to see Tristyan's vision for the garden come good.

Clara had been devastated to learn about her father, though thrilled to discover she had a niece in the shape of Flick. It had been a very confusing time for them all, and there had been many awkward family reunions and memorials and for a while it had felt as though Strangeworlds was a counselling centre rather than a travel agency.

Isaac Hudson had finally met the twin sister he hadn't seen for practically his whole life, and, though their friendship had started rather stiltedly, they were now regularly meeting for coffees and chats. It wasn't always easy – not yet – but there was plenty of time. Clara was going to be around a lot, now.

Jonathan came into the kitchen, still hanging on to Freddy. 'Don't you ever feed this child?' He picked up a biscuit and shoved it into the toddler's open mouth.

Flick laughed. 'You keep moaning and groaning about it, but you're going to be a great big brother, you know.'

'We'll see,' he said darkly. 'Depends how stuck they get on naming it Tamarisk. Or Anchusa. Or Carpatica. The poor thing's going to be bullied off the face of the planet.'

Freddy waved his arms to be put down, and promptly toddled away back into the travel agency, where he started using one of the suitcases as a drum.

'Would it make you feel better, or worse,' Jonathan asked Flick, 'if he did have magic?'

'I don't know,' Flick said. 'In some ways, both.

I'd like him to have adventures, but . . . if there was ever any trouble, I can't help him out any more. I'm . . . not special.'

Jonathan gave her a small smile. 'You didn't use to want to be special.'

'I know.' Flick peered through the now clean magnifying glass. A soft golden haze swam in her vision, like a blurred metallic cloud. She hadn't seen the glittering sparkles or particles since the battle in Pendularbor. She could still see magic, she could still stay a member of The Strangeworlds Society, but she knew she would never manipulate a schism again. Though she had walked away from the battle, a part of herself had been left behind, its purpose fulfilled.

The front door banged, and Avery came in, holding four dangerously drippy Mr Whippy cones. 'Hurry up,' she said, holding them at arm's length.

Everyone snatched for them, and Flick handed one to Freddy, and they all sat in the relative cool of the shop, silently eating the ice creams.

'You know,' Jonathan said, after a few minutes, 'there's a really excellent ice cream shop in the world of Lenaria. They get honeycomb into it without it going soft. Quite remarkable.'

Flick caught Avery's eye, and they both grinned. 'Think we should check it out?' Flick asked.

The friends leapt up. Jonathan checked the new suitcase-filing system to find the location of the right suitcase, and then pulled it off the shelves, before Flick shouted –

'Wait!'

Everyone paused.

'What about Freddy?' she asked.

Avery shrugged. Jonathan leaned down and caught the toddler's attention. 'Freddy,' he said, 'would you like to come on an adventure?'

The toddler's face lit up. Whether he understood or not Flick wasn't sure, but if Jonathan was offering him something, Freddy usually wanted it. He reached, to be picked up.

'Wait.' Jonathan picked the magnifying glass off the desk. 'You need to look through this, first. Peepo, what can you see?' He demonstrated, and then held it out.

'What if he never sees anything?' Avery asked.

Flick shrugged, and took her hand. 'I'll take him anyway. He's my brother. You shouldn't be kept from magic just because you can't see it. That's the sort of thinking Azarus would have liked.'

Avery beamed at her.

Freddy took the magnifying glass from Jonathan and held it up in front of his face. There was a pause, as the heavy instrument made his arm wobble, but then he held it still, and peered through it seriously, just like Jonathan had.

Flick grinned as she watched his little mouth drop open.

It was time to pack their bags for another adventure.

ACKNOWLEDGEMENTS

As always, it took a team of people to bring *The Strangeworlds Travel Agency* to life, and I am grateful to every single person involved. First and foremost, thanks must go to my agent, Claire Wilson, to whom I owe a thousand debts of gratitude and snacks. Strangeworlds wouldn't exist without you, Claire, and I am so grateful that you, like Jonathan, gave me the nudge I needed to set off on this adventure.

Heartfelt thanks must also go to my editor, Lena McCauley, for all her hard work and wondrous enthusiasm – you make me want to be a better writer for you, and I can't wait for the next voyage into the unexpected! To my marketing and publicity bods, Beth McWilliams and Dom Kingston, thank you for all the support, the beautiful images to use online, and for helping me to shout as loudly as possible about the series. Merci, gracias and danke schön to the Rights team, for all the hard work sending Flick and her friends around the world. Gratitude must go as well to Writers and Artists (in particular Clare Povey), and to OwlCrate Jr for your support. And a thousand thank yous, and heaps of promised cake, to Natalie Smillie and Samuel Perrett for once again knocking my socks off with a book cover to die for.

Thank you as always to booksellers across the land and sea for all the support, for all the window displays, the hand-selling, events and dealing with me popping in randomly to sign things! Thanks especially to Helen at Wonderland Bookshop, Gavin Heatherington, Tsam Potts, Louise Inniss, Daniel Riding, and Dion and Fliss over the other side of the world. You guys are awesome! And to the book-bloggers, particularly Steph, Jo and Imi, thank you for giving up your time to tweet, write, and shout about the *Strangeworlds* books. I appreciate it more than I can say.

To my writing-world pals – Darran, Alice S-H, Alice O, Louie S, Non P, El Lam, Sophie A, Hux, Harry W, Mia K, and especially to my accomplice in all things not-suitable-to-list-in-the-back-of-this-book Nicole, thank you for not ghosting me in the horrors of this year and for all the memes. Sorry not sorry for the spam.

But the biggest thanks of all must go to you – the readers. Thank you for taking Flick, Jonathan and Avery into your hearts, and for joining them on their escapades. Though I am sad to see the series come to an end, I am thrilled to have been able to share the stories with you. Keep your eyes out for magic – you never know when it will appear.

And to Anton and Joseph, you have my love now, forever, and always.

ABOUT THE
AUTHOR

L. D. Lapinski lives just outside Sherwood Forest
with her family, a lot of books and a cat called Hector.
When she isn't writing, L. D. can be found cosplaying,
drinking cherry cola and taking care of a forest
of succulent plants. *The Strangeworlds Travel Agency*
is her first series for children.

AT THE
STRANGEWORLDS
· TRAVEL AGENCY ·

**EACH SUITCASE TRANSPORTS YOU TO
A DIFFERENT WORLD. ALL YOU HAVE
TO DO IS STEP INSIDE . . .**